QUEST FOR LOVE

The Sisters of Rosefield Book 2

EMMA EASTER

Quest For Love
by Emma Easter

Paperback Edition

CKN Christian Publishing
An Imprint of Wolfpack Publishing

6032 Wheat Penny Avenue
Las Vegas, NV 89122

Paperback ISBN: 978-1-64734-005-6
Ebook ISBN: 978-1-64119-881-3
Library of Congress Control Number: 2019956882

QUEST FOR LOVE

To my dear son, Jimmy.

ONE

Audrey smiled sadly at Ken as they sat talking on her couch.

He put a hand on her shoulder and said, "Don't worry, baby. We might not be able to get married now, but the wait will only make it sweeter. You'll see!"

Audrey sighed and tried to cheer up. Without a doubt, Ken was as disappointed as she was about the fact that the wedding had to be postponed, but, unlike her, he wasn't letting it get to him. As usual, he was optimistic. Unable to resist any longer, she pulled him close and kissed him passionately.

When they finally came up for air, he gave her a crooked grin and said, "What was that for, Audrey? Do you want me to lose my head and decide to spend the night here?"

She shook her head. "It's exactly what we don't want." She gave him a rueful smile. "If we were already married, you wouldn't have to return to your hotel room tonight." She kissed him again; it was a slow, lingering kiss.

He shook his head when they finally separated. "You are going to get me in trouble. This is really fun" -- he waved his hand between them -- "but you remember we decided to reduce the amount of time we spend kissing, especially when we are alone... just so we keep on the straight and narrow."

"Okay... okay!" She thinned her lips, got up from the couch and went to sit on the armchair across from him. She took a deep breath as she curled up on her seat.

"Much better," he said.

She gazed wistfully at him. It took everything in her to stop herself from joining him on the couch again, just so she could cuddle up to him. These days, they were constantly facing a dilemma. Because of the wedding planning, they had to spend lots of time alone together, sometimes late into the night. And every time, they ended up snuggling and kissing. Before long, they almost always started to push the boundaries, until one of them broke it off before it was too late.

She said to him, "If we can't keep our hands off each other here, what will happen when we get to Madrid for our vacation and our guards are down?"

He lifted a brow. "We would probably have to ask Bryan and Sienna, or Trisha, to be our chaperone. That's the best thing we can do."

"Or we could just elope now," she chuckled.

"We could... but then your sisters wouldn't be at the wedding."

She shrugged. "Well, Bryan and Sienna did it." She sighed. "But I want my sisters at my wedding. And I also want my brother to be there."

He nodded and said, "Yes, and that's why we can't

elope or get married right now. Plus," he grinned at her, "we have so many guests because your guest list is getting out of hand."

She laughed at the teasing smile he gave her. "My guest list is half the size of yours, Ken, and you know it. I think you are inviting everyone in Miami."

"Because I want everyone to see me married to the love of my life." He winked at her and patted the space beside him on the couch.

She shook her head. "No... no... Ken. I am staying right here."

He huffed playfully. "Okay, then. Anyway, we need to set a date for the wedding."

"What about three months from now? I think that might be enough time to find Rafael. Also, Trisha would have given birth to her baby by then and we will be able to plan the kind of wedding we want . . ."

She shrugged when he raised his brows at her. "Okay, the kind of wedding I want. But just like you said, I want it to be memorable... though, I would marry you tomorrow if it wasn't for the fact that we need to find my brother now." Audrey frowned as a thread of worry went through her. For a long moment, she hesitated to say what was on her mind, and then she spoke. "What... what if he's... dead, Ken? I've been thinking about that for a while. Even though I didn't know he existed until a few weeks ago, the thought still terrifies me."

Ken gave her a sympathetic smile and said, "I think he's alive. And I think God wants us to find him. But you can't worry about things you have no control over. Just trust that it will all work out for good in the end."

She tried to smile, but she couldn't. "He could be in prison. All my life, I've been hauling others off to jail, but my own brother could be…"

"Stop, Audrey! Stop worrying. We've hired the best investigator, after all. He'll find Rafael in no time. You'll see." He gave her a lopsided grin. "Are you sure you don't want me to come over and give you a comforting hug?"

She shook her head quickly. "You know where that hug might lead. We are trying to prevent that from happening. 'Sides, weren't you the one who told me to sit here?"

He groaned. "That I did."

She got up. "I'm hungry. Let me go get dinner. We can continue to talk about the wedding while we eat." He started to get up to follow her, but she shook her head and he sat back down.

She hurriedly rustled up some spaghetti and meatballs and brought it to the dining table.

They sat facing each other as they ate and talked about the wedding and their trip to Spain.

"I booked rooms for all of us at the Citadel Hotel Madrid," she told him excitedly. "I can't wait for the trip. We'll have such a great time."

An hour later, she drove him back to Hattie's Bed & Breakfast.

He kissed her before opening the car and getting out.

She smiled as he stuck his head back in the window for another kiss. When he straightened, he tapped her nose and said, "See you tomorrow, sweetie."

She waved to him and watched him walk into

the bed and breakfast. When he was out of sight, she exhaled and started the car. As she drove home, she prayed that the months before their wedding would fly by quickly, because it was getting harder and harder to wait.

Her heart thudded as she prayed. Hopefully, they would make it to their wedding night with no regrets.

*****

Faizan stood up after his morning prayers and turned to look at the men beside him. They'd all just finished their prayers as well—two dozen men side-by-side. They were all his men now. Since Mustafa had died a month before, he'd taken over as leader of their group, Al-Muharib. He was eager to prove himself a capable leader. He would carry out the final wishes of his mentor. All infidels would feel the wrath of God.

He picked up his prayer mat from the hard, rocky ground, folded it, and said to the lean, muscular man next to him, "Are the men ready to leave Algeria for Spain as soon as possible?"

Hassan, his second in command, answered, "Yes, and all the weapons are ready to be carried onto the plane."

"And are the men ready to give their lives for the cause if need be?"

"They are."

Faizan smiled. "Good." He waved over one of the men and handed him his prayer mat. Turning back to Hassan, he said, "Come and show me the weapons. We will carry them onto the private plane once it arrives from our sponsors . . ."

"Who are these sponsors, Faizan?" Hassan interrupted. "I would like..."

Faizan turned on him with a cold stare, and he immediately stopped speaking. "Don't ever interrupt me when I am speaking! Is that understood?"

"I'm sorry, Faizan. It will not happen again."

Faizan glared at him for a few seconds and then said, "It had better not. Now, show me the weapons."

Hassan led the way out of the massive cave that was the operation center of their group. The cave, located amidst cavernous mountain ranges and surrounded by the Arabian Desert, also served as a temporary residential space for members of the group.

They passed some of the men guarding the vicinity, and Faizan made a mental note to place more guards around the area. They walked for a long time until they came to a spot where three trucks were parked. Hassan opened the trucks, and Faizan smiled. Their sponsors had come through, providing everything they would ever need for this mission in Madrid.

He hefted one of the rifles and inspected it closely. Hassan lifted another.

Two men approached them carrying a big box. They placed the box in the back of the truck and Faizan opened it. He nodded with satisfaction.

The bombs. Good. This was what he'd been preparing for ever since his mentor, Mustafa, had told him about his plan for a huge attack, starting with Spain. Unfortunately, Mustafa had died prematurely, but Faizan had been glad to finally take his place. He'd gone on a few of the jihad missions, but they were small. This was big and might be his last. If it turned out they needed it to be a suicide mission, he was ready to give his life for the cause of the group— to make Allah's name feared amongst the infidels.

Hassan asked, "Have you finally decided on the specific targets?"

Faizan nodded. "I have." He started to make his way back to the cave, dust swirling around his feet, while Hassan followed from behind.

Entering the cave, he led the way to a section where only leaders of Al-Muharib were allowed. He opened a small map and pointed at a spot which he had circled with a red pen. "This is the first train station where we are going to detonate a bomb," he said. He pointed at another spot, also marked in red. "This is the second one. We are also going to position men in these two hotels," he pointed at two spots on the map. "And we will be planting bombs in them. The Regal Hotel, here, and the Citadel Hotel Madrid, right here."

Hassan nodded. "So, the men taking out the trains will be giving their lives?"

"Yes, the others will be waiting at strategic points close to the hotels. Anyone who survives the bomb blast will be shot by our men." He looked at Hassan. "It goes without saying that none of the men can leave this place until we are ready to go on the mission. And none of the men can breathe a word of our plans to anybody outside this place. Anyone who does will be shot immediately. Is that understood?"

Hassan nodded. "Definitely."

Faizan waved his hand dismissively, and once Hassan left, he went to the chamber that had been his private sanctuary since they'd moved there two years previously. Al-Muharib had been a part of a larger group, but Mustafa had chosen to leave because they were straying from the cause. He had followed Mustafa, of course, as he owed his mentor his life.

He picked up a jug of water, poured it into a wash bowl, and washed his hands and face. He ran his fingers through his beard as he sat on a mat on the floor and thought about his life. Soon, he would start the true mission for which he had been born. He was thirty-four years old and it was about time. If he died while carrying it out, he would be a martyr and his death would be a worthy one.

*****

Trisha placed the dishes she'd just finished washing on the drying rack. She picked up a clean kitchen rag and began to wipe down the cabinets.

Her cell phone began to ring, and she quickly dried her hands on her apron and picked it up from the kitchen island. When she saw it was her lawyer calling, she clicked the answer button.

"Hello," she said, her heart thudding. Hopefully, the woman was calling with good news.

"Hello, Trisha," her lawyer said chirpily. "I've got great news for you."

"Yes, I'm listening." Trisha held her breath.

"Stan has finally relented and agreed not to delay the process any longer. In a few days, you will be a single woman."

Trisha lifted her hands and gave a happy yelp. At last, the news she'd been waiting to hear for months now. This long drawn out divorce would finally end. She would be free from Stan.

She exhaled. A small part of her was sad. She'd put so much into her marriage; plus, their unborn child would not be raised with both her parents present in the same home. She shrugged. There was nothing she could do about that now.

"Trisha, are you still there?"

"Yes. Thank you so much." She breathed a deep sigh of relief. "I'll finally be at peace. This divorce has taken so much of my strength and peace of mind."

She talked with her lawyer for another minute and then ended the call. She dialed Audrey's number, her heart soaring with happiness, and waited as it rang.

"Trish?" Audrey said as her voice came on the line.

"Hey, Audrey! I have good news."

"What is it?"

"I'll share when I get to your house. When did Sienna say she was coming?"

"Umm... she and Bryan said they would leave Green Valley at about three o'clock. That's an hour from now. They should be here in two hours or so. Ken will also come about that time."

"Okay... I'll be there in two hours. I'll see you then."

The call ended, and she continued cleaning the kitchen. She smiled as she imagined being at Audrey's with her sisters and their partners. Unfortunately, she would be the odd woman out, with no spouse of her own. However, that wasn't terribly important right now. All she wanted was freedom and a new beginning.

She finished with the kitchen, went to her room, and shed her clothes. Entering the bathroom, she went into the shower.

For a long time, she stayed under the shower's flow, reminiscing about her life with Stan. She felt as though the water pouring over her was washing her from within; washing away her past. For a long time after she'd found out about Stan's adulterous relationships, she'd felt unclean. She had been sharing him with many other women. Now, she felt whole again. She smiled, took a deep breath, and exhaled.

She stepped out of the bathroom about thirty minutes later, cradling her belly. At eight months pregnant, her belly was huge. She put on a pair of loose jeans and an old T-shirt and put her hair in a messy bun. She grinned as she looked at herself in the mirror. One of the perks of not living with Stan anymore was that she was free to let herself go... at least for a while. Stan had wanted her to look good at all times, and she had constantly made the effort to please him. But that had not kept him from bedding other women.

She sighed and went to the kitchen to make a dill pickle sandwich for herself. She carried the sandwich to the living room and ate while she read her new novel. Like her sisters and their significant others, she'd taken a long break from work. The money they had inherited from their late father afforded them the opportunity.

None of their lives had really changed because

of the money. They hadn't splurged on anything except, of course, for the lavish vacation they were planning to take to Spain, which was also a search mission. She'd decided for now to stay in the home she had shared with Stan for over a decade. Audrey had decided to continue to keep their parents' home as hers. When she and Ken got married, they would start to look for a bigger house, but for now, she was still living there.

Bryan and Sienna still lived in their tiny new home in Green Valley. They planned to stay there until they both graduated from the Bible school and then they would move to a bigger house.

Trisha gradually became absorbed with her novel. After some time, she glanced at the clock on the wall and her eyes widened in surprise. It was almost four o'clock. Time to go to Audrey's. She slowly got up from the couch.

She went into the bedroom, slipped on a pair of ballet flats, and picked up her purse. She grabbed her car keys from the bedside table and left the house.

Bryan and Sienna's blue Honda was parked in front of Audrey's when she got there. She parked beside the car and exited hers. Ken was probably here, too. Their evening would most likely be spent talking about plans for their trip. But first, she would share her good news with all of them.

She walked up the stairs and opened the front door. Just as she'd guessed, Ken had arrived. He was sitting beside Bryan, and both men were chatting about something. Sienna and Audrey had their heads together, laughing and whispering. They all looked up and smiled as she entered.

"Hey, Trish!" Audrey and Sienna chorused.

She went to them and they hugged. She reached out and hugged the guys as well, and then sat between her sisters on the couch.

"So," she began, "my lawyer called earlier today to say that I will be a free woman in less than a week."

Audrey whooped. "Yay, Trish! That's great news. Finally, Stan will be out of your life for good." She frowned. "Talking about Stan, I haven't even seen him for weeks. Where has he been hiding?"

Trisha shrugged. "I don't know, and I don't particularly care."

Sienna put her hand on Trisha's shoulder. "Are you okay, though, Trish? Even though Stan was a scoundrel, you were married to him for years and you loved him."

Trisha gave her a sad smile. "Unfortunately, seeing him in our matrimonial bed with another woman and knowing it was probably not the first time killed most of that love. He'll always have a place in my heart, but I can genuinely say I don't love him anymore."

Ken said, "I guess congratulations are in order, then."

Audrey winked at her. "Now maybe you can give our Frank a chance. I don't know why he isn't married or even dating, but I think it might be because he hasn't found someone he loves as much as he loves you."

"Who is Frank?" Bryan asked.

"A good friend of our family's," Sienna answered. "He has loved Trish since we were kids."

Trisha cringed. "Please, guys, no more talk about

dating. Can't you see I am pregnant? Besides, I am not in that place at all."

And even if I was, Frank would not be on my list of guys to date.

She changed the topic quickly before anyone could say anything else about Frank. "About our flights, Audrey; you have our tickets, right?"

Audrey nodded. "Yes. Three more days. I can't wait."

Trisha smiled. "I can't, either. I have to take it easy with the excitement, so…" she gasped as a piercing pain hit her stomach.

"What is it, Trish?" Sienna asked, looking worried.

Audrey put her hand on her shoulder. "Are you okay?"

Trish nodded. "I'm sure it's nothing. Probably just…" She gasped again as another wave of pain hit her, and then she felt something wet trickling down her legs. "Oh, Lord!" she exclaimed. She looked down at her thighs and saw that her jeans were soaked. "It can't be! My baby is supposed to be due in four weeks."

Audrey and Sienna shot up from the couch.

Audrey's eyes grew round, and then she looked at the men and said in her take-charge way, "Guys, call 911. I think Trisha is going to have her baby now!"

*****

Trisha cradled her precious bundle in her arms as she lay on the hospital bed. Her heart overflowed with love as she gazed down at her beautiful daughter. She looked up at her sisters and let out a happy sob. "She's so beautiful!"

Sienna had tears in her eyes. "She's gorgeous, like her mom."

Audrey looked down into the baby's face and beamed. "I think she looks just like you. I hope she doesn't suddenly start to look like Stan as she gets older."

Trisha chuckled. "She might. She's his daughter, after all. As long as she doesn't acquire any of his bad behavior, I'm okay with that." She looked at the baby and kissed her cheeks. "You are going to be a great girl, aren't you, my love?"

Sienna lifted her fingers, kissed them, and gave a long sigh. Her expression turned wistful as she gazed at the baby. "I can't wait for the day Bryan and I have our own baby. You are so blessed, Trish."

Trish smiled at her. "You guys will have yours in no time."

Ken and Bryan came in. After they both cooed over the baby, Ken said, "The doctor says you can leave the hospital tomorrow, Trish." He smiled sadly at her. "That means you won't get to come with us."

Audrey looked at him as though he were nuts. "We can't leave now that Trish just had a baby! We will have to postpone our trip."

Sienna nodded. "That goes without saying."

Trisha shook her head. "You guys will do no such thing. You are going. I'll be fine."

Audrey ran her hand over Trish's hair. "Stop, Trish. We are not going anywhere without you."

Trisha looked up at her. "I will feel so guilty if you guys put off the trip because of me. 'Sides, do you really want to postpone your wedding again,

Audrey? You want our long-lost brother to be at your wedding, don't you?"

Audrey nodded.

"Then go find him now." Trisha looked at Sienna and Bryan. "Just have fun. You guys can tell me all about the trip when you come back. And I'm sure we will have many other trips in the future."

Audrey started to shake her head, but Trisha said, "No more, Audrey. You are all going. I insist!"

*****

Lauren Patterson sat up on the bed as her cell phone rang. She rubbed her eyes and picked up the phone. Her heart skipped a beat as she stared at the caller ID. It was Richie.

She frowned. What does he want?

She kept staring at her cell phone until it stopped ringing. She bit her lip and leaned back against her pillow. She'd not spoken to her husband in weeks. Since Ken had brought her to Rosefield, she'd experienced the kind of peace she had long yearned for. The small town had a way of filling her mind with a sense of serenity every time she was on the verge of worrying about her marriage. All she needed to do was take a walk around the town and she would feel good again.

But best of all was the kind couple she was staying with.

She glanced around the small room that she'd occupied since she had come to live with the Gibsons. The room was tiny, with only a single bed, a wardrobe, and a dressing mirror. Compared to the room she'd shared with her husband in Miami, this room was like a pauper's. Still, she would not give it up for the world. The Gibsons, along with the few other girls who also lived there and had similar issues to hers, had taught her so much about valuing herself.

But she couldn't stop thinking about Richie. A deep sadness overwhelmed her the more she thought about him. She still loved him, in spite of how he'd constantly abused her. She felt slightly ashamed of the fact, but she couldn't deny her feelings for him. She missed him. When he wasn't angry and abusive, he was actually a good husband—funny, accommodating, and romantic.

She sighed. If only her marriage had gone the way she thought it would. But it hadn't. Instead, it had turned out to be a nightmare.

She turned on her bed, and for the umpteenth time since she'd met Ken again at the police station, she wondered how her life would have turned out if she hadn't ended their engagement; if she had gone ahead and married him. Without a doubt, she knew he would have been a good and loving husband. He would certainly never have been like Richie. She had been young and foolish when she'd broken up with him.

He's kinda boring, she had said to herself when she'd broken off their engagement. What kind of life will I have with him?

But Ken had not been boring at all. She had fallen in love with another man, a bad boy who'd made Ken seem uninteresting. Now she regretted her decision every day.

She gazed at the missed call on her phone and resisted the urge to call Richie back, the way she had since she'd left him months ago.

She pressed her lips together. She had to forget about Richie. Going for a walk might help, but it was only five o'clock in the morning. It was too early to go for her daily walks.

She sighed and forcefully pressed away all thoughts of Richie and Ken from her mind so she could go back to sleep.

Just as she started to doze off again, her phone rang. She groaned and opened her eyes. She hesitated for a few seconds, fearing it was Richie again, and then picked up her phone from the bedside table. She looked at it and then shook her head as her stomach clenched in anxiety. It was Richie... again.

She considered ignoring the call, but she just couldn't. She answered and said, "Hello, Richie!"

"Lauren, where are you, babe?"

She shut her eyes, imagining him at their house, holding his phone tightly and pacing their bedroom floor. She had to be careful how she answered him. She wouldn't give away any information about her whereabouts, but she didn't want him to go into a rage. Even over the phone, he made her nervous. "Umm... I'm somewhere safe, Richie."

He didn't say anything for a long moment and she wondered if he was still there. At last, he said, "You don't need to hide from me, Lauren. I am getting help now. Please come back home. I promise never to hurt you again."

She shook her head, even though she knew he couldn't see her. "I can't!"

"Please, Lauren," he said in a voice laden with desperation. "At least think about it. I still love you, honey."

She sighed loudly. "I don't know, Richie. You've hurt me so many times, physically and emotionally."

"I am changing," he said. "Right now, I am attending anger management classes and it's helping me. But I need your help if I am going to completely change and become the man you need me to be. I need you to be here with me."

She sighed again, worry coursing through her. She wanted to be there for him, but she wasn't sure she could risk it.

"Many spouses come to the meetings too, just to support their better halves. I need my wife there with me as well."

For a minute, she said nothing. She bit her bottom lip until the pain made her stop.

"Lauren, baby, are you still there?"

"Umm… yes, I am." She gripped the phone tightly and said, "I will think about it, Richie. That's the best I can do for now."

"Okay."

He sounded disappointed, and she wondered what he had expected. Did he think he would just ask her to come home after he'd brutalized her, and she would come running back to him?

"Please let me know what you decide to do as soon as possible," he said.

She didn't say anything.

"Lauren?"

"Yes, Richie?"

"I love you. Remember that. I want us to be together, and I will do whatever it takes to make that happen."

"I've heard that before," she told him.

"I mean it this time. I want you back in my life, and I won't give up until I do."

After the call ended, Lauren sat staring at the wall opposite her bed. Confusing thoughts and emotions ran through her mind. She wanted to stay in the comfort of the Gibsons' home, but she couldn't stop thinking about the good times she had shared with her husband.

She lay back down and stared at the ceiling. Like Richie had asked her to do, she needed to make a decision now, but not the one he had in mind. She needed to decide right away to either go back to him or divorce him. She shut her eyes tightly. The thought of going forward with either decision made her sick to her stomach.

TWO

Zainah Keita walked to the front of the prayer tent where everyone had gathered for the evening prayers. She looked at the small crowd of women and children sitting on the hand-woven rugs on the desert ground. All of them looked eager to hear God's word. She felt honored that Miriam, the oldest woman in the camp, had chosen her to share the word today, and whispered a prayer for help before opening her Bible.

She began to read Matthew chapter five out loud, emphasizing some of the words as she read. When she got to the eleventh verse, she stopped as a sob rose in her throat. It had been more than a decade since she had been ostracized and chased out of her community in Mali because of her faith. Thankfully, she had been brought here after a kind Christian woman had found her roaming the streets. Still, she'd not forgotten her beloved family. She missed them every day.

She continued reading, "Blessed are ye, when men shall revile you, and persecute you, and say all manner of evil against you falsely for my sake."

After she'd finished reading the passage, she began to teach on the beatitudes. She reminded the women, and even the children, why they had all come. "Some of you came here because you ran away from forced marriages, some because you were persecuted for your faith and you wanted it to stop. Others, like me, were disowned by their own families. But, however you came here, we are united now. Our purpose is to live only for the Lord who saved us, to pray constantly for the souls of those who do not know him, and to pray for our brothers and sisters who are still persecuted all over the world for His sake."

She looked at their faces. Most of them were from surrounding Arab countries. Like her, most of them had families they had left behind. They were brought, or chose to come here, to this desert, in order to practice their faith without fear.

She reminded them of the need to forgive and pray for their persecutors. She continued speaking for another ten minutes, and then she rounded up the sermonette with a prayer.

Another sister, Fatima, came and led the prayers. As each of them prayed, some quietly and others crying out loudly to God, Zainah remembered the months after she'd been brought here. She'd been miserable, yearning for her family. She had left behind seven brothers and five sisters, and the thought that she might never see them again had been way too much for her. But the Lord had brought her through, and she'd found a new family amongst these women.

Her mind strayed to a dream she'd had a few

months before.

Before she'd come, she'd dreamt of getting married and having a large family of her own, like other girls. Even after she gave her life to Christ through some missionaries who came to her small community when she was eighteen, she prayed constantly for a godly man. But when she came to the desert and saw there were no men, she knew the dream would never come to pass. This women's camp was where she would spend the rest of her life.

She'd grown to love this place and had gradually put away her childish dream of a husband and children… until three months before. She had dreamt of a man with fair skin so different from her own. Though she had not seen his face clearly in the dream, she had heard the words, "That's him, the man you will marry." When she'd woken up, the dream had felt so real. Yet, she knew it couldn't be. Not only was the camp occupied by only women, she had taken a vow of chastity some time ago, which she would never break. Still, the dream had stayed with her.

For the hundredth time since that night, she'd had the strange dream, and she lifted it to the Lord, asking to know what it meant.

"Lord, I am twenty-eight and I am not searching for a husband. You know I made a vow of chastity to you. Besides, there are no grown men anywhere in sight, so that dream probably meant something else… but what, Lord? Please help me understand."

She listened, but heard nothing.

She blinked with guilt as Fatima began to round up the prayers. She had not been paying attention.

Soon everyone began to troop out of the prayer

tent to finish their chores. Before long, it would get dark, and then most of the women would either retire to their individual tents or stay outside, chatting in the desert night.

Zainah chose to retire to her tent early that day. She just wanted to spend a bit of time with the Lord, eat her dinner, and go to bed. But her closest friend, Leila, entered her tent just as she did. Leila had an olive complexion and wavy, long, dark hair. She always wore a smile, but the smile was missing today.

"What is it?" Zainah asked, concerned.

Leila shrugged as she sat on one of the brightly colored hand-woven rugs on the floor. Most of the women in the camp wove the rugs. A few people who had vowed to keep the camp secret came from the city every month and collected the rugs. They paid a handsome sum of money on which the members of the camp lived.

Zainah sat next to her and put her hand on Leila's shoulder.

"It's not so important. It's just that sometimes, especially since I turned thirty, when I see some of the children here, I wonder how it would have been if I'd had a husband and children of my own. But that will never happen."

Zainah pressed her lips tightly together. She'd just been thinking the same thing. How strange. She considered telling Leila about her dream, but immediately changed her mind. She didn't want to distress her friend any more with dreams about a husband or children. She smiled at Leila and said, "We are really blessed to be part of a family that loves God. Even though we don't have some of the things those outside here do, I wouldn't trade my life here for anything. We have all dedicated our lives fully to our Lord, and He is our husband now."

Leila nodded and smiled. "You always know what to say to make me feel better, Zainah."

Zainah smiled, but groaned inwardly. If only her friend knew she was struggling as well. She'd been content to remain unmarried and childless for the rest of her life, until the dream had brought a deep discontentment that she was now fighting every day.

She immediately changed the topic. They chatted about different things, from their lives before the camp to their future plans. It was past midnight before Leila went back to her own tent.

Long after she did, Zainah lay on her sleeping mat, praying through the night that the Lord would take away her discontentment.

*****

Audrey stopped in front of the hotel room and smiled. "Whew! Finally, in Madrid! All I want to do now is take a really long nap."

They had booked a penthouse suite with three separate bedrooms. She couldn't wait to take a shower, lie down on a bed, and go to sleep.

Ken beamed. He stood with his luggage next to hers, while Bryan and Sienna stood apart, whispering in each other's ears. "You can't do that, though," Ken said to her.

Sienna looked at her. "We are supposed to schedule a meeting with the investigator immediately and then have dinner together."

"I know," Audrey said. "Well, maybe I can take a short nap."

The concierge opened the door to their room, and after they had generously tipped him, they all walked in.

Audrey strode through the hotel room, or more appropriately, luxury apartment, marveling at how beautiful and spacious it was. Her mouth fell open as she looked around her. There was a large living room with marble floors, cream and gold furnishings, a Persian rug, and two massive crystal chandeliers hanging from the ceiling. Audrey walked into the dining area and kitchenette. Everything was well appointed. The dining table could have seated eight people, and there were only four of them.

Sienna squealed and said, "Audrey, come see the view!"

Audrey went out to the balcony and stared at the breathtaking view. Clear blue waters and sand almost as white as snow stretched out before her. She couldn't wait to go out and take a dive in the water. But that would have to be the next day.

She turned to say something to Sienna, but her sister had already left. Sienna called her name and Audrey went into the room again.

"I guess this room is for Bryan and I?" she heard Sienna's voice from somewhere in the apartment.

She followed the sound of her sister's voice and entered an opulent room with an oversized king bed. "Wow!" she exclaimed.

Sienna took her hand. "Look at the bathroom."

She followed her sister in and glanced round the massive marble bathroom with a huge bath that could easily contain four people. She grinned at Sienna.

Her sister turned to look at her husband with a sly smile, and Audrey immediately knew what was on Sienna's mind. It saddened her a little. If she and Ken were married now, they would be in a room together, enjoying the space like Sienna and Bryan, rather than in separate rooms.

Audrey walked out to give Bryan and her sister some privacy and went to find her own room. Ken was standing at the door of the connecting rooms, looking from one to the other. They had the same lavish look as Bryan and Sienna's, except for the fact that they were smaller.

Ken turned to her as she approached him. "I was waiting for you to come and choose a room so I can take the other." He beamed at her. "This place is astounding."

She smiled at the look of wonder on his face. "It is. And thanks for waiting for me." This was just one of the reasons why she loved him. He always put her first. She walked up to him, sighed, and kissed him. She started to draw back, but he hugged her to himself.

"Another kiss." He smiled and planted a firm kiss on her lips before letting her go.

Both rooms looked almost identical. She said to him, "Let's just pick the ones nearest to us now. I'll take this one on the left and you take the one on the right."

He nodded and went to get his luggage from the living room.

Five minutes later, she was unpacking for their two-week stay. When she'd finished, she showered and took a nap. Her phone rang about fifteen minutes into her nap, and she roused. She answered the phone and found it was the investigator.

"Can you hold on a second?" she said. She got out of bed, slipped her feet into a pair of fuzzy slippers, and knocked on Ken's door. When she heard him say "come in," she entered and found him sitting on the bed, watching a soccer match on the TV set. He turned down the volume and looked inquisitively at her.

"It's the investigator," she mouthed, and then turned on the speaker.

"About your brother, I'm on to something," the investigator said. "I think I'll know more by tomorrow. Do you want to meet me then?"

They agreed that the man would meet them at the hotel lobby the next evening, and then she ended the call.

Her heart soared as she smiled at Ken. "I'm sure it's good news," she said. "Hopefully he has found Rafael."

Ken nodded.

"I was so afraid the info Dad left us about him wouldn't be enough. I mean, he left us with just the birth name his mother had given him, his Mom's name, and the town where they met." Audrey sat down beside Ken and looked at him. "My poor Mom. She didn't even have any idea my father had a love child. It would've broken her heart."

Ken put his arm around her shoulders.

"Anyway, it wasn't Rafael's fault. I can't wait to see him… and see if he looks like Dad." A thread of worry ran through her. She searched Ken's eyes. "He'll want to come to our wedding, won't he?"

"Yes, I'm sure he will." Ken shook his head and said, "Stop worrying, Audrey. You've started with the doubts. Of course he'll want to come."

She smiled. "You always know what to say to calm me down." She looked deep into his eyes for a few seconds and then said, "I better go now." She stood up from the bed, walked to her room, and shut the door firmly.

She sat on the bed and prayed. She prayed that the investigator had truly found Rafael and that their brother would want to meet and get to know her and her sisters. There was a chance he might not want to have anything to do with the children of the father he never knew. If he didn't want them in his life, she would be heartbroken, and so would Trish and Sienna.

*****

Faizan watched closely as his men carried the weapons into the private plane that had arrived only the evening before. After they'd finished, he waited for his men to board. Hassan was standing a few feet away; the other men that were not going on the mission were also watching them. Faizan beckoned to Hassan.

"I can trust you to take care of the camp while we are gone?"

Hassan nodded.

Faizan looked at him intently, and for the first time since he'd known the man, put his hand on his shoulder. He said, "You know what to do if I don't return. You will take over as the new leader of our group."

Hassan smiled and nodded again.

Faizan looked over the remaining men, shouldered his rifle, and began to board the plane.

"May Allah be with you," Hassan called out.

Faizan turned, returned the salute, and then entered the plane. He immediately went to the cockpit where the pilot was, looked around to make sure everything was good, and then went to take his seat with the men.

He began to address his men, briefing them about their activities once they landed at the airport in Madrid. They already had contacts at the airport, people who would make sure their passages through security went without a hitch. And people who would help transport the weapons to their destinations.

"We will enforce God's will on this earth as his servants, and if we die while doing that, we will have our reward in paradise."

The men applauded and screamed their approval.

He talked for about an hour, and then he sat, contemplating their mission. He recalled clearly that years after joining their old group, he'd been held with some suspicion. Even though his birth mother, who was Spanish, had given him partly dark features, he still looked discernibly white.

He'd had to prove himself constantly to rise to the position he was in today. But there was one secret he had kept from everyone. Only Mustafa had known. His birth father was an American. With the hatred the leaders in the old group had for America, he'd kept that information buried deep within him.

He hated America himself. Maybe one day, if it

was in Allah's plan and if he survived this mission, he would go there and mete out God's judgment on the country.

He looked out the window at the Arabian Desert and the undulating mountains. In some hours, they would be…

His eyes widened as sand suddenly began to lift from the earth and swirl swiftly around like a tornado. The faster the sand swirled, the darker the sky became, until he couldn't see anything. The plane began to shake.

He stood and went to the cockpit as his men began to murmur amongst themselves. When he opened the door to the cockpit to ask the pilot what was happening, he was suddenly knocked off his feet. He fell back onto one of the plane seats. He felt a throbbing pain in his right arm, but he ignored it.

He stood up again and tried to get to the pilot, but he was knocked down again. He shook his head as he began to lose consciousness.

He screamed, hoping the pilot would hear him. "What is happening?"

But there was no answer. He looked around him. The men were shouting, and chaos reigned as the plane jerked and then nose-dived. His stomach roiled, and he held on tightly to the seat as the plane began to plummet to the ground.

Faster and faster the plane fell, and all he could do was pray they would make it out alive. But somehow, he doubted it. Just as he braced himself for impact, the plane hit the ground with a force that sent him sailing into the air. His entire life passed through his eyes for the few seconds he was in the air, and then he fell and screamed in agony at the excruciating pain he felt. He heard the men screaming too, and then he began to fade away.

Just before he blacked out, he felt an overwhelming regret at the fact that he would die without completing his mission.

*****

"You can't be thinking of going back to that beast. After everything he did to you, Lauren," Sally said with concern clearly written on her face. "Please tell me you're only joking!"

Lauren sighed and replied, "I'm not joking. I have already packed my things." She looked at her new friend. There were four girls living now in the Gibsons' house; girls who had come seeking refuge from an abusive spouse. Sally, however, was the only girl she had truly formed a bond with. "Don't worry about it, Sally. I really think he has changed or I would not be going back to him. He's even attending anger management classes now."

Sally turned away. "I should get Diane to talk to you."

Lauren stood up from the Gibsons' living room sofa and decided to leave immediately. There were only two people who could get her to change her mind about going back to Richie. One of them was Diane Gibson, and the other, Ken. She didn't want anyone to stop her now. She quickly made her way to her bedroom to get her things, but Sally followed.

Lauren brought out her packed suitcase from behind the bed and began to roll it out of the room. Again, Sally followed her.

"Don't go!" Sally said.

Lauren stopped and looked at her. "I have to go. I need to be with Richie as he goes through his classes. He's depending on me to provide moral support, and I can't let him down. I want to see him transformed into the man I know he can be."

Sally sighed loudly and nodded. "You leave me no choice." She brought out her cell phone and began to dial a number Lauren knew was Diane's.

Diane had gone to a social function at the city hall with her husband, Paul. Lauren had decided to take the opportunity to leave the house when they left.

Lauren hastened out of the house and stood to wait for the taxi she had called earlier. Her heart raced as she waited and hoped that the taxi would arrive quickly, before Diane or Paul came home.

Sally came out of the house and held out the phone to her. "Diane wants to speak with you, Lauren."

Lauren ignored Sally and folded her arms. Where is that taxi?

"Lauren, please speak with her!"

"No," Lauren said sullenly. She was an adult and she had made the decision she believed was best for her. She would not answer the phone and give Diane the chance to talk her out of her decision.

She breathed a sigh of relief when the taxi finally came to a stop in front of her. The driver came out and put her suitcase in the trunk. He reentered the taxi, and she got into the back. She looked out the window at her friend. Sally had a mournful look on her face.

"Don't look so sad, Sally. I'll be fine."

"Will you? How are you sure of that?"

Lauren smiled sadly. "I'll miss you. I left a note for Paul and Diane, letting them know how grateful I am for their kindness." She put her hand out the window and held her breath, hoping Sally would take it.

Sally looked at her hand for a long moment and then took hold of it. "I'll miss you, Lauren," she said with tears shimmering in her eyes. "Please be careful… and remember that I am praying for you."

Lauren felt her insides turn. The religious talk in the house was the only thing she wouldn't miss about the place. She smiled at Sally. "I'll try to call when I'm in Miami." The taxi started to move and she waved to Sally, then turned around. She took a deep breath, leaned back on her seat and shut her eyes. She sighed as a feeling of uncertainty came over her. Hopefully, she had made the right decision to go back to Richie.

She fell asleep on the long drive to Boise and didn't awaken until they'd reached the airport. Throughout the flight to Miami, she fell in and out of sleep. Every time she was awoken, a small voice in her head kept scolding her, telling her she was making a huge mistake. The only thing that silenced it was sleep, so she tried to snooze as much as possible throughout the journey.

Richie was waiting for her at the airport when she arrived. Her heart pounded as she slowly walked to him with her suitcase. She studied his handsome face closely for any signs of hostility. When she found none, she hurried up to him.

He swept her off her feet and hugged her tightly. "I've missed you so much, Lauren," he said. He kissed her and then hugged her again.

"I've missed you too," she said, smiling.

He handed her a bouquet of flowers and said happily, "Welcome home, honey."

She wanted to tell him that this was a probation period for him, to see if he had truly changed, but she held her peace. This wasn't the time.

She followed him to his Mercedes and sat beside him in the passenger seat. On the way home, they chatted about everything; from her stay at the Gibsons' home to his anger management classes. When he brought up the one topic she didn't want to talk about, she suddenly became quiet.

"Lauren, I really think we should start thinking about that again."

She shook her head. "I'm tired, Richie. Can't we talk about it tomorrow? I've had a long day."

"You know that I really want a child," he said. He looked at her briefly before facing the road again. "You aren't getting any younger."

She winced but said nothing. When they'd gotten married, they had decided to wait a few years before trying to have children. But when Richie had become abusive, or rather, his abusive nature had started to show, she'd decided she didn't want a child with him; at least, not until he had changed his ways. Since she still wasn't sure he had, this talk about trying to have kids now was making her uncomfortable.

He said nothing until they drove into their driveway. She exited the car and waited while he got out her suitcase. When he opened the front door, she walked in and sat on the couch. Memories of their last fight in the house flooded her mind, and she bit her lip.

Did I make the right decision? She asked herself again.

He sat beside her and she held her breath, afraid he would restart their earlier discussion about having a baby. She shut her eyes in relief when he said, "Tomorrow is another anger management class. Will you be able to come with me?"

She smiled and nodded. "Yes, definitely."

Soon, they snuggled up together before the fireplace. She became drowsy and shut her eyes. He pulled her even closer and kissed her hair, and she sighed in contentment. This was the side of Richie she loved. The tender, romantic guy. If only he could be like this all the time.

She smiled as she finally dozed off, knowing she had made the right decision to return to him.

THREE

Zainah opened her eyes as the sound of howling wind invaded her prayer time. Some of the women in the prayer tent also lifted their heads. A few were on their feet. The wind began to scream and she heard the sounds of crashing drums and poles.

She immediately ran out of the tent with the other women. Some of the children had been playing outside and they needed to get everyone into the general tent. It was built much stronger than the others and had withstood two sandstorms since Zainah had come.

As they quickly gathered the little children, sand swirled around and about them, while the wind blew their hair and clothes about. They herded the kids into the tent just as the sky darkened. Zainah thanked God they had all gotten inside and out of the way of the storm.

The tent shook and the wind continued to shriek as they all sat down waiting for the sandstorm to be over.

Suddenly, they heard a loud, horrific sound, like

an earthquake and a huge house crashing to the ground. They all screamed. Some of the children started to cry and many of the women began to pray.

Zainah frowned, wondering what had caused the horrible sound.

The commotion outside continued, while prayers went up in the tent. After about ten minutes, everything suddenly stopped. Everyone began to murmur and a few women asked Zainah what she thought the scary crashing sound was. She told them she was just as clueless about it as they were.

They all stood and made to leave the tent, but Miriam's voice stopped them.

"We don't know what that sound was," she said. "I think only a few of us should go. The rest should stay here and watch over the children and our things."

She looked around the tent and then said, "Nadia, Zainah, Leila, and I will go."

Zainah went out of the tent with the other three women. She fell into step with Leila as they waded through the sand towards where they believed the sound had come from.

Leila asked her, "What do you think it was?"

Zainah shrugged. "I don't know. But we'll find out soon."

"I hope we aren't walking into some kind of danger," Leila said, trying to dust away the sand from her hair. They were all covered in sand, but it was strange Zainah had not noticed until now.

"Maybe someone has discovered our location," Leila added.

Zainah shook her head. "I don't think so. The

Lord would not allow that." But on the inside, she trembled. What if Leila was right? The Lord had kept them safe for such a long time, they had all come to take it for granted. What if a group of zealots found out about their camp with its group of Christian converts and decided to destroy them? What would happen to the children?

She pushed away her fears. The Lord had kept them safe for a long time. He would continue to do so.

They walked on and then Zainah spotted something in the distance. Leila gasped beside her.

Zainah's eyes widened in astonishment. A fiery plane was some feet away from them.

"A plane!" Leila exclaimed.

Zainah said, "That's what we heard. A plane crashing." As they neared the wreck, her heart raced. She prayed with all her heart that there weren't people there or if there were, that they would be alive.

But when they finally got to the plane, her stomach roiled and she felt nauseated. Scattered around the area were charred bodies.

Leila and Nadia threw up, and Zainah began to hyperventilate. If it wasn't for the short nursing training she'd had before she came, a training which had proven useful for helping the sick or injured in the camp, she would be throwing up too.

"We have to quickly check and see if any of these people are alive," Miriam said.

Zainah immediately noticed a part of the plane that was leaking what she'd earlier assumed was water. Now she realized it was jet fuel. At any minute, the plane would blow up. They were in danger.

Her pulse quickened as she went around the plane searching for any whole bodies and holding in her horror at the sight of so many body parts.

"We need to leave now!" Miriam yelled.

Zainah went into the plane. She didn't want to leave immediately, as she felt a tug in her heart.

Someone is alive, I can feel it.

Leila came inside and screamed. "Zainah, we need to leave right now!"

"I'm coming," Zainah said.

"The plane will blow up any moment from now, Zainah!"

"Someone is alive," she said as her eyes traveled through the wreck. I can feel it.

Lord, where?

She instantly felt a pull towards the back of the plane. She went there and searched but found nothing. And then she noticed a bright red cloth under the wreckage. She began to frantically dig through, and then smiled in gratitude when Leila came and started helping her.

"We need to leave now," Miriam said as she dashed over to where they were digging.

Zainah gasped as a hand appeared. They continued digging, and soon the full body of a man, untouched by the fire, emerged. Zainah almost cried with relief when she felt the man's pulse and found he was still alive.

Miriam bent down and helped them carry him out of the plane.

They maneuvered through all the debris, trying to carry him out quickly without injuring themselves in the process. At last they came out of the fuselage.

"Let's hurry up and leave this place!" Miriam yelled with urgency. "We will have to come back later to bury the bodies."

They carried him away as fast as they could, knowing the plane would explode soon. Just as they got to the entrance of the camp, a loud explosion rocked the ground and threw them off their feet. Zainah tried to hold on to the man as she fell, but she couldn't. When at last, she got up with the others, she felt the man's pulse again to make sure he was still alive.

He suddenly opened his eyes, and she drew back in surprise. He looked at her, mumbled something, and then shut his eyes again.

Her heart raced as she stared at him. Something about him looked familiar, but she couldn't place it. His face, in spite of the blood trailing down it, was handsome, and he was a strongly built man. But what caught her attention were his eyes. They were hard and cold.

She came out of her reverie quickly and began to lift him up again. And then she realized there was nowhere to put him. There were only women and a few small children here. There was no place for a grown man.

As if she could read her mind, Miriam said, "Zainah, since you are our resident nurse, I need to ask: where are we going to place him as you tend to him?"

Zainah immediately knew. "In my tent," she said. "It will be easy for me to tend to him there."

"Are you sure that's a good idea?" Miriam asked, even as they carried him towards her tent.

"As you said, there is no other place to keep him.

My tent is the best place."

"And where will you be sleeping… or changing, if he is in your tent?" Leila asked.

Zainah shrugged. "I don't know yet," she answered. In spite of herself, she smiled at her friend, "Maybe yours?"

Leila smiled back.

They finally entered her tent and Zainah said, "Place him on his back. He has a gash on his chest." She knelt beside the man and tore open his shirt. He was wearing a necklace with a heart locket. She thought about removing it, but changed her mind. She examined the wound on his chest where blood was seeping out and saw it wasn't as deep as she had thought.

She immediately took a small scarf from the cushion beside her and applied pressure on the wound. She said, "Nadia, there are bandages behind that loom there; please get them for me. And Leila, please get some warm water, soap, and a clean towel. Also bring the antibiotic ointment inside that box over there, Nadia."

When they brought what she'd asked for, she worked quickly on the injured man while she prayed silently that he would heal quickly. He was alive, but out in this desert, his wounds could get infected quickly if care wasn't taken. That could be fatal.

She had her work cut out for the next few days. She wanted this man well and alive. For some reason, there was nothing she wanted more right at that moment.

*****

Audrey left the room with Ken, Sienna, and Bryan. They entered the elevator together and Audrey held Sienna's hand. Her emotions roiled with a mix of anxiety and anticipation.

She looked at Sienna and squeezed her hand. "We will finally find out where our brother is," she said. "At least I hope so."

Sienna squealed. "I am so excited!"

The elevator doors opened again and they exited into the mesmerizing hotel lobby with the huge raindrop-inspired chandelier. They strode through the lobby and found seats near the reception desk.

Audrey looked up and saw a man in a buttoned-down white shirt and graying hair enter the lobby. She recognized him as the investigator they had hired to find their brother. She had spoken a few times with him over Skype back in Rosefield. When he turned in their direction, she smiled and waved him over.

He sat on the sofa facing her and Ken. Sienna and Bryan were on the couch next to theirs.

Audrey looked at him and took a deep breath. She took Ken's hand for support and then asked, "So, you have news for us about our brother, Rafael?"

The man nodded and his expression turned grim. "It's not good news."

Audrey's heart plummeted.

Sienna said, "What do you mean?"

The man answered, "From my investigation, I found out Rafael was adopted when he was five. His birth mother is long dead, and I couldn't find any trace of him after that. It's very likely he was taken out of the country after his adoption."

Audrey shook her head. "No… Does that mean we won't ever be able to find him?"

The man said, "I can't help any more… However, I know someone who specializes in these kinds of cases. He might be able to help."

Hope reentered Audrey's heart and she asked, "How can we contact this person?"

The man brought out a card from his shirt pocket and handed it to her. "Here is all of his information. You can call him and then set up a meeting."

Audrey took the card and thanked the man. When he'd left, she said, "Well, it could have been worse. Let's call this guy immediately. Hopefully, he can truly help."

Audrey took out her phone from her purse and immediately called the number on the card. When the investigator picked up the phone, she introduced herself.

"I was given your number by the investigator I hired, Mr. Sanchez."

She told the man about her brother and what her investigator had said. She finally took a deep breath and asked if he thought he could find her brother.

"I think I might be able to find him," the man said in a thick Spanish accent.

They set a date and time to meet, and Audrey thanked him before ending the call. She smiled. "He said he can help. We will meet him here tomorrow, at about this time."

She took Ken's hand again and looked at Bryan and Sienna. "So, guys, now that we have hired this investigator, Ken and I have decided to hire you guys."

Sienna lifted her brows and Bryan tilted his head toward her.

"Hire us as what?" Sienna asked.

"As chaperones," Audrey answered.

Bryan laughed and Sienna giggled.

Ken shook his head. "We are serious, guys. We both decided we need your help, especially now we are on this vacation."

Sienna's smile faded. "I didn't know you guys were struggling. You seem so strong." She faced Bryan. "I remember what it was like, babe. We struggled with staying pure, didn't we?"

Bryan smiled. "We sure did." He looked at Sienna. "I think I struggled more than you did, though."

She shook her head. "No... you have no idea how much I was struggling with my thoughts." She sighed loudly. "I'm so glad that's over, and I can have you all to myself whenever I want."

He beamed and kissed her softly.

Audrey coughed. "You guys aren't helping at all. It's talk like this that makes things worse." She eyed them. "Are you both going to be our chaperones or not?"

Sienna looked at her and said, "Okay, okay, we will be your chaperones. But what exactly does that even entail? Are we supposed to follow both of you everywhere, even at night?"

"Just knowing you aren't far away will suffice," Ken answered. "You don't have to follow us everywhere all the time."

"Good," Bryan said and smiled naughtily. "Because we intend to use this vacation to try to make a baby. Don't we, Sienna?"

Sienna nodded.

Audrey groaned. "Guys! It's not funny!"

Sienna giggled. "Sorry."

Ken moaned. "Please, no more talk about making babies."

"Alright," Bryan said. "We won't talk about that anymore. But get ready for us to be in your business all the time."

"That's exactly what we want," Audrey said.

"This does remind me of our Bible school and the rules there."

"It isn't a rule… we just want to make sure we don't do anything before our wedding that we will regret," Audrey quipped.

Bryan said, "I know." He looked at Sienna and added, "We understand how you guys feel and we will try our best to help."

"Thanks," Audrey smiled. "We need all the help we can get."

*****

Richie's anger management class was made up of ten people seated in a circle facing each other. The class counselor sat with the group. Lauren and a few of the spouses sat outside the circle, quietly watching.

Lauren listened as a man whose wife sat next to her told how he used to scream at his wife all the time. "I knew I needed help the day I hit her. It was the first time, and I felt horrible after I'd done it." He looked down, shame clouding his features. "I promised my wife I would get help immediately.

That was how I came here. Since I started attending the classes, I have stopped shouting at Irene. Whenever I get angry, I use the techniques Jack taught us, and my anger gradually subsides."

Lauren discreetly turned to look at Irene, the man's wife. She had tears in her eyes. Lauren wasn't sure if they were tears of hurt or of pride in her husband's progress.

Each person in the group told how they were managing their anger better since they had begun to attend the class. When Richie's turn came, Lauren held her breath, anxiously waiting for him to speak.

"Since I started attending the classes," he began, "they have helped me realize how badly I treated my wife, Lauren." He pointed at her. "I called her and told her how the classes were helping me, and she decided to come back."

He went on to speak about the mess he'd made of their marriage and how he intended to make things better. Lauren listened, her heart swelling with love for him. They would start anew from today and build a marriage that would be better than anything they had ever dreamed of.

After everyone had spoken, the counselor reminded them of their breathing exercises and all they had been taught in the previous class.

The class ended an hour later, and Lauren drove home with Richie. They sat in the living room together, and she turned to him and smiled. "I am so proud of you for beginning to make the necessary changes we need in order to make our relationship better."

He turned to her, and she blinked at the angry

glint in his eyes. "I'm not the only one who needs to make changes, Lauren. You do too."

Lauren raised her brows. "I didn't say you were the only one who needed to make a change." She studied his face. Even though his anger had put her in the hospital a couple of times, he still thought that she was partly to blame for the breakdown of their marriage. This was the time to be careful with what she said so his anger wouldn't flare up. She sighed. "I just wanted…"

He interrupted her. "If you hadn't been shacking up with that Ken guy, who I learned was your ex that last time, I wouldn't have gotten so angry."

Her jaw dropped. She'd thought he was only partly blaming her for the breakdown of their marriage, when in actual fact he fully blamed her for it. She stared at him for a brief moment. To him, she was the reason why he had gotten so angry that he'd beat her up and left her injured. If Ken hadn't scared him off by pointing a gun at him, who knew what more he would have done to her. Ken had rushed her to the hospital that day because Richie had succeeded in opening up her wounds and leaving her with a broken leg.

She reminded him of what he'd done that day, and he looked away. "You should never have moved to your ex-fiancé's house. It just wasn't right."

"I had no choice," she said to him. "I couldn't take any of your rage anymore, and I had nowhere else to go."

He turned back to her and the look in his eyes caused her to shift away from him. Her heart thudded in fear and she shook her head. She knew where this look had led before.

He snarled. "You are actually justifying living with your ex even though you are a married woman?"

"No, Richie," she shrunk back from him. Her voice shook as she said, "Remember what you were taught in your anger management class. Take a deep breath and try to let go of your..."

He grabbed her hand. "Don't tell me what I should or shouldn't do!"

"You're hurting me, Richie," she cried out. She tried to pull her hand away but his grip was too strong.

He stared into her eyes for a full minute, his blazing with anger. At last, he let her go and sighed loudly.

She sprang up and looked down at him. "I don't think returning to you was a good idea. Maybe I should leave."

He looked up at her with sad eyes. "I'm really sorry, Lauren. I'm trying. Please don't go. I need you."

"You are still the same angry man..."

"No... I am changing. Can't you see? I would have let my anger take over before and it would have ended really badly. But today, I didn't let it get the best of me. I didn't hit you, did I? I would have before."

She started to shake her head, and he pleaded again. "Please, Lauren. Don't go!"

She didn't say anything for a long moment and then she gave a long sigh. "Alright. I'll stay. But that has to be the last time you get so angry that you hurt me in any way."

He nodded vigorously.

She sat beside him again, but at the edge of the seat.

He shifted closer to her and took her in his arms. "What can I do to make it up to you?" he asked.

"Just promise that you will keep putting into practice everything you're taught in your class."

"I promise I will." He kissed her passionately until she melted in his arms and kissed him back. When they came up for air, she smiled and said, "And there is another thing you can do to make it up to me."

"What?"

"I want to be kissed every day the way you just kissed me now. Can you do that?"

He smiled and nodded. "I definitely can." He drew her close and claimed her lips once more.

*****

"Trisha, I'm here," Paula said. "Ruby will be fine. Go to your bookstore."

Trisha picked up her car keys from the coffee table and her purse from the sofa. She kissed her baby daughter cradled in her best friend's arms one more time. "It's not that I don't trust you to watch her, Paula, but…"

"I understand how you feel. You are leaving her for the first time, but she will be fine." Paula gave her a reassuring smile.

Trisha nodded. "Remember to call me if you need anything. I'll be back in two hours."

Paula nodded and bent to kiss Ruby on her forehead.

Trisha sighed longingly, and then quickly left the

house before she would change her mind. Like Paula had said, she hadn't left the house or her baby girl since she'd come back from the hospital. She'd been blessed with friends who had rallied around her to help with virtually everything. She was grateful to them, especially to Paula, who came almost every day to help her out. Paula was a housewife with two children. When her husband went to work and her kids to school, she had come to watch Ruby while Trisha did some housework.

Trisha entered her car and started it. She had to go to the bookstore because some of the books she'd ordered before she gave birth would arrive today. They were supposed to be brought directly to the store, and she had to be there when they arrived. Nothing short of that would have convinced her to leave the house. And, thankfully, Paula was there to help, or she would have had to take her baby with her.

She finally got to the store, exited her car, and opened her purse to get the front keys. She gasped when she bumped into something. She raised her head and her eyes widened in surprise.

"Trisha!"

She smiled hesitantly. "Frank! How are you?"

He nodded. "I'm good." He looked her over in that same way he did whenever she saw him—like she was a precious and fragile work of art that needed to be handled with care. It made her uncomfortable, the way he always looked at her. Every time she saw him, she had a vague feeling of guilt because of what had happened when they were teenagers. It was such a long time ago, yet the guilt hadn't completely disappeared. She didn't have much of a relationship with him anymore, but he was still good friends with Audrey.

He grinned. "You look great, Trisha. As always. I heard you had your baby. I would have come to visit, but…" His voice trailed off.

She knew what he wanted to say. He didn't want to come because of Stan. Without thinking it through, she said, "Stan isn't in the house anymore. We are divorced now."

A light entered his eyes that made her want to groan. The light disappeared almost immediately, and he looked at her and said, "I'm sorry to hear that, Trisha."

"It's okay." She couldn't resist looking into his eyes. He seemed genuinely sorry, which was baffling considering how he felt about her. She quickly turned away and went to unlock the bookstore. She felt his eyes on her as she opened the door and entered.

Turning around, she smiled and invited him in.

He entered and looked around. "I haven't been in here in years."

She studied him as he picked up a spy novel and opened it. He'd been gangly and pimply when they were teenagers, and for some reason that image had stayed in her mind. As she studied him, she noticed that not only had he filled out and was brawny now, he'd become quite a handsome man. She had been so absorbed with Stan through the years that she had never really noticed . . . or had never wanted to.

He suddenly turned, and she quickly looked away, embarrassed.

He probably saw me gaping at him. That's not good.

To defer the awkwardness, she asked, "So, how is your police work going?"

He shook his head. "I left there four months ago. I have my own restaurant now. It's in Green Valley."

Another thing I didn't know about him. She smiled warmly. "Oh wow, I didn't know that you had a major career change. Congrats on the restaurant."

He nodded and then said, "I guess I'll leave now. It was really nice seeing you again, Trish."

"It was," she said. He started to walk out the door, and for some reason she said, "You can come to the house and see the baby whenever you like."

He turned around and beamed. "I will."

When he left, she scolded herself for inviting him to the house. Knowing he still liked her, she might as well have asked him out. Why… oh why did I invite him? Hopefully, he wouldn't take her up on her offer. The last thing she needed now, after just finalizing her divorce, was another relationship. And certainly not a relationship with Frank.

Why not? A small voice whispered in her ear.

She sighed. Starting another relationship now seemed really wrong to her. And after what she did to Frank when they were younger, stringing him on when she didn't feel the same way about him as he did her, was not what she was prepared to do.

She brushed aside every thought of romance and relationships. Heading to the sofa at the far end of the store, she sat and opened her novel to read while she waited for her books to arrive.

FOUR

Hassan paced back and forth, running his hands frantically through his hair as he did. He kicked the rock in front of him, ignoring the pain the action brought, and sighed loudly in frustration. It had been three days since Faizan and the men had left for Spain, and still there was no news of them or of any bombing in Madrid.

He looked into the distance as though at any minute he would see Faizan walking up to him with his usual arrogant strut, and then he sighed again.

What has become of them?

Two days after they had left, he had asked one of the men to find out about them. The man had returned to tell him he'd heard nothing. It was as if they'd just disappeared into thin air. He had been distraught and had decided to send for a famed tracker. The man was already on his way. Hopefully, he would be able to find out what had happened to Faizan and the men. If there was any chance any of them were alive, or if the weapons could be recovered, he would take it.

A stranger walked up to him with one of the guards, and he guessed it was the tracker he had sent for. The men reached him, and he waved the guard away.

"You are Ahmed, the tracker?" he asked the stranger.

The diminutive man nodded.

Hassan said, "You've been briefed about my people who went missing a few days ago?"

Ahmed nodded again. He seemed a man of few words. As long as he could find Faizan and the other men, Hassan was fine with that.

"And you are sure you can find them?"

"I am."

"Then go. You will be rewarded handsomely when you do find them."

Ahmed nodded again, turned around, and walked away.

Hassan kept staring into the distance long after he was gone. Allah's will had not yet been done and half of their manpower and boxes of ammunition were missing. It was imperative that the men be found as soon as possible, dead or alive.

*****

Zainah deftly cleaned the injured man's wounds and then changed the bandages on his chest and arm. As she cleaned the wound on his forehead, she studied his face. He was indeed a handsome man, with lush, dark hair and a manly, sculptured face with a bushy beard. The color of his eyes, whenever he opened them briefly, was a curious combination of gold and green.

For the past three days, she'd tried to nurse him back to health as he lay on her sleeping mat. She mostly fell asleep on the other side of the room. He woke up at very brief intervals, and she gave him water to drink and a bit of food, which he mostly refused. He slipped back into sleep almost immediately after.

Even though Leila had agreed to have her stay in her room, Zainah didn't want to impose on her friend, as the individual tents were tiny. Apart from that, she felt more comfortable staying in her room and watching over this man as he slept.

And it was a good thing that she had. The wound on his chest had somehow become infected, and he'd been delirious. But she had it under control now and he was getting better. She gazed at him, wondering what his story was. Were the other men he had been traveling with friends of his or were they strangers? If they were friends, he would be distraught when he awoke and discovered they were all dead.

She looked up as someone came into the tent.

"Leila, what are you doing up at this time? It's late."

"I could ask you the same question," Leila said, sitting down across from Zainah and her unconscious visitor.

"Since the infection," Zainah said, "I try to clean his wounds more regularly."

"I couldn't sleep. Since the evening prayers ended, I've been thinking."

"About what?" Zainah asked. She went out of the tent for a second, poured out the water she'd used to clean the stranger's wounds and came back in.

"About what we were discussing the other day. The more I think about it, the more I am beginning to realize that I do want a family of my own… before it's too late."

Zainah sat beside her friend on the red-and-gold rug opposite the sleeping man. She looked at Leila with concern and said, "But you know that is almost impossible here." She smiled and said in jest, "Unless you want to marry that man over there."

Leila looked at the man and then turned back to Zainah. "I wish I could. He's really handsome, but I don't know if he's a Christian or married."

Zainah shook her head and chuckled. "I was just joking, Leila. Are you really serious about wanting to get married? How do you intend to make that happen when there are no men here…" she nodded at the man, "apart from him?"

"I am thinking of leaving the camp."

Zainah gasped. "You can't, Leila! This place is a safe haven for people like us. Where will you go?"

"I don't know yet, but I'm seriously thinking about it." Her eyes searched Zainah's. "Haven't you ever thought about having a family of your own, Zainah?"

Zainah sighed. Not again. She'd been trying to forget all about that, but the presence of this handsome man in her tent had made it virtually impossible. Now Leila was adding to the difficulty. Again, she considered telling Leila about the dream and what the voice in her dream had told her, but she changed her mind once more. Instead, she said, "I think about it sometimes, but since I know it's impossible, I don't dwell on it. Why should I spend precious time worrying about things I have no control over? Besides, I love this place. I would never consider leaving."

She put her hand on Leila's arm. "I think you should seriously pray about how you are feeling. The Lord cares about us. If having a husband and children are in His plan for your life, then He will bring it to pass no matter how impossible it seems."

Leila smiled sadly and then nodded.

Zainah pressed her lips together thoughtfully. The words she'd just spoken caused her emotions to churn. Was it God's plan for her life as well? Did she really believe that, in spite of how impossible it seemed, she might one day get married and have her own children?

Instinctively, she looked over at the man on the mat and her heart thudded. What if the Lord had sent him and he was the one for her?

No, that cannot be. I made a vow to God.

Her eyes widened when his suddenly snapped open.

He turned, looked her in the eye and murmured something she couldn't make out.

Leila gasped. "He's awake! What does he want?"

Zainah stood up and went to stoop beside him. "What did you say?" she asked him.

He shut his eyes and then opened them again. He frowned as his eyes searched her face, as though he was trying to figure out if she was someone he knew.

"Do you want some water?" she asked him.

His expression became puzzled and he murmured again.

She took the jug of water beside his sleeping mat,

poured some into a cup and put it to his lips. He drank a little, lay back again, shut his eyes and went back to sleep.

Zainah stood and went to sit beside Leila again. "He awakens like this at odd times and murmurs something. Sometimes, he drinks the water I offer him and other times he doesn't. He always goes back to sleep almost immediately after."

"And does he eat?" Leila asked.

"Once in a while… and very little. I am hoping he comes out of this state soon so he can start to eat well and regain his strength."

"I wonder where he's from," Leila said.

Zainah shrugged, but she'd wondered about that numerous times since they had found him at the wreck.

Leila whispered, "Maybe you will marry him after he's completely well."

"Leila! Stop that! He's not some toy that was dropped here so he could be my husband."

"I didn't say he was. But miracles can happen." She chuckled. "Maybe he will be so grateful that you saved his life that he will fall in love with you and profess his undying love. Besides, look at you. You are a beautiful girl. How can any man resist falling for you when they see you every day?"

"Leila!"

"If you don't want him though, can I have him?"

"Oh Lord, please help me!" Zainah exclaimed. "I thought this place was for women who had totally dedicated their lives to following the Lord. We aren't supposed to be thinking of all this."

Leila shrugged and stood up. "I have to go. It's my turn to prepare this evening's meal. I'll see you after the prayers." Leila began to leave the tent.

"Leila?"

She turned back. "Yes?"

"About what you said earlier, please reconsider. I'd miss you terribly if you left."

Leila looked up, her face thoughtful. She looked at Zainah again and said, "I don't know, Zainah. I think we have to find our priorities in this world. If it's not part of God's plan for me to get married, I will submit to it. But I think I owe it to myself to at least try and see what is out there."

"You already know what's out there, Leila. Greed, lasciviousness and persecution for us who believe in Jesus."

Leila turned around and left the tent.

Zainah stooped down again and watched the sleeping man as his chest rose and fell. She groaned and stood abruptly. If only Leila had not planted this idea into her mind. Now all she could think about as she looked at him was having this good-looking man fall for her.

She sighed again. Who was she deceiving? She'd been thinking about that even before Leila said anything. Or more accurately, she'd been trying to prevent herself from falling for him. She knew nothing about him, and yet she sometimes stayed watching him for hours as he slept.

Lord, why did you bring him here, and to me? Why?

She gasped when she heard a clear whisper in her ear, "To save his life."

"I have tried to do that, Lord," she said. "He's on his way to full recovery."

She shut her eyes as it dawned on her that it

wasn't only his physical life God wanted her to save. Contrary to what Leila had said, God hadn't brought him here to be her husband. He had been brought here because, whoever he was, his soul needed to be saved. She was certain of that.

*****

Faizan opened his eyes and for the first time in what seemed like months, he didn't feel nauseated or like he was in a fog. He groaned as he licked his lips. His mouth felt parched, and he looked around him. He'd groggily noted the room he was in some time before. It was a small room with bright red and gold furnishings, mostly rugs and cushions. But it wasn't the room furnishings that interested him. It was the beautiful dark-skinned woman who gave him water and food every time he woke up. He couldn't see her anywhere. Usually she was standing beside him whenever he awoke.

He lifted his head and tried to sit up, but he couldn't. He coughed and said weakly, "Water."

The woman appeared by his side almost like a miracle, and he said again, "Water!"

She went and poured a cup of water for him. When she brought it and placed it on his lips like she usually did, he tried to grab the cup from her. He grumbled, "Let me hold it!" He didn't like being treated like a child.

She beamed at him. "You can talk now!" she exclaimed with an excited expression on her face.

He ignored her and took the cup, but he felt too weak to hold it, and the water spilled on the ground. He groaned in frustration and shut his eyes briefly. When he opened them, she had refilled the cup with more water. She placed it to his lips, and he swallowed his pride and drank.

He drained the cup and she smiled again. "Good. You finished your water."

He watched her as she placed the cup back on the jug beside his sleeping mat. When she came and stooped beside him again, he looked at her face and asked, "Where am I?" It was the question he'd been dying to ask her for a long time but had not been able to.

She smiled sadly. "You are somewhere safe."

He scowled at her, dissatisfied with the answer she had given him. He was used to plain answers to his questions and did not appreciate her response. He tried again, "Who are you and how did I get here?"

"My name is Zainah," she said. "We found you in a plane wreck not far from here."

His eyes suddenly grew round as he remembered the mission and then the plane falling to the ground on their way there. Panic took over his heart. Where were the men? Were they alive? He had to complete the mission no matter what. He had to fulfill God's will.

"I have to go," he muttered, more to himself than to her.

"You can't leave! You're not well enough."

He ignored her and tried to lift his head. He immediately became nauseated and moaned.

"Lie back down," she said softly and touched his shoulder.

He turned on her and said, "Don't try to tell me what to do!" He struggled again to rise and felt himself begin to slip back into unconsciousness. He muttered a curse word and then lay back on the rug.

She looked down at him, frowning. "I told you that you weren't strong enough to leave."

His heart filled with rage. "Who are you to tell me what I can or cannot do?" He cursed her.

She blinked rapidly and then backed away from him... but she didn't leave the tent. She sat across from him and stared.

He felt a small sense of satisfaction at the wariness he saw on her face. Good. Let her fear me. No one, especially not a mere woman, tells me what to do!

After a minute, he was surprised when she came to sit beside him with a bowl of water and started to change his bandages. He frowned again. So, maybe she isn't that afraid of me.

His heart pounded as he looked up at her cleaning his wound. She was truly beautiful. He noticed she wasn't wearing a hijab or any head covering. Her curly dark hair was held back in a single braid, reaching to her waist. He asked her why her head wasn't covered.

She shrugged, but didn't answer.

"Answer me!" he barked, and then sighed as weakness overwhelmed him.

She shook her head at him, a grimace on her face. "Why are you so angry?" And then her face suddenly softened. "Were those men on the plane your friends?"

He blinked. "My men! What happened to them? Are they somewhere here as well?"

The expression on her face caused panic to rise

up in him again. He asked firmly, "What has become of them?"

She didn't say a word.

He snarled. "Tell me!"

She shut her eyes and shook her head. "They are… they are all gone."

He stared at her, trying to contain his anger. "Gone where?"

"They are all dead. I'm sorry."

His heart twisted and he felt like passing out again, but he drew himself together. The men had been dedicated members of the group. They could have died as noble martyrs. Instead, they had perished in a plane crash.

He turned away from the woman as fury overwhelmed him. Not only had he not been able to complete his mission, he was weakly lying in this strange woman's tent while his men were all dead. He felt her hand on his shoulder and turned.

"I'm so sorry for your loss," she said. "I've been praying for you. The Lord Jesus heals every broken heart."

His eyes widened in astonishment and then outrage. She was a filthy Christian! No wonder she hadn't answered when he'd asked about the hijab. He turned to her and said coldly, "So, you are a Christian, are you?"

She hesitated for a beat and her eyes filled with fear. And then the fear disappeared, and she answered, "Yes, I am. I am a lover of Jesus."

He cursed her again, shut his eyes and laughed. "So, all this time, I have been in a Christian's tent, eating your filthy food and drinking your accursed water." He opened his eyes, and for a brief second he thought about wrapping his hand around her throat and snuffing her life out, but he put away the thought. He didn't have the strength to do that, and there was something about her that made the thought seem repulsive. Instead, he lifted his head. This time, he was determined to leave this place or die trying. He couldn't go on staying there. He had to leave and find a way to complete his mission or at least go back to the caves and try again soon.

He sat up with the little strength in him and struggled to rise, fighting the dizziness he was feeling. He was surprised the woman hadn't tried to make him lie down again. Maybe she was now truly afraid of him. For some reason, the thought didn't give him the same satisfaction it had earlier.

He finally rose to his feet and shut his eyes as waves of nausea went through him. He staggered forward and then fell back. Just before he landed on the floor, the woman caught him. He saw the strain with which she held him from falling, and he sighed. He rolled away from her onto the mat.

He shut his eyes and felt himself beginning to black out. The struggle to rise had been way too much for him.

The last thing he saw before he faded away was the woman touching his forehead and whispering a prayer for him.

*****

Lauren put on a simple A-line dress as she got ready to go to the counseling class Richie had told her about. She didn't know anything about the marriage counselor except for what Richie had told her—that the man had been recommended to him by a friend of his. He had already attended a session with the man, but he wanted her to go with him so they could start the process of seriously repairing their relationship.

When Richie had brought up the counseling the day before, she had been happy about it. He'd said, "I want to make everything between us better." She was excited about going for counseling with him. As much as their physical intimacy was good, the emotional part needed lots of work.

Lauren slipped a pair of black sandals on her feet and went to sit in the living room to wait for Richie. He had gone to his job at the law firm very early that morning, but he'd promised her that he would come back early so they could go to the counselor's office. She had started to think about working again. She'd been an elementary school teacher before all the problems with Richie had started. After being asked a few times about all the scars she'd tried so hard to hide, and after many absent days, she had quit. Somehow, that had even pacified Richie for some time and his violence had abated… until it started again after a few nights out with his friends. She had to bring up the topic of going back to work soon with him, but she wasn't looking forward to doing that.

The front door opened and Richie walked in with a big smile on his face. Her heart skipped a beat. He looked so handsome and happy. She couldn't resist standing to kiss him. He held her for a few seconds.,

"I can see you are ready. Give me a few minutes to freshen up and I will be too," he said, loosening his tie and unbuttoning his dress shirt. He smiled at her again and left the living room.

Twenty minutes later, he came back wearing a navy-blue t-shirt and black jeans. "Ready," he said.

She got into his car, and he drove to the counselor's office. She was surprised it was just a five-minute drive away from their house.

Entering the counselor's office, a one-story brick building, they waited at the reception area. There was only one other couple waiting—an older pair who looked like they were about to come to blows any second. Lauren surreptitiously watched them and hoped with all her heart that when she and Richie were their ages, they would not be like them. That was why they were here; to make sure that did not happen.

The older couple was called in first, and Lauren glanced at them as they left the waiting area. She whispered to Richie as they did, "Did you see the way that couple was with each other just now? I hope we are not like them when we are older."

Richie shook his head and then looked up at the TV set showing a game of football.

Bored, her mind soon drifted to the Gibsons. They had called twice since she'd left Rosefield. She had answered neither of their calls. Hopefully, Ken did not yet know that she had gone back to Richie. She shuddered, thinking about how disappointed he would be if he knew.

She shrank as she thought about it, and then she shook the feeling of guilt off. It was her life, and this was what she'd decided was the best path to take. She loved Richie and she wanted to give him another chance. Everyone deserved that.

About forty-five minutes later, the older couple

came out looking and acting a lot less hostile. The counseling session had clearly helped them. Lauren hoped hers and Richie's would do the same.

The receptionist finally beckoned to them and told them they could go into the counselor's office. "The second door down that hallway." She pointed at a hallway to her right.

Lauren and Richie stood in front of the door and knocked. A male voice called out, "Come in," and they entered.

A middle-aged, clean-shaven man looked up from his computer and smiled at them. "Welcome. Mr. and Mrs. Patterson?"

They nodded.

He extended his hand out to them. Richie shook it first and then she did.

"I'm Peter Lester," he said to them. "He looked down briefly at his computer and then looked up at them. "I see a domestic violence case here?"

Lauren didn't say anything, but Richie said "Yes."

Peter Lester looked at her and smiled. "You decided to stay with him. That is what I like to see. I usually counsel the women involved in cases like this not to totally give up on the men. They could be going through a lot at work or it could be a problem on the inside that they are trying to sort out. They lash out at you because you are the closest person to them, but it really isn't about you."

Lauren blinked in surprise as she listened to the man. This wasn't what she had expected to hear when Richie had told her they were going for marriage counseling. Her stomach twisted with worry. This man was essentially saying that she had to stay with Richie even when he hurt her. He was removing the blame of Richie's actions from him.

He kept on talking, but she stopped listening to him. She wouldn't listen to a man who was supposed to help make their relationship better but, in truth was actually going to make it worse if his advice was followed. From the corner of her eye, she saw Richie soaking up everything the man was saying.

Of course he would. He'd found someone who was taking the responsibility of dealing with his anger away from him. Where did Richie even find this counselor?

She suddenly tuned the counselor in again when he said something about "giving your husband everything he wants." She looked at the man and found he was looking at her. She said to him, "Umm... sorry, I didn't get what you just said."

The man smiled. "I said that as a wife, you are supposed to cater to all your husband's needs, all the time. It's your duty. In that way, he will always be satisfied and have no cause to resort to violence."

Her jaw dropped at the man's words, but she quickly recovered. She pressed her lips tightly together so she wouldn't say something she would regret and waited in silence for the man to finish speaking.

He did, twenty minutes later, and asked if they had any questions to ask him. Richie said he did, but she shook her head.

Richie said, "I've wanted children for a long time, but my wife has always been hesitant about it."

Lauren shot him a surprised, angry look, but he went on.

"We decided early on in our marriage that we

would wait for a few years before starting a family… but it's been years since we got married and we
still don't have any kids."

Lauren's stomach boiled with anger. How could
Richie just bring this up here without talking to
her about it first?

"I've been telling my wife for some time that I
want kids and that it's time for us to start a family,
but she won't budge. I just wanna know what to
do." Richie turned to her. "Is there any advice you
can give to my wife about it or is there anything I
can do to help her take it seriously?"

Lauren folded her arms across her chest as embarrassment settled on her. She listened with growing anger as the counselor listed what her duties as
a wife was. He basically told her she had to listen to
Richie all the time, it wasn't fair on Richie, and that
her husband was justified in wanting children now.
Maybe Richie's violent behavior was in reaction to
her refusal to give him the kids he wanted so badly.

Everything was about Richie. She wanted to
scream, "What about me?" but she held her peace.
Once she got home, she would confront Richie
about this and ask where he had found this counselor.

The man finished his strange talk minutes later.
and at last he told them they could go and return
next week for another session. Lauren couldn't
wait to get out of the office and out of the building.
She didn't shake the man's hand when he extended
it this time.

In the car, on the way home, she changed her
mind about confronting Richie. Demanding that
he tell her where he'd found the counselor might

trigger his anger. It would be the wrong thing to do. Maybe she could tease him about it and then gently suggest they find another counselor because if she had to return to Peter Lester's office again, she might be the one who needed to start attending anger management classes.

When they got home, she searched her mind for the best way to let him know what she had decided—that she would not attend the sessions again and that they needed to get another marriage counselor.

He turned to her as they went up to their bedroom and said, "It was a good session, wasn't it?"

She studied his face. Even though he was smiling, there was a look in his eyes that was challenging; like he was daring her to say anything bad about the counselor and the mess that had spilled out of the man's mouth. Lauren sighed. If she said anything negative now, he would get angry, and who knew what that would lead to, especially now that he'd been told his anger was not his fault.

She decided to say nothing today. Instead, she would search out another counselor and then tell him she wanted them to try a different one.

He asked his question again, his mouth turned up in anger this time.

She smiled and nodded.

Her non-verbal acquiescence seemed to satisfy him and he grinned at her. "I can't wait for the next session," he said.

She nodded again and decided to start searching immediately for a replacement so she wouldn't have to return to that unbearable counselor.

FIVE

Audrey listened as Bryan spoke about the so-called 'watchers' at the Bible college. They were having dinner in a restaurant at their hotel and its cheery ambience matched their moods.

"A few days after our wedding," Bryan said, looking at her and then at Ken, "I came to Sienna's class to get something from her. We decided to leave the class together. Outside, we saw that guy who reported Sienna and I to the provost. He scowled at us when he saw we were holding hands. He probably didn't know we'd gotten married." Bryan shook his head. He turned to Sienna. "Tell Ken and Audrey what you did, my love."

Sienna chuckled. "Well, I pulled Bryan into my arms and kissed him passionately in front of the guy."

Audrey and Ken roared with laughter.

Audrey exclaimed, "You didn't, Sienna!"

"I did. You should have seen his face."

"You've become such a naughty girl, Sienna! I didn't know you had it in you." Audrey turned to look at Bryan. "What have you done to my sister?" she asked, smiling.

Bryan took Sienna's hand from the table and kissed it. "I've always known she had a naughty streak. But she's also the nicest person I know." He looked into his wife's eyes. "I can't wait for us to have kids so they can have your mischievous personality."

Audrey sighed as she watched them. So much for making them chaperones, she thought almost sullenly. The way they were looking at each other, as though they couldn't get to their room fast enough so they could be alone, made her slightly uncomfortable. She turned her eyes away from them. She had to remember that they were newlyweds. It wasn't their fault that she and Ken had had to postpone their wedding.

She turned to look at Ken. He was watching them with interest. He finally said to them, "I would have said you both should get a room, but we haven't even had dinner yet."

Sienna looked at Ken and shrugged.

The waiter came with their starters and placed the food in front of them. Ken brought up the discussions they'd already had with the investigator. They were supposed to meet up with him again the next day to discuss any new leads.

Forty minutes later, the waiter brought their main course—a massive seafood platter.

They all continued to chat while they ate, moving from one topic to the other. By the third course, Audrey was feeling a little sleepy. They'd had a long day, visiting some tourist sites before finally coming back to the hotel to change and then hurrying here for dinner.

Half an hour later, Bryan and Sienna got up to leave.

Ken frowned at them. "You guys are the worst chaperones in the whole world."

They sat down again. "We should be leaving now." Sienna pointed at Audrey. "Look at Audrey. Any minute from now, she'll be fast asleep with her head on the table."

Audrey smiled. "Ken, I think they are right. We should definitely leave now."

They all got up and left the restaurant. Once they got to their apartment, instead of going to sleep, they all sat in the living room and continued chatting. Ken told them one story after another about his hairy adventures at the Miami police department.

They talked late into the night. Audrey soon drifted off to sleep. She awoke when Ken lightly tapped her on the shoulder and called her name.

She looked at him through sleepy eyes and mumbled, "I'm so tired. I think I'll just sleep here." She shut her eyes and heard Ken chuckle. She felt herself being lifted from the couch and then placed on her soft mattress. She opened her eyes and smiled at Ken as he stood over her.

"Thanks, Ken," she said, yawning. She raised her hand with her eyes closed and said, "A good night kiss, please."

She felt his lips on hers, but just as he started to pull away, she held on to him and kissed him again. "For being such a great fiancé."

He kissed her nose. "You look so cute with one eye open."

She opened both her eyes and kissed his cheeks and then his lips. He returned her kiss with fervor.

She shifted on the bed to give him more space and then held on tightly to him as they continued to kiss. As she drew even closer to him, it occurred to her that he was on her bed and that they were playing with fire now. She told herself to pull away, but instead, she wrapped her body tightly around his.

And then he thankfully tore himself away from her. He shook his head as though trying to clear it, sprang up from the bed and looked down at her. His eyes were glazed with desire, probably mirroring hers. "I had better leave now," he said huskily and backed away. "I'll see you tomorrow, Audrey." He turned around and walked out the door.

For more than an hour, she tossed and turned, knowing he was just next door. She could go to him right now and no one would know.

She shut her eyes and begged God to take away the raging desire in her. After another agonizing hour, she finally fell asleep.

*****

Zainah looked down at Faizan as he lay staring at the tent ceiling, a troubled look on his face. She clutched her Bible as though for protection from him and then gingerly sat down beside him. She'd made up her mind in spite of his outburst the day before to start reading the Bible to him. She instinctively knew that beyond all the rage was a man who needed to hear about the God who loved him dearly.

She was scared of what he would say when she started reading God's word to him. However, she was even more scared about what would happen if she didn't speak to him about his eternal soul. From his constant angry outbursts, it was clear that most Christians would be afraid of him and very few would have the courage to preach the gospel to him. But now, he was a captive audience because of his injuries and weakness. There was no better time to tell him about Christ's love.

He didn't move or acknowledge her presence as she sat watching him. She adjusted her scarf, having worn it so as not to offend him, and turned away to open her Bible. She quickly found the scripture she was looking for—John chapter three—and began to read the passage out loud.

He suddenly turned and barked at her, "Leave, now!"

She continued to read. When she got to verse sixteen, she emphasized each word, wanting him to understand God's love.

For God so loved the world that he gave his one and only Son, that whoever believes in him shall not perish but have eternal life.

He swore and began to curse her.

She stopped reading, shocked by his vehement attack. But he didn't stop cursing her.

At last, after a full minute of hate-filled words, he stopped, and snarled at her. "I would kill you if I could get up from here," he said coldly.

She stared at him in shock. The hatred in his eyes chilled her to the bone. She finally turned away from him, stood and left the tent.

Outside, she felt tears stinging her eyes. She

wanted him to be saved so badly, but how could she continue to speak to him about God's love when he spewed out such hatred and didn't allow her to talk at all? What sort of person said words like that? She shut her eyes for a second.

Lord, I don't know if I can do this.

She decided to speak with Miriam about it and headed for the woman's tent. She found Miriam in front of her tent, working on her loom.

"Miriam, I need to speak to you about something," she said.

Miriam looked up at her. "Does that something have anything to do with your injured visitor? I haven't even gone to your tent for some time to see how he is doing."

Zainah glanced at the children who were playing a game of hide and seek a few feet away and then turned back to Miriam. "He is fully awake now, getting better, and as angry as the devil himself." She blinked back her tears and continued. "I was trying to read to him from the scriptures today and teach him about God's love, but he wouldn't listen. He said unprintable words to me. How can I reach him when he won't listen and is so full of hatred?"

"You have to be patient, Zainah. You just started sharing the gospel with him and you expect him to act like a saint? How is that possible?"

"I don't expect him to act like a saint. Just a normal human being. He seems so ..."

"So like a sinner? That's because he is. Our Lord said that those who are well have no need of a physician, but those who are sick do. He said he didn't come to call the righteous but sinners to repentance. If that man in your tent acted like 'a normal human being' like you just said, then maybe he would not need someone like you."

"But I can't go on when he curses me so violently."

Miriam smiled at her. "The Lord has entrusted him to you because he knows you can handle everything he throws at you."

Zainah sighed. Miriam was right, of course. And it wasn't that she was about to give up. The man's words just hurt her more than she would ever care to admit. She smiled at Miriam in spite of herself. "Well… I guess I better get back to the tent. My visitor eagerly awaits me."

"That's the spirit," Miriam said, grinning. "And remember what I said. Don't give up on him no matter what. God's grace is enough for you."

Zainah nodded and went back to the tent, ready to face whatever the man threw at her. But before she entered, she prayed for patience. Most of all, she asked that God would fill her heart with His love—the same love she was trying to tell the angry man about.

*****

Faizan glanced around the feminine-looking tent that had been his abode for what seemed like an eternity. He just wanted to leave this place, but he couldn't. Now that woman had begun to read her book to him. He laughed without humor. She was really trying to convert him.

He noticed her Bible a few feet from where he lay and wished he could reach it so he could tear it to pieces. Then she would not be able to read to him from it any longer.

His heart filled with anger. She knew he was a captive here and couldn't move, so she was taking the opportunity to try to make him a Christian. The thought seemed so perverse to him. Yet there was something about her that inexplicably drew him every time he saw her. Maybe it was why he had cursed her so vehemently. He was trying to expel whatever it was that drew him to her.

He looked down at the wound on his chest. It was almost fully healed thanks to her. Because of her, he was alive. It puzzled him why she still took care of him when all he'd done was curse her. If their roles were reversed, he probably would have had her killed.

He took in a deep breath. Christians were such disgustingly weak people. If only he could leave this accursed place right now.

He looked up as she entered the room and glowered at her. "Get out, now!" he roared.

"I'm not leaving! This is my tent, in case you have forgotten." She went and picked up the Bible and opened it. She started to read from it again, a story about the prodigal son told by the prophet Isa who they claimed was the son of God. He tried to shut his ears from listening to the story, but somehow, he couldn't. Her voice reminded him of something he couldn't quite place. Something that shook him to the very core. He groaned and then turned his back to her.

The story somehow reminded him of how he'd yearned for the love of a father as a child. He remembered his adoptive parents. His mother, may Allah rest her soul in Jannah, was kind to him and he had loved her. But the one who had called himself his father hadn't particularly cared for him. He had never been present at home. And when he was, he'd made life difficult because he was always angry at his mother and at him.

A small voice whispered in his ear, "The way you are always angry now?"

Anger was necessary to survive where he had grown up. And in what he did now. He pushed the voice away. He continued to listen even though his back was still turned to her. When his parents had died and Mustafa took him, the man became not just his mentor but also a father figure. From him and the group they had belonged, he received the love of a father he'd never had. And because he was an only child and had always craved siblings, the members of the group became his brothers.

The woman began to speak about knowing the father in the story, a father who loved in spite of all the wrong the child had done. A father who loved unconditionally. His heart twisted as she talked. For some reason, he yearned to have that.

And then she said the father in the story, the one who had run to his unfaithful son, was God. He shook his head and finally blocked his ears from her lies. What sort of God loved like that?

The kind you have been yearning to know all your life.

He nearly gasped at the clear whisper in his ear. He shut his eyes and pressed away the confusing thought. Once again, for the umpteenth time that day, he prayed that Allah would grant him the strength to leave this tent so he could finally go and complete his mission in Spain.

*****

Lauren stirred in her sleep and mumbled. She felt someone shaking her shoulders again and then opened her eyes. Richie was standing over her, a notebook in his hands. She groaned. "I need to go back to sleep, Richie. I'm tired."

She shut her eyes again, but opened them when he roared, "Look at what I have in my hand!"

"What is it? You have a note..." She stopped talking when she saw it was her notebook. He had opened it to a page where she had written down the names of a few marriage counselors that she'd found on the internet. She sat up as her heart began to thud.

"What is this, Lauren?"

She wanted to ask him in a sarcastic voice what he thought the names and addresses looked like, but she thought better of it. From the furious expression on his face, that would be the wrong thing to do. She said nothing, and just stared at him.

"Why are you searching for other counselors when we already have one that is perfect?"

She couldn't hold back her anger anymore. "Perfect for whom, Richie? That guy doesn't know what he's talking about. I'm never going back to him again."

Richie's eyes flashed with anger. He sat beside her and said coldly, "We are going back... you and I." She opened her mouth to say "No," but he covered her mouth with his hand. "You will do exactly as I tell you, Lauren. I found that counselor personally and you insult me by saying he isn't good enough."

She grabbed his hand to take it off her mouth, but he shoved it away. He pressed his hand tightly over her mouth and grabbed her with his other hand. "Listen to me!" he shouted as she struggled to escape from him. "We have an appointment with the counselor tomorrow evening and you are coming with me. Do you understand?"

She shook her head.

His hand went around her neck and he tightened his grip until she felt herself choking. He asked again and she nodded, her eyes wide with fear and panic.

"Good!"

He released her and she held her throat, coughing and trying to get her breath back.

He stared her down. "Now, I don't want to ever find you trying to change our counselor." He picked up her notebook from the ground and tore out the page she'd written on. He crumpled the paper in his hand and then spat out, "It's time to get up! It's Saturday, and you remember that the counselor advised us to spend more time together during the weekends."

She nodded and scrambled out of bed.

He regarded her and said, "Get dressed! We are going out." He left the room, and she slid down on the floor and wept quietly. She had made a big mistake coming back. If only she had listened to Sally. She glanced around their bedroom and bit her lip. Tonight, she would secretly pack her things and leave him.

She thought about going to Ken's but decided against it. The last time she did, things had gone really badly in every way. Richie would probably trace her and find her there. And then he would do something that would get him thrown in jail for sure. She didn't want that for him. Also, she didn't want Ken to have any problems with his fiancé the way he had when she had stayed in his house the year before. She didn't even want him to know she'd come back to Richie. The only place she could go was back to Rosefield and the Gibsons'. Hopefully, they wouldn't be too angry with her for leaving without letting them know.

She ran her plan through her mind. Tonight, she would call a taxi and go to the airport. There, she would fly to Boise and then to Rosefield.

She heard Richie's footsteps approaching again and quickly stood up. She couldn't afford to get him angry again. She would pretend and cater to him until she could secretly leave tonight. And once she did, she would never return again.

*****

That night, while Richie was asleep, she quietly brought out a small duffel bag from her closet and began to throw a few of her clothes into it. She tiptoed to the bathroom and grabbed her toothbrush and toiletries. Coming back into the room, she glanced at him and saw he was still sleeping. She put the toiletries into the bag and zipped it up. She couldn't afford to take a lot more than she had, as she was afraid he would wake up and find her about to leave him.

She lifted the bag, tiptoed to the door, and then turned briefly to look at him. Her heart twisted when he turned, and then settled into its normal rhythm when he became still again. She went out of the room and went down the stairs as quickly and quietly as she could.

She got to the bottom of the stairs and then reached out to open the front door. And then she gasped. The door was locked, but the key, usually in the keyhole, wasn't there. Richie must have taken it out before they'd gone to bed.

Panicking, she went to the back door and found the key was not in that keyhole either. She blinked and then almost cried out in frustration.

What in the world am I going to do?

She took a deep breath to try to calm down. Where would Richie have kept the keys? she thought.

She went into the living room and searched everywhere to see if she would find the front or back keys. She didn't. She straightened and bit her lip, wondering where he could have kept them. Their bedroom was the most likely place, but if she woke him up by mistake while searching there, her escape would be thwarted. She decided to search the kitchen first while she bolstered up the courage to search the bedroom.

She started to head to the kitchen and then froze when she heard his footsteps coming down the stairs. Quickly, she went and hid her duffel bag under the couch. She sat and picked up the TV remote control.

He entered the living room just as she turned the television on.

"Lauren, why are you not in bed?"

She forced a smile. "I couldn't sleep so I decided to come down here to watch some TV."

He frowned and then came to sit beside her. "What do you want to watch?"

She inwardly winced but managed to keep her smile. "Umm… I don't know yet. But I'll find something."

He nodded. "I can't sleep either. I guess we'll watch TV together." He grinned at her and then put his hand around her shoulders.

She snuggled up to him while her mind raced. Clearly, she couldn't leave tonight. But on Monday, when he left for work, she would not hesitate to go. In the meantime, she had to do everything he said so he wouldn't hurt her again, the way he had the day before.

SIX

Audrey walked back into the hotel holding Ken's hand. Sienna and Bryan walked ahead of them. They had just returned from a day spent at Retiro Park. Just as they entered the elevator going up to their room, her cell phone rang. She brought it out of her purse and saw it was their private investigator. Her heart skipped a beat. Does he have good news for us?

"Hello," she said as she answered the call.

"Hello, Miss Gardner. I have news for you about your brother."

She held her breath, praying it was good news. She would be ecstatic if he'd found their brother. She put the phone on speaker so they could all hear what the man was going to say.

"I'm sorry to tell you that it's not very good news."

Her heart sank. "What did you find out?"

The man began to speak about what he had discovered. He'd found out that the couple who had adopted Rafael in Italy died when he was twelve.

After that, all he could find out was that Rafael had been taken out of the country.

Audrey felt the tears swimming in her eyes as her heart broke. She walked out of the elevator, the others behind her. "So, does that mean you weren't able to find out anything else about him?" she asked the investigator.

"I couldn't find any trace of him anywhere after that. It's like he just disappeared from the face of the earth."

Ken opened the door to their room and they all entered. Audrey took a deep breath and swallowed the sob threatening to escape her lips. "But do you think he's still alive?"

The man answered, "It's hard to tell. I really don't know at this time."

Sienna let out a sob, and Bryan held her close.

The man told her he was sorry and then the call ended. Audrey stood staring at the living room wall. She barely noticed the lavish surroundings. Sienna was in Bryan's arms, weeping. Finally, she couldn't take it anymore and fell into Ken's arms.

He held her and stroked her back as she cried. She had placed all her hope on this investigator, while praying fervently that their brother would be found. From what the investigator had just told them, it appeared their brother was dead as there was no trace of him. The thought broke her heart.

Her shoulders shook as she cried while Ken held her. She had really wanted Rafael to be at her wedding. In fact, she'd been imagining him there since the day they'd decided to search for him. Now they would never meet him.

Ken led her to the sofa while Bryan and Sienna went away, probably to their room.

Ten minutes later, she raised her head off Ken's chest and said, "I have to call Trish and tell her."

Ken nodded, his expression grim and sympathetic.

Audrey dialed Trisha's number and, when she picked up, asked if she was home.

"I am," Trish said. "What's up?"

"Is there anyone there with you?"

"Paula and Hannah are here."

Audrey exhaled and then told her about the news the investigator had given them. She bit her lip as Trish sniffled and then asked, her voice choked with emotion, what they planned to do next.

"What else can we do? We will stay for the remainder of our trip and then come back to Rosefield," Audrey answered.

She ended the call a minute later and exhaled again. She looked up at Ken. "Thanks for being here for me."

He frowned. "Where else would I be, Audrey? I'll always be here for you, no matter what."

She smiled at him and placed her head on his shoulder.

He kissed her hair. "I love you with all my heart." He whispered to her, "Everything will be fine. You'll see."

She looked up at him. Forever optimistic. She drew herself up and kissed him. "I love you, too." She stood, gazed longingly at him for a few seconds, and then went to her room with a heavy heart.

*****

Trisha gently placed Ruby in the stroller and smiled down at her. She took her daughter's hand, kissed it and then suddenly noticed how Ruby's eyes reminded her of Stan's. She hadn't seen him for weeks now. He hadn't even come to see his child since Trisha had given birth. He had gone AWOL. But she didn't care. She didn't want to see him right now, as she was enjoying this peaceful time taking care of her daughter.

She sighed sadly. The only thing that marred her serenity was the news about their brother, Rafael. She had been heartbroken after Audrey had told her he had disappeared following his adopted parents' deaths.

She looked up from the pram when the doorbell rang and frowned slightly. She wasn't expecting anyone today.

Maybe it's Paula, she thought. Once in a while, her friend dropped by without telling her, though she hardly came on the weekends.

Trisha lifted Ruby from her pram and carried her to the living room. She opened the door, expecting to see one of her friends. Her eyes widened in surprise when she saw the unexpected visitor at the door.

"Frank!"

"Hi, Audrey!" His eyes skimmed her, and then he searched her eyes. "If this isn't a good time, I can leave."

She shook her head. "No... I'm sorry. You can come in." She held the door wide open so he could enter.

He smiled at the baby in her arms. "How is she? She looks beautiful, just like her mother."

Trisha smiled back at him. "She is beautiful. And she's quite a good baby. She hardly cries." Trisha motioned for him to take a seat on the sofa and he did. When he asked if he could carry Ruby, Trisha was slightly surprised, but gently handed her to him. Her surprise increased when he carried her properly, like a newborn should be carried, without any instructions from her. Many of her visitors, especially the men, didn't know how to carry a newborn properly.

She sat next to him and said, "I'm impressed, Frank. You are carrying her like a pro."

Frank's eyes were on Ruby as he said, "After college, I lived with my brother and his wife for some time. She had a newborn that I adored and babysat many times."

They began to talk about their childhood and the times he and his brother, Michael, had come to their house to visit with his parents. They had been close family friends, then. She'd not known that he'd liked her until the Christmas he'd revealed his feelings for her in a grand way. The Christmas she and Stan had started dating.

Every time she remembered that day and how she had treated him, guilt wrapped itself around her. Even now as they talked, she felt slightly guilty. The fact that she and Stan were now divorced because Stan had proven an unfaithful husband made the guilt worse. Without a doubt, she had chosen the wrong guy.

As they talked, Trisha noted how easy it was to talk to him. She'd not imagined that it would be. She kept watching him holding and rocking Ruby while her heart twisted. If she had chosen him instead of Stan, she would probably still have a marriage now and a faithful father for her daughter. He was clearly good with kids. She had let youthful lust blind her.

He stopped talking and studied her as though he knew she was thinking about him rather than what he was saying. She told herself to look away as he scrutinized her face, but she couldn't. There was something entrancing about the way he was watching her now. His eyes held everything he felt for her, and she somehow felt special and safe. In a way, she knew he would give everything, including his life for her if need be.

Her heart thudded with a mixture of guilt and excitement. Maybe it was time to let her guard down and let him in. But Stan's many moral indiscretions suddenly flooded her mind and she looked away from him. She wasn't ready for another relationship, and maybe she never would be. She had married a dog rather than choose the saint before her. She had no right now to pull him in. She still didn't really like him as he did her. It would be wrong to tag him along and then break his heart for a second time. She didn't deserve him. He should be with someone who did. Someone who would love him as much as he loved her.

She brought up another topic about their high school days and breathed a sigh of relief when he stopped scrutinizing her. She would have to find a way to discourage him from coming here without being rude. It bothered her that he had never married. She had never even heard that he was in a serious relationship. Maybe she would try to find someone for him; secretly, of course. She could ask Audrey what type of girl he would like. She had many single friends looking for a good man. It was the least she could do for him.

A small measure of peace settled in her heart as

she made that decision. As soon as Audrey came back, she would make it her goal to get him a girlfriend. That might alleviate her guilt and also help him to find someone who would love him.

*****

Lauren entered the car with Richie after another annoying marriage counseling session. She sat in the passenger seat and buckled her seatbelt while she fumed. That idiotic counselor had given them even more preposterous counsel than the last time. Now she was pretty sure he was a stooge hired by Richie to be his 'yes man' and tell her what she needed to do for her husband. There wasn't a single piece of advice for Richie about what he should do for her.

She folded her arms across her chest as Richie got into the car, whistling. He turned to smile briefly at her before starting the car and driving out of the parking lot.

As they drove home, she recalled what the counselor had said. This time, he'd told her she wasn't supposed to ever deny her husband anything. When Richie brought up once again the disagreements they had about having children, she wasn't surprised when the counselor told her it was time to give in to Richie's request.

She'd wanted to laugh out loud when he'd said the word "request." Clearly, it wasn't a request. Richie was demanding that she have children for him now, even though she didn't want to. Was it wrong for her to want a stable, non-violent home before bringing a child into it?

She stared out of the window at the cars racing past them and remembered her failed attempt to leave Richie the night before. She had removed her duffel bag from under the couch very early in the morning and placed it in the kitchen cabinet where he would not find it. She would try once again to leave the next day, after he'd left for work.

They got home, and after she'd prepared dinner and they had eaten together, she waited for him to go to bed. As usual, he locked the front and back door, took the keys, and went upstairs. She sat in the living room, hesitant to go up to the bedroom. But she knew she eventually had to or he would come down soon to ask why she wasn't in bed.

Upstairs, she climbed into the bed beside him and bit her lip when he drew her close and held her firmly. Eventually, she fell asleep still in his arms.

The next morning, she woke up and found that he had already left for work. She sighed in relief and then got out of the bed quickly. She showered hastily, threw a few more clothes into another bag, and carried it down the stairs. She called a taxi, went into the kitchen, and brought out her bag from the cabinet where she had put it. Carrying it to the living room, she placed it beside the other bag. She sat down to wait for the taxi and then sighed when she heard the sound of a car stopping in front of the house. She smiled.

That was quick.

She stood, glanced around the living room, and smiled sadly. She would miss this house, but she couldn't stay here anymore. She had made a big mistake coming back.

She packed her luggage. One was full of her

clothes and the other held her toiletries. She then carried her bags to the door and opened it. Immediately, her eyes widened in terror. Richie was standing in front of her, staring at her with a surprised look on his face. He was dressed in jeans and an old t-shirt and he had a bouquet of wild roses in his hand. He looked down at her bags and then frowned deeply.

"Where are you going, Lauren?"

Her mouth turned dry and she couldn't speak. She looked at his face. He was still staring at the bags in her hands. His face had turned red and his forehead was furrowed. He looked up at her and asked again, "I said where are you going, Lauren?"

She searched her mind for something to say and then muttered, "Umm… I just wanted to go to the dry cleaners… my clothes… to give them my clothes, I mean." She hid a sigh at how jumbled her words were. He would read through her feeble excuse without difficulty.

He raised his brows. "You want to dry-clean two bags of clothes?"

She nodded dumbly.

"Okay… I'll take you there."

She shook her head. "No… no need. I called a taxi." Thankfully, the taxi she had called to pick her up rolled into the driveway just then and she pointed at it.

"Tell him he can go," Richie said, in a voice that clearly told her he would entertain no arguments. "I'll take you myself."

He took the bag from her and she went to the taxi, quickly told the driver she didn't need him anymore and then slowly returned to where Richie was standing. She wondered as she got into the car beside him what he would say when she opened her bags and he saw not just her clothes, but her toiletries and shoes as well. He handed her the flowers as he entered the car and she begrudgingly thanked him for them. The car instantly filled with the smell of roses.

What is he even doing home at this time? she asked herself as she put the flowers to her nose and inhaled its scent deeply. Finally overcome with curiosity, she turned and asked him about it.

"I took some time off work to be with you and work on our marriage," he answered. "I just decided to go to the florist this morning and get you some flowers."

He drove into the parking lot of the drycleaners.

They entered together while her heart beat quickly. When the petite lady at the desk asked for the clothes she wanted dry-cleaned, Richie watched closely as she opened her bag. She sighed with relief when she saw it was the bag that contained only her clothes.

She smiled at the lady and said loudly for Richie's sake, "I think I will only have the clothes in this bag dry-cleaned. I'll keep this other bag for another time."

The lady nodded and took the bag. Lauren was glad when Richie didn't ask why she'd decided not to dry-clean the clothes in the other bag. She was also relieved when he walked to the door with a bored look on his face and waited for her there.

She ignored the odd look the lady gave her as she grabbed all her underwear and face towels and snuck them into the other bag. She smiled at Richie when he turned his eyes to her.

After she was through with the lady, she quickly joined her husband at the entrance of the drycleaners and they walked to the car together.

As they drove home, she cursed her luck. Now that he was on vacation, he would not let her out of his sight. Her heart filled with worry. She didn't know how long his impromptu vacation was. It could very well be for a month, and that probably meant she wouldn't be able to leave him until then.

She shut her eyes as her head began to pound. She couldn't remain with him for that long. She wasn't even sure she could survive another day with him. She wanted to ask him how long his vacation would last, but she didn't want to give him any cause to suspect that she was planning to leave him. All she could hope for was that his "time off" would only be for a few days. And then she could leave him forever.

*****

Zainah stood in the camp kitchen, stirring a big pot of stew. She wiped her brow with her sleeve and then turned to Leila, who was cutting vegetables next to her. "I had a strange dream. You have to promise you won't laugh or judge me if I tell you."

Leila smiled. "I can't promise I won't laugh, Zainah. But of course I won't judge you. You know me better than that."

Zainah frowned at her friend. "But you will laugh."

"Maybe."

Zainah stared at Leila for a few seconds, shook

her head at the naughty expression on her friend's face, and then sighed. "Okay. I dreamt that..." she hesitated. Now that she was saying it out loud, she was a little embarrassed by her dream. Did it mean she was falling for that hot-tempered man or was it a symbolic dream? She continued. "I dreamt that... I... I married him."

Leila looked at her. She'd expected her friend to laugh or at least tease her, but there was no smile on her face. "By him, you mean the handsome man who has been in your tent for more than a week now? That's not strange. If he was in my tent for that long, I would be planning our wedding by now."

"But I don't even sleep in that tent anymore. I only go there to take his food to him and tend to his wounds. I avoid him as much as possible because he is so angry."

"That is enough time to fall for him."

Zainah eyed Leila. "Except I haven't fallen for him. I think the dream might be symbolic."

Leila shrugged. "You still don't know his name?"

"He won't tell me. And maybe it's for the best."

Leila said nothing and went on cutting the vegetables. Zainah looked at Leila and once again wondered if she should tell her about the dream she'd had months ago; the one that had felt so real that she was almost certain it was from God. At last, she decided against it. It was one thing to tell Leila the silly dream she'd had about marrying a handsome man, but it was another to tell her about hearing God say she was supposed to marry him. If only she'd clearly seen the dream groom's face.

And what if you had? she scolded herself. Do

you really believe that dream was from God? What about your vow? Haven't you given up on the idea of marriage?

She held back a groan and brushed away all thoughts about dreams and marriage from her mind. They continued cooking, she and Leila, but they changed the topic to the chores they needed to do the coming week. Zainah had to finish weaving a mat she had started the week before but hadn't been able to continue because she'd been tending to the man in her tent.

Talking about that brought him back to the forefront of her mind. She had to take his food to him soon. This time, she was determined to do two things when she went into the tent with his meal. Firstly, she would read the Bible to him while he ate and no matter what he said, she wouldn't let it get to her. Secondly, she would find out what his name was.

She and Leila finished preparing the meal for the camp. She ladled chicken soup into a bowl for him, while Leila went to tell Miriam that lunch was ready.

Zainah put the bowl of food onto a tray and carried it to her tent. For modesty purposes as well as to avoid his caustic temper, she had stopped staying in the tent. He was sitting up now and even standing, but still too weak to walk.

She entered her tent and found him sitting down on the sleeping rug and staring at the wall opposite him, his expression bleak. She placed the tray of food in front of him and then went to pick up her Bible.She watched him eating for a few seconds, and then she opened the Bible to First John chapter four, and started to read from verse sixteen.

Immediately, he leveled his gaze at her and said angrily, "No… no! Don't start reading that again."

She looked up at him and raised her brows. "Just like I said to you the last time, this is my tent. I can do whatever I want in it."

He barked at her. "No, you can't! And can you not read it silently?"

She gave him a sly smile. "I can't. I need to meditate on the words and so I want to hear it out loud."

He glared at her for a full minute, but she didn't let it faze her. She lowered her head again and continued to read the passage out loud. As she read, she prayed in her heart that the Lord would somehow use the passage about His love to reveal Himself to this angry but very needy man. She was surprised when he didn't say anything more.

Hopefully he is listening, and the Spirit of God can use this word to capture his heart.

She blinked when he suddenly roared with laughter and said, "Why do you always read about God's love? You serve a weak god."

Her heart thudded as she looked up at him. This might be the opening she'd been asking the Lord for. She prayed silently that God would give her the right words to say in answer to his question. "I read about God's love all the time because that's His most important attribute. We all want to be loved, and the fact that the God who made the universe loves us is beyond anything we could possibly imagine."

He chuckled. "You aren't going to convert many people with that message."

She raised her brows questioningly at him. "In what way do you think many people would be converted?"

"People need to be persuaded in a different way..." he suddenly stopped speaking and looked away from her.

She frowned, curious as to what he meant, but she decided against asking him. Instead she said, "It was love that caused God to send his only son to die on the cross for you and me. Jesus suffered a horrible death so we could be reconciled to God."

"Stop trying to spread your lies to me! The God you speak about is weak, and I want nothing to do with Him."

"He isn't weak. It takes strength to love like that," she said. She started to speak in detail about the purpose of Christ's death and resurrection. As she talked, he remained silent, and she thanked God for that. At least he was listening.

She jerked when he jumped to his feet and roared, "Stop now!" A string of curses came out of his mouth and she recoiled.

"Get out!" he barked and cursed her again.

She shut her eyes from the hurt she felt at his words. Standing, she left the tent. Once she was outside, she let the tears come. "Lord, I can't do this any longer. He isn't listening. His heart is set against You, and I can't keep swallowing his hurtful words." Tears streamed down her face. "I'm sorry, Lord. Please forgive me, but I can't!" She hastened away, as far away from the tent as she possibly could.

SEVEN

Long after Zainah had left, Faizan kept watching the entrance to the tent. For the second time that week, he felt strangely guilty for how he had spoken to her. She'd obviously been hurt by his words. He wondered at his guilt. He had never cared who he hurt before. Why did he care about this woman's feelings? It was weird.

He sat up. What was even weirder was why she kept tending to him, feeding him, even giving her sleeping space over to him, in spite of the way he treated her. Why hadn't she just left him to himself? Why had she kept nursing him back to health even when he had threatened her? If not for her, he would be dead.

He continued to think about it, perplexed. If the roles had been reversed, the scenario would be completely different. And it wasn't just her. The other Christians here had been kind to him. They had come into the tent to visit him from time to time. He had either just ignored them or even cursed them. Yet, they still let him live amongst them.

As if to buttress his point, two little boys, not older than around seven, came into the tent, playing and laughing. When they saw him, they stopped laughing and stared at him with fascinated intensity. He knew he was the reason why they had come here. The camp was made up of only women. He was the sole man here. Without a doubt, as boys, the presence of a grown man had to be captivating to them.

They whispered amongst themselves, and for a brief moment he felt like calling to them and asking if they wanted to play a manly game of arm wrestling. And then he came to himself. What has gotten into you, Faizan? These were Christian children, bred in falsehood. He turned to glare at them angrily but they didn't run away or even flinch.

You've lost it, Faizan.

He sighed, lay back down, exhausted, and tried his best to ignore them. Conflicting thoughts and emotions warred in his mind. He'd been taught since he was twelve that Christians were misguided and needed to be subjugated or eliminated. But the kindness of these people made him start to question everything.

Thoughts about Mustafa's instructions to him suddenly flooded his mind, and he pressed his lips tightly together. Why was his heart softening toward these people? They were unbelievers, infidels. They were only kind to him because they were determined to convert him. They didn't understand that their efforts were futile.

He prayed again that Allah would give him strength quickly so he could leave and complete his mission. Maybe once he was totally well, he would even start from here.

He turned to the children who were now sitting opposite him, chatting and giggling. He suddenly felt nauseated at the thought of harming them. His mind traveled to Zainah; sweet, kind, beautiful Zainah. The thought of even the slightest harm coming to her agitated him. He couldn't possibly comprehend harming her himself. It felt completely despicable to even think about it.

The children stood up and left, and he sighed. What had gotten into him? Why had he suddenly turned into a weak person? This place was changing him. If he stayed here any longer, he would not be able to go back to being the leader of Al-Muharib. His men would sniff out even the slightest weakness. That would not be good. The earlier he left this place and forgot about that Zainah woman, the better for him.

*****

Audrey walked into the clothing store, Sienna next to her. She walked through rows of clothes, picking up one item and then putting it back again. Sienna had already chosen a number of clothes to buy, but she just couldn't bring herself to buy any.

Sienna shook her head. "Audrey, you have only bought one shirt since we started shopping. So much for our only girls' shopping trip today."

Audrey smiled at her. "You know the only reason I agreed to this girls-only shopping trip was to spend time with you."

Sienna beamed. "I know. I miss Trisha. Our girls' trip isn't complete without her."

"I know," Audrey said. She picked up a sky-blue shirt, examined it, and then decided it would be her second purchase of the day. She placed it over her shoulder and then looked up when Sienna called her name and frowned at her. "What is it?"

"That shirt is hideous, Audrey! Put it back."

"It's not!"

"It is. Look at it. What about it do you like?"

"It's functional and… well, it's something I can wear."

"Something you used to wear. Think about Ken. What do you think he would like to see you in?"

Audrey shrugged. "Ken likes me the way I am."

"I know he does. But still, he might appreciate you putting on something special for him from time to time. Maybe we should get evening dresses and have dinner this evening." Sienna rubbed her hands in glee and smiled. "We will order room service before the boys get back from their soccer game, get all dolled up, and then surprise them. What do you think, Audrey?"

Audrey smiled. "I like the idea… except for the dolled-up thing. But I guess Ken would appreciate that, so why not? Let's do it." She looked at Sienna as they went to find evening dresses for their surprise dinner. "Talking about the boys, I'm glad we're going back soon so I can finalize plans for the wedding. I've enjoyed this vacation, but there have been way too many close calls."

Sienna smiled curiously at her. "What do you mean by close calls?"

"I mean that Ken and I need to get married as soon as possible… before we do something we might regret."

Sienna laughed.

"It's not funny, Sienna. It's been a huge struggle having Ken sleeping in the room right next to me. I can't wait until we get back to Rosefield. I'll miss him for the few weeks he's away in Miami, but at least there will be no temptation to do the wrong thing."

Sienna picked up a strapless black dress and then looked at her. "I know what you mean, Audrey. Just like I told you some days ago, I understand. I went through the same thing before Bryan and I got married, but I guess this is worse. Both of you are practically staying in the same house now." She sighed. "I don't know what I would have done if it was me, but I know you and Ken are strong. Most of all, God's grace is sufficient. You'll both be fine."

Audrey shrugged, but she didn't know if Sienna was right. She changed the subject and said sadly, "I really thought we would find Rafael. I just wanted to make Dad's dream come true."

The moment felt depressing, and Audrey changed the topic again. They talked about the dinner they were planning to have and about keeping the guys away from the room until they were ready.

After an hour of going through clothes and Sienna trying on different dresses, they finally bought two gowns. Audrey had selected a plain, navy blue dress but Sienna took it away. At last she'd agreed for Audrey to get a burgundy pleated gown while she bought a one-shoulder mustard dress.

They left the store and Sienna said excitedly, "Off to the spa and salon! We'll get our hair and makeup done as well."

Audrey sighed wearily. "Fine! But I'm only going

to get a simple hair and makeup look."

Sienna smiled but didn't answer.

They got into a taxi, and as it set off, Audrey thought of something and then turned worriedly to Sienna. "Considering what I told you about Ken's and my struggle, do you really think it's a good idea for me to wear that dress you chose for me? Isn't it a little too sexy? And I'm getting my hair and make-up done as well. Ken and I already struggle with me looking as plain as I do. I don't know if…"

"Audrey!" Sienna interrupted. "Just like I said earlier, you'll both be fine. Besides, Bryan and I will be there. We won't let you guys do anything stupid."

Audrey nodded, but on the inside, her worry remained.

*****

Once they got to their hotel rooms, Audrey and Sienna ordered an extravagant feast for their double dinner dates. Audrey had called Ken when they were coming back from the salon and asked where they were. The guys had gone to the soccer stadium to watch one of Ken's favorite soccer teams, Real Madrid, play with another team. When Ken told her they were on their way back, she sent him on an errand to get toiletries.

Audrey and Sienna had changed into their new dresses at the spa, after their hair and makeup were done. They waited for the food to arrive while hoping the guys would not come back too early.

"Maybe you should call Bryan and tell him to get you something at the mall," Audrey said to Sienna as they sat in the living room. "Just to buy us more time."

"They might start to suspect something if we send them on another errand," Sienna replied.

"But if we don't, they might come back now and the surprise will be ruined!"

Sienna called Bryan and asked if he and Ken could get them groceries from the mall. He sounded a bit surprised, but he agreed quickly.

The girls breathed a sigh of relief when their food arrived thirty minutes later. After the table had been set and the steward had left, they sat at the table and chatted while they waited.

Not long after, Audrey heard the door open, and she put her hands on her lips to let Sienna know the guys were back. They had turned off the regular lights and turned on the lamps, so that the dining room took on a soft, romantic glow.

Ken and Bryan were chatting loudly about something as they entered the dining room. The girls stood in front of the dining table. When they yelled, "Surprise!" Ken and Bryan jumped and then laughed.

Bryan came near and exclaimed. "Wow! A surprise dinner date." When he saw Sienna, his jaw dropped. "You look amazing, sweetie!" He kissed her.

Ken stared at Audrey, and she laughed at the mesmerized look on his face. After a long moment, he shook his head and exclaimed, "You look absolutely stunning, Audrey! You always look great, but now…" He didn't finish his sentence.

Audrey melted under his gaze. She was pleased that she had taken Sienna's advice and done the makeover.

They chatted as they ate. Ken took Audrey's hand,

and from time to time he gazed at her throughout the dinner. After they had all eaten, they continued their conversation in the living room.

A few hours later, Bryan and Sienna stood. "Will you guys be OK?" Sienna asked. "We're going to bed."

Bryan looked at Ken and then at Audrey. "Do you want us to stay here?"

Audrey was about to nod and say she wouldn't mind them staying, but Ken shook his head. "It's okay. You can go."

They left and Audrey looked at Ken. "Maybe they could have stayed a while longer."

Ken stood. "They don't have to." He stood as well. "I need to go to bed now."

"So soon?" she asked.

He nodded. "It's best for both of us."

She ruefully watched him leave and then went into her own room.

*****

Lauren finally finished cleaning the kitchen and stretched. She was tired but satisfied. She'd spent the day spring cleaning the entire house and now she was through.

She hung up the kitchen rag and then went up to the bedroom to take a nap. Richie had gone to the store to get some groceries ten minutes before. He'd told her he would also stop by the hardware store. She figured he would be away from the house for thirty or forty minutes. She could nap until he got back. She lay down on the bed and went to sleep almost immediately.

It seemed like she had only slept for ten minutes when someone began to unbutton her blouse. She immediately sat up and saw it was Richie. Shaking her head, she brushed away his hand. "You're back already?"

He nodded and then came at her again.

She shook her head again and lay back down. "Not now, Richie. I'm tired."

He pulled her up forcefully, and she gasped. "What are you doing?"

He sneered and said, "You've forgotten what you were told by our marriage counselor. As a good wife, you are not supposed to deny me anything."

She glared at him. "I only said I was tired. I've been cleaning the house all day. You can wait for a few hours, can't you?"

He shook his head. "I can't. I want you now." He lunged for her, but she sprang up from the bed.

He fell on the bed and yelled in outrage.

She tried to leave the room, but he caught a hold of her arm and slapped her hard on the cheek.

She gasped in pain and then glared at him, angry and defiant. She said, "I'm not doing this anymore, Richie. I'm leaving you right now!"

He looked slightly shocked and apologetic. He let go of her arm and pleaded, "I'm sorry, Lauren. I shouldn't have done that. Please, don't go."

She laughed bitterly. "What shouldn't you have done? You've done nothing but abuse me since I came back. I can't stay here anymore. I thought you were truly changing, just as you told me over the phone, but it was a lie. You are still exactly the same." She wanted to let go and spill out her anger, but she controlled herself. "I'm leaving you for good this time."

He shook his head vigorously. "I am changing." He looked into her eyes. "Please… just give me another chance to prove to you that I am different now."

"You aren't, Richie! Stop deceiving yourself. You haven't put into practice one single thing you've been taught in your anger management classes. You are still as angry as ever and you try to blame me for your anger all the time." She'd had enough. She was going to leave with the clothes on her back. With grim determination, she started to walk past him. She gasped in pain when he grabbed her hand and held on tightly.

"You can't leave me!" he yelled. She tried to wrench her hand away, but his grip was too strong. "You aren't going anywhere."

"Let go of me!" she screamed.

He shook his head and then said, "Please, Lauren. For the sake of our love and marriage."

"You can't force me to stay with you," she said to him. "It's not right!"

"Please, Lauren, just give me one more chance. I'll never hit you again."

She said again, but weakly this time, "I can't stay."

"Lauren," he held her hands and looked her in the eye, "Do you still love me?"

She looked away and didn't answer.

He turned her face back to face his. "Tell me, Lauren. Do you still love me?"

She sighed loudly and nodded. She still did, in spite of everything he had done to her.

"And I still love you," he said. "Please don't give up on me. I promise never to hit you again. In fact, you can hold me to this promise. If I ever lay my hands on you again, you are free to leave me immediately and I will not try to stop you."

She searched his eyes to see if he really meant what he'd just said. He looked sincere. Maybe she could give him just one more chance. He was right. If you loved someone, you didn't just give up on them. She sighed again and then nodded. "Okay, Richie. I'll hold you to your word. I'll give you one more chance."

He smiled widely, and she added, "If you go against your word this time, I'll leave for good. Even if you try to stop me, I'll eventually find a way to leave."

He nodded again and gently laid his hand on her cheek, the one he had slapped. "I'm so sorry," he said, looking into her eyes. "Please forgive me."

She didn't say anything and he hugged her, probably taking her silence as proof that she had forgiven him. After a long moment, he let her go and said, "To show you how sorry I am, I'm going to make you a special dinner. Just sit... or sleep, whichever you decide to do. When it's ready, I'll let you know."

He left and she sat heavily on the bed. Once again, she questioned the logic behind her decision to stay with him.

There is no logic, she told herself. She stayed because she loved him. There was also a part of her that was afraid to completely leave him; afraid that if she did, he would harm himself irreversibly. But maybe that fear came as a result of continuously being made to believe that it was her duty to keep him happy all the time.

She shut her eyes and thought about Ken again.

If only I had married him.

He was getting married to someone else in a few weeks, someone who had seen his true worth. Maybe the many trials in her marriage were a sort of punishment for how she had treated him. Well, she had promised to give her husband one more chance and she would keep that promise. But if he messed up again, she would leave, no matter how much she still loved him.

EIGHT

Trisha stood at the window of her bookstore, looking out. It felt as though she was waiting for her sisters to come into the store. She missed them so. Thankfully, they would be back very soon. She couldn't wait to see them and also for them to see how much Ruby had grown since they'd seen her as a newborn. It was only a few weeks before, but she'd gotten bigger since then.

She moved away from the window and went to check briefly on her baby daughter. Ruby was still fast asleep, her precious mouth turned up in what looked like a smile.

Trisha touched her tiny toes and hands. She couldn't believe this precious bundle belonged to her. She looked up when someone walked in, prepared to attend to the customer. She moved closer and her heart suddenly skipped a beat when she saw it was Frank. She sighed, wondering at her strange reaction to him.

"Hi, Trisha," he said to her as she walked up to him.

"Hey, Frank! How are you doing today?"

"Good! I just came by to pick up a book."

She nodded, but she knew why he had actually come. He'd come to see her.

His eyes regarded her the way they always did and he frowned slightly. "How are you feeling? You look a little stressed."

She studied his face for just a second and then looked away. Of course he would notice that she was slightly stressed. Ruby had kept her up for the last two nights. "I'm okay. I just haven't slept for a while now," she said, smiling at him. "It's part of the routine of having a newborn."

"Is she here?" he asked.

"She's asleep back there," Trisha answered, pointing to the back of the store.

Frank went to the cookery book section and began to peruse a few of the books. She watched him as he did and remembered she had decided to get him a girlfriend who might hopefully become his wife one day, if everything went well. She hadn't gotten to it yet, but she had to before he became a regular at the bookstore and began to expect more from her than she wanted to give.

He left the cookery section and went to the shelf where she'd arranged all the fiction books. He turned to her and said, "Can you recommend a good book? I am taking a short leave from work for a week and I want a good novel."

She nodded, joined him in the fiction section and began to look for the kind of book she knew he might like. She found the one she was looking for, a Gary Stone novel. As she handed it to him, their hands brushed, and she felt a small spark of electricity go through her fingers. She gasped and quickly withdrew her hands. The book fell on the floor, and she winced. "I'm sorry."

He bent and picked it up. "No need to apologize."

He opened the book, and as he scanned it, she wondered what had gotten into her.

Get yourself together! She scolded herself silently.

He looked up at her. "I'll take this one."

She nodded and took it from him to package it.

As he brought out his wallet to pay, she kept wondering why she'd felt the way she had as she handed the book to him minutes before.

You should look for that girlfriend for him now.

After he had paid, he looked at her, and before he opened his mouth to speak, she immediately knew what he was going to say. He was about to ask her out. She quickly searched her mind for an appropriate single friend that might be interested in dating someone like him.

"Trisha, I was wondering if…"

She interrupted him. "Umm… Frank, I know this sounds a little invasive, but would you be interested in going out with one of my friends… on a blind date?" He frowned and she added, "She's a really nice girl and very pretty. You will like her."

His frown deepened and he shook his head. "Umm… I don't know." He studied her face for a few seconds while she silently prayed he would agree. Finally, he said, "I don't think I can, Trish. I have my eyes on only one girl."

Her heart beat fast as he gazed at her and said, "But I won't pressure her to date me. She might not even want to."

She watched him walk out of the store with the book he'd bought and then shut her eyes when he'd disappeared from sight. Her heart thudded and her emotions roiled. She didn't want to turn him down if he ever asked again because of how she'd blown him off when they were teenagers. She'd treated him badly, ditching him for Stan while they were on a date. Still, she couldn't go out with him, or anyone for that matter. She just wasn't interested in him.

A small voice whispered in her ear, Why, then, did you feel the way you did when your hands touched?

She sighed in confusion and tried to push away all thoughts of Frank from her mind. But his face stayed with her for the rest of the day.

*****

Faizan listened as Zainah read the Bible to him. For the past week, she'd come into the tent every day without fail to read to him. Each time, his resolve to block his ears from the words she read had grown weaker and weaker. That day, he had no more strength to tell her to stop or go away. Her determination was amazing to him.

She was reading now about the good shepherd going after the one lost sheep. The story churned in his mind. Why would this shepherd decide to leave his ninety-nine sheep to look for just one? And then she read the explanation and he understood. He also knew why she was reading this particular passage to him. In her mind, he was the lost sheep, the sinner who needed to repent. He found it ironic that she saw him the same way he saw her—as an unbeliever.

The thought pricked at his conscience as a strange voice whispered in his ear. The difference between you two is that while she wants to convert you by showing you kindness, you want to destroy everyone that is not like you.

He frowned at the thought and tried to push it away, but it remained, filling his heart with dread. He shut his eyes, trying to fall asleep so he could shut out her voice, but sleep would not come. At last, he decided to stop evading the troubling thoughts. That wasn't who he was. He never hid from a challenge.

He looked up at her, determined to tear apart the scriptures she was reading and send her away in tears the way he had done some days before. But what he saw on her face gave him pause. As she looked up from her reading and gazed at him, the concern on her face for him took his breath away. Even though he knew she was misguided for believing he was a lost sheep that needed to be saved, he couldn't help but be touched.

She had tears in her eyes as she spoke about how much her Jesus loved him. He wanted to look away from her, but he couldn't. His heart quivered as she spoke about the God who loved him so much that He wanted a personal relationship with him. He kept listening to her, mesmerized by the sweet sound of her voice and the earnest expression on her face.

And then he finally shook himself out of his strange stupor. He decided to tear at her confidence or ridicule her so she would flee from him.

He was surprised when he did neither. Instead he heard himself say, "I haven't seen any men here." He waved his hand around the tent. "Which means you are unmarried." He chided himself for speaking those words after they escaped his lips. Why had he said them anyway?

She looked at him with alarm on her face, and his eyebrows lifted. So, what he had said had made her uncomfortable after all. He smiled scornfully at her and twisted the verbal knife he had stuck in. "Wouldn't it be better to have the love of a man than the love you speak of?"

She blinked rapidly and then told him to stop teasing her.

His smiled widened. He was happy she was finally discomfited. At last, he'd found a way to shut her up anytime she decided to read her Bible stories to him. He would mock her mercilessly about love and marriage. He regarded her closely. She was probably a virgin. Maybe he would jeer at her about it. That would certainly do her in.

His eyes stayed on her, perusing her body boldly. She looked down at her Bible, but he kept his eyes on her. After a minute, she raised her head and looked at him.

"Can you stop looking at me like that?" she asked him in a slightly shaky voice.

"Why should I? I like what I see."

She gasped audibly, and he forced himself not to laugh. It would spoil his plan.

She stood up and went to get her first aid box. When she came back and reached out to change his bandage, he grabbed her hand. He looked deep into her eyes just to make her even more uncomfortable, but his heart began to pound at the look in her eyes. Apart from the discomfort he expected to see, he saw no fear. Instead, her eyes held a deep unexpected affection for him.

He blinked in surprise as he stared into her eyes. They reminded him of something, or someone...

He suddenly remembered. Her eyes reminded him of his mother. Not that her eyes physically looked like his late mother's, but it was the love in them. His adopted mother had had that same love and concern in her eyes whenever she looked at him.

A sob rose in his throat and he released her hand more from surprise than anything else. He hadn't cried or felt like crying since he was twelve. What was happening to him?

It was definitely time to go. He could get up now and move about some.

I doubt you can get far in the wilderness before you collapse and die in the heat, he scolded himself.

He looked away from her and said hoarsely, "Leave me."

He was both relieved and troubled when she stood and left the tent.

*****

Hassan went around the perimeter of the camp, checking for any security loopholes. His sandals were covered in dust and his mood was no better. His hand went to his gun as one of the men approached him. A force of habit. He exhaled and stood at ease again.

"The tracker is here," the man said.

"Bring him."

A minute later, Ahmed, the pint-sized tracker who he had hired to track down the whereabouts of Faizan and the other men, walked up to him.

He nodded at the man in greeting and immediately asked, "So, have you found them?"

"I have," Ahmed answered with a grim expression on his face.

Hassan frowned deeply. "Well? Out with it!"

"They are all dead," Ahmed said, with no inflection in his voice.

Hassan groaned inwardly. They are all dead, and yet there was no news of a bomb explosion in Spain. What happened to them? He asked Ahmed, "Where did you find them? How did they die?"

"Their plane crashed," Ahmed answered. He explained to Hassan where exactly he had found the plane. It was a location on the border between Algeria and Morocco.

"So, they didn't even manage to go very far," Hassan said, more to himself than to Ahmed. "And what about their bodies?"

"They were buried in shallow graves."

Hassan shook his head and looked away from Ahmed for a short moment. So much loss. He suddenly thought of something and turned to Ahmed again. "Did you bury them or were they already buried by the time you found them?"

"They were already buried."

Hassan felt himself shaking with anger. Someone or some people had buried them. Did the plane crash happen naturally or had someone shot down that plane and then had them buried?

Ahmed continued. "I had my men exhume them. All eight of them."

Hassan stared at him, frowning. "Eight? There were nine of them, including our leader. Are you sure there were only eight bodies?"

"Very sure. We counted them twice."

Hassan began to pace. "How can there be eight bodies when nine of them, including the pilot, left here?" He stopped in front of Ahmed and said, "Someone must have taken one of them, dead or alive."

Ahmed nodded. "It's what I believe as well. And I also think I know who took the missing person and buried the bodies."

Hassan blinked rapidly. "You do? Who?"

"There is a small community of Christian women I found living secretly in that area. I have no doubt that they were the ones who did it."

Hassan clenched his jaw in rage. He looked back and motioned to one of his men behind him. The man came, and Hassan said, "Call me Sadiq."

The man quickly went away, and Hassan started pacing the desert ground again. The messenger came back five minutes later with Sadiq, one of their skilled assassins.

Hassan glanced at the tracker and then the assassin and said, "Sadiq, you will go with Ahmed to where a group of filthy Christian women are hiding out. They have one of our men. When you get there, kill them all and get our man, whether he is dead or alive. Don't let even one of them escape you. Is that understood?"

Sadiq, burly, with reddish eyes, nodded.

"Go now!" Hassan ordered. He watched the men leave to do his bidding, and for a few minutes he kept pacing in anger. At last, he stood still and took a deep breath. The sooner Sadiq completed his mission, the sooner they could have their revenge. Then, as the new leader of Al-Muharib, he would organize another terror mission in Spain. And this time, they would not fail.

*****

Audrey gazed ruefully at the hotel room one more time before she went out the door with her travel bag. Bryan, Ken and Sienna were already headed to the elevator. She joined them as they entered.

"I'm going to miss this place," she said to them. "But I can't wait to finally get home."

"True that," Bryan said. "This has been a great vacation, but it would be nice to go home."

Sienna smiled. "It's been so much fun!" She turned to Bryan. "We have to take another one soon, just the two of us."

Bryan nodded.

Ken shrugged and looked at Audrey. "By God's grace, we should be on our honeymoon in a couple of months."

Audrey grinned and walked out of the elevator with the others as the door opened. "Now, I can't wait for that. We haven't even talked about where we want to go for our honeymoon. Where would you like us to go, Ken?"

Ken tapped her nose and said affectionately, "Wherever you want, my love."

"How about you guys honeymoon in Venice?" Sienna said excitedly. "I went there once when I was a model. It's a beautiful place."

Audrey smiled. "We will consider it." She turned

to Ken. "We definitely need to add 'finding the best honeymoon location' to the list of things we have yet to do for our wedding." She laughed. "The list is growing longer and longer every day."

"If it wasn't for my classes at the Bible college, Audrey, I would help more with the planning," Sienna said. "Anyway, Trisha will help you guys out. Especially you, Audrey. I know it won't be easy once Ken goes back to Miami."

Audrey went with Ken to the check-out counter. Sienna's words rang in her mind as she stood waiting for the receptionist to check them all out. She would miss Ken terribly once he left. She looked at him as he handed their key to the lady and sighed.

He turned to her and winked. "All set to go," he said.

"I'll miss you," she said, trying not to cry.

"What are you talking about, Audrey? We are all going back to Rosefield together."

"Yes, but you will only be staying there for a week before you have to go back to Florida."

"And then I will come back again in less than a month." He took her hand as they made their way back to Sienna and Bryan. "This vacation with you, Bryan and Sienna has been so memorable. Best of all, I have loved every minute living in the same house with you . . . even though it was very tough. I can't wait for the day we will actually get to live together for the rest of our lives. Imagine what fun we'll have!"

She felt herself blushing and shook her head at him. "Okay, let's wait until then before we start talking about having fun." She leaned in and kissed him and then wrapped her arm around his waist.

They reached Bryan and Sienna, and as they all walked out of the hotel to go to the airport, Ken said to Audrey, "Promise me you will not be sad anymore... even when I leave for Miami in a week."

"I can't promise that," she said, entering the car and sitting beside him. Sienna sat next to her, while Bryan sat in the front seat.

"Okay, at least promise that the remaining week we have before I leave will be spent enjoying each other's company instead of worrying about my imminent departure."

She nodded and smiled at him. "I can promise that."

*****

Lauren smiled up at Richie as he stood beside the bed with a tray of croissants and some coffee brewed just the way she liked it. He sat next to her. and when she sat up, he placed the tray before her.

"Breakfast, honey," he said, smiling at her.

She beamed, leaned forward and kissed him. She looked down at the food. "Thanks, Richie."

He nodded.

"So, what do you want to do today, my love?"

She shook her head, still smiling. "I don't know. Whatever you want to do."

"I have an idea. We will leave this morning," he stood up, and she smiled at the eager expression on his face. "As soon as you've finished your breakfast, prepare to go out."

She gave him a mock salute. "Yes sir!"

He went out of the room and she grinned. Since he'd made the promise never to hit her again, he'd kept his word. In fact, he had become sort of a model husband. Many days, just like now, he'd brought her breakfast in bed, given her flowers almost daily, and taken her out to picnics and restaurants. He'd become the man she'd fallen so desperately in love with and married years before.

She finished her breakfast, stood up and went to take a quick shower. Since Richie had not mentioned anything about a fancy restaurant and it was still morning, she decided to wear something casual and comfortable.

She rummaged through her closet and finally brought out a pair of white shorts and a mint green top. She put the shorts and blouse on and put her hair in a high ponytail. After that, she regarded herself in the mirror. She smiled, satisfied with the way she looked. The outfit was very comfortable but somewhat chic at the same time. She slung a small beige purse over her shoulder and wore flat gold sandals on her feet.

She stared at herself a moment longer. Her decision to continue to stay with Richie had been a risky one, but it seemed to be paying off. Richie was now putting into practice the things he had learned in his anger management classes. Thankfully, they hadn't returned to that quack counselor, and neither had Richie bugged her again about having children.

She touched her stomach as she looked in the mirror and imagined what it would feel like to have a baby growing inside her. Now that Richie was getting better, she had started considering having a baby with him. It wasn't yet time of course, but if he continued on this peaceful and loving path, in a few months she would probably be ready to start trying again.

The bedroom door opened and Richie walked in. "You are ready?" he asked.

"Yes." She asked curiously, "Where are we heading today?"

"Umm, somewhere not too far from here," was all he said.

She followed him downstairs and out of the house. They got into the car, and he drove out of their driveway onto the road.

As they headed to the mysterious place, Lauren thought about how her life had changed over the past few weeks. She'd gone from being an abused wife sheltered in a kind couple's home to a loved wife living with her husband again. She smiled at Richie and he turned to smile back at her before facing the road again.

Richie drove into a residential area, and Lauren frowned. The street definitely looked familiar. And then she knew where they were going. It was to one of their old friends' houses; a couple who Richie had had a falling out with. He had banned her from communicating with them a few years before. Since they were initially his friends and she wasn't that close to them, she had not complained.

She lifted her brows in surprise and turned to him. "We are going to see Andy and Gina?"

"Yes."

She frowned deeply. "I thought you never wanted to see them again."

"I saw them at the country club the other day and we reconciled. I promised them I would bring you to their house for a visit soon. So, here we are."

As he said that, he drove into the driveway of Andy and Gina's large, Spanish–style home. Palm trees surrounded the house and a spiraling flight of stairs took them up to the front door.

Richie knocked on the door and they waited. Soon, a woman dressed in a maid's uniform came and opened the door for them. They were shown to the downstairs living room—a lavishly decorated space that Lauren thought was way too extravagant. They sat down on the ornate cream sofa and were offered refreshments. Lauren refused, while Richie was poured a glass of cognac.

Gina and Andy came into the living room a minute later and hugged Lauren and Richie. Gina was a petite woman with golden blonde hair and bright blue eyes. Andy was the very opposite of his wife in physical stature. He was tall and huge, with dark hair and light green eyes.

Lauren smiled at the couple. They were nice people from what she remembered, but somehow, she'd felt as though Richie was a little jealous of them. He always went on about how they lived in such a huge house when they had no kids or about whatever new car the couple had bought.

Richie shook Andy's hand and hugged Gina. "I told you I would bring Lauren for a visit, and here she is," he said.

Gina smiled warmly. "I'm glad you did." She looked at Lauren and said, "We've missed you both, Lauren. I hope our friendship gets back to how it used to be."

Lauren nodded. "I'd like that."

They all sat down and chatted about old times. Soon the men were talking about the stock market.

Gina and Lauren wandered out of the house and soon sat in the sweet-smelling garden, proliferated by different types of bright flowers. They talked about random things at first, and then more intimate things. Lauren told her that Richie wanted kids, but she wasn't quite ready for a baby.

Gina said in her usual sweet voice, "Richie loves you, Lauren. I'm sure he'll wait patiently for you until you are ready."

Lauren hid a smile. Clearly this woman didn't know Richie well… or, more likely, Richie had hidden his true character from Gina and Andy. He was anything but an easy-going man and waiting patiently for a baby wasn't what he'd done since she'd come back to him, or before she'd left him either. Hopefully, things would be different now. as she couldn't deal with any more pressure to have children.

She asked Gina tentatively why she didn't have kids either.

"I wanted them so badly when Andy and I got married, but I couldn't have children. The doctors found out I had a damaged fallopian tube. We decided to adopt after that, but it just never seemed to be the right time. I guess we just got used to living without the responsibilities that kids would require. I'm basically happy with the way things are now, but I haven't completely given up on adopting a child one day."

Lauren smiled at her and then thought about it. Maybe she needed to just give in now and have a baby. It had been her husband's dream since they'd gotten married. She shouldn't keep that from him.

They continued to chat for another thirty

minutes, and then they went back into the house. Fifteen minutes later, Lauren got into the car with Richie and they began the drive home.

All through the drive, he didn't speak to her, even when she asked him a specific question. She nervously sat looking out the window while searching her mind for what she might have said or done that would have offended him.

They finally got home.

Her heart raced as he opened the front door. His anger was very apparent from the look on his face and she worried about what he would do. She entered the house with her palms sweaty and her pulse racing. He entered after her and locked the door.

She looked up at him with dread. His eyes were flashing with anger. When he grabbed her shoulders and shook her, she cried out. "What is it, Richie? What have I done now?"

He roared, "What have you done? You have no shame!" He slapped her hard and pushed her down.

She screamed in pain as she fell to the ground. He hovered threateningly over her, his eyes hard as he stared down at her. "How could you, Lauren?"

She moved back from him. "I didn't do anything."

He yelled, "Liar! You were flirting with Andy. I saw you!"

Her jaw dropped. "When? I spent most of our time there with Gina. How could I have been flirting with Andy?"

He bent down and glared at her. "I saw the way you looked at him, and that hug you gave him..." His eyes flashed again. "I'm going to kill you!"

He raised his hand to hit her again, and she

shook her head. "You promised you wouldn't hit me again!" she said quickly as her heart pounded with fear. "You already hit me. Are you going to do it again?"

He stared at her as though she was the most disgusting thing he'd ever seen and then he brought down his hand. He stood, glared at her for another minute and then huffed away angrily.

She exhaled and then decided she would leave that night, no matter what. He had broken his promise to her. He'd slapped her now in a jealous rage even though he'd told her he would never hit her again. Who knew what he would do the next time he felt she was being too friendly with a guy? He might kill her, just as he had said.

She got up and sat on the couch. She would bide her time. Once it was night, she would make sure she was there when he locked the doors. She would follow him up and watch where he kept the keys. When he went to the bathroom for his usual bath before bed, she would take the keys and leave. Hopefully, she would never see him again after she did.

*****

That night, after he'd locked the doors, she followed him up the stairs in a conciliatory manner. He had not spoken to her since their fight in the afternoon. She'd continued to speak to him however, pretending she was sorry for what he was accusing her of.

When they entered the room, she changed into her pajamas and got into the bed. Slightly turning her body away from him, she stretched out on the bed and shut her eyes. She opened it again a few seconds later and saw him put the keys to the doors in the top compartment of their wardrobe. He started to turn around, and she immediately shut her eyes and pretended she was already asleep.

Some minutes later, he went into the bathroom. She waited until she heard the shower running and then stood up and quietly walked to the wardrobe. She stood on her tiptoes and stretched her hand to the top. Searching with her hands, she instantly found the bunch of keys and grabbed it.

She quickly grabbed her purse from the bedside table and a long-sleeved top from her closet. She ran down the stairs as fast as she could, praying the noise from the shower would mask her hasty steps. This time she took no clothes with her.

Her heart pounded as she reached the living room door and put the key into the keyhole. But it wouldn't enter. Frowning, she tried the next key, but it still didn't enter. She fumbled for the third key and tried it, but it was still the same thing. She paused as her heartbeat increased and tried to gather herself together. She looked at the keys again, closely this time.

She groaned. None of these was the front door key. The backdoor key was not there, either. Frustrated, she shut her eyes and swore. Had Richie changed the keys? But she had seen him lock the door with them before they'd gone up to their bedroom.

In desperation, she hurried to the back door and tried all the keys, but none of them worked. She nearly screamed in frustration. She stood and pondered what to do next.

"How can none of these keys open any of the doors?" she muttered angrily.

"Because I planted fake keys on top of the wardrobe for you to find!"

Her eyes widened in horror.

Richie!

Richie walked up to her and glared at her.

She bit her bottom lip as she looked at him. He looked really mad.

"After our fight, I saw the way you looked at me and the way you were acting. Your eyes told me you wanted to hurt me, but your actions were loving and totally compliant. I knew almost immediately that you were going to try to run away tonight or tomorrow. That was why I planted those keys where I did. So you would not be able to." He gave her an evil grin. "I was right, but thankfully, my plan worked."

She trembled as she looked at him. The combination of fury in his eyes and his wicked smile gave him an evil look that terrified her. But she decided not to show her fear and shook her head. She said to him, "How can you force me to stay with you when I don't want to? You can't make someone love you, you know."

He raised his brows. "But you do love me. You even told me that not long ago."

"No, I don't," she lied. "You have killed all the love I have for you now." She walked closer to him, even though her heart was pounding with fear, and said softly, "Where are the keys, Richie? You know it's not right to hold me against my will. If you love someone, you let them go. Isn't that how the saying goes?"

A look of confusion briefly passed through his eyes, and then he smiled again. "No, you are trying to deceive me. You still love me. I'm pretty sure of that. And that saying is wrong. If you love someone, you hold on for dear life."

She shuddered at his words and the look on his face. He wasn't ever going to let her go. Even when his vacation had ended and he'd started working again, he would find a way to keep her captive. Fear grabbed and squeezed her tight until she became dizzy. She was her husband's prisoner. The only way out was to secretly call Ken to come and get her out. She would beg him not to hurt Richie or arrest him. All she wanted now was to leave and go back to Rosefield. She had learned her lesson. Her husband was a monster and he was never going to change.

She forced a smile and nodded. "Okay… you are right. I still love you. I'll stay, but you have to keep attending your anger management classes." Maybe Ken could come when Richie was out so there would be no confrontation, which would almost surely end up with one or both of them getting hurt.

Richie smiled. "Of course. But you will always go with me, won't you?"

She suppressed a sigh. "I'll try."

"No. If you don't go with me, I won't go."

"Okay, I'll always go with you."

"Good. But I am still angry with you about what happened with Andy. Only a kiss will make it better."

She cringed on the inside but smiled. "You want a kiss?"

"Yes. One that will convince me that you have no

designs whatsoever on Andy."

She forced herself to lean in and give him a brief kiss on the lips.

He laughed and looked at her with an incredulous expression on his face. "Is that all you've got? That wasn't a real kiss, Lauren."

She sighed. "Okay, how about this one?" She kissed him once more, as passionately as she could this time. When she stepped back, he smiled.

"That's better." He took her in his arms, kissed her again and then let her go. "I can't wait for us to start trying to make a baby."

He grinned and she forced a smile, even though everything in her was revolted at the idea of having a baby with him.

He thankfully went upstairs again and she walked to the living room. She grabbed a throw pillow, screamed into it, and shut her eyes as tears ran down her cheeks. He had thwarted her plan to leave again and now he was talking about making babies. The sooner she could leave this house, the better for her.

The next evening, while Richie was asleep upstairs, she dialed Ken's number.

"Hello, Ken," Lauren said when he answered his phone.

"Hi, Lauren. How are you? I shouldn't even be asking. Diane just told me you left and went back to Miami. Why didn't you tell me you were going to leave?"

She ignored his question and asked, "Umm... Ken, you said Diane just told you I had left?"

"Yes. This morning."

Her heart sank. He was in Rosefield. She'd

wanted him to come get her from there. She sighed. "You're in Rosefield."

"Yes." He sounded slightly angry. "I have a wedding to plan."

"I forgot about that. Congratulations on…"

"Lauren, tell me you didn't go back to your husband!"

Lauren sighed loudly. "Yes. I went back to him."

"After all he did to you? I can't believe it!"

Lauren shut her eyes. Since Ken was in Rosefield and she didn't know when he would be back, there was no need to tell him about Richie's violent behavior. Besides, she didn't want to disrupt his marriage plans after the previous year's confusion with his fiancé. She said, "Richie and I are trying to work on our marriage."

"Really?" Ken didn't say anything more for some seconds, and then he spoke again. "And he hasn't hit you since you went back to him?"

Lauren pressed her lips together and then said, "Umm… he hasn't. Not really."

"What do you mean by 'not really?' Either he has or he hasn't!"

"He hasn't," she said hastily. "Ken, I just wanted to find out how you are doing. Call me when you get back to Miami. Okay?"

"Lauren, is there something you're not telling me?"

"Nothing." she answered.

"Okay. I hope you know you can tell me anything. If he hurts you in any way, I want to know about it."

She didn't say anything and he spoke again, "Lauren, promise me you will let me know if he ever hits you again."

 Guilt blanketed her as she said, "I promise."

"Good. I'll call you once I'm back."

When the call ended, an intense feeling of hopelessness overwhelmed her. She covered her face with her hands and wept softly.

NINE

Zainah finished changing Faizan's bandage while her heart beat wildly. From time to time, she scolded herself for her racing heart. Why was it drumming so madly, as though it were about to jump out of her chest? Why did he have such an effect on her?

She poured a little water into a cup and handed it to him. She avoided looking at his face as he drank. When he'd finished, he handed her the cup and she took it without looking at him. She went to drop it in the corner of the tent, and then made her way out.

As she exited the tent, she frowned, troubled. If she was beginning to feel this lightheaded around that angry man, how could she continue to speak God's word to him and bring him to Christ? She was supposed to read the Bible to him before she left the tent that day, but she just couldn't bear to stay longer than she had. Every time she was with him, she felt herself falling for him, which made his constant angry words hurt even more than she could have imagined.

She went to the large cooking tent where Fatima and Aisha had started dinner. She greeted them and took the earthen pot in the corner. She went out and headed for the well at the edge of the camp, which they had dug only a week before.

As she fetched water for the women to cook dinner with, she continued to think about Faizan. She had not been able to get him out of her mind since he'd arrived at the camp. But the last few days had been even worse.

Lord, please help me not to fall in love with him, she prayed silently.

She finished filling the big pot and carried it on her shoulder. Reaching the cooking tent, she dropped it in the corner and then decided to head to Leila's. That day, she would not go to her tent to read to him, she decided. He never listened anyway. And she needed the break. Just for today.

She got to Leila's tent, but before she entered, she heard a clear voice in her spirit asking her to move away from Leila's tent and go to hers.

Lord, please, I don't want to go today, she pleaded. If I keep away for a while, maybe I can break these feelings I am beginning to develop for him. Besides, you know I took that vow of chastity last month. I'm afraid going there will make it hard for me to continue to keep my vow.

She sighed wearily as she heard the Lord's gentle voice urging her to go to her tent and continue to read the Bible to the angry man.

She turned around and headed for her tent.

*****

Faizan looked up as Zainah entered the tent, and his heart did a violent flip. He shut his eyes in anger. Why did she affect him so?

She is a Christian and your enemy; remember that.

But he couldn't wrap his mind around that fact. She didn't seem like his enemy. She had done nothing but care and tend to him since he'd arrived.

She sat across from him and looked at him, and he told his heart to be still. When she had changed his bandage earlier, he had held his breath until she'd left, afraid he would move or say something wrong. That had puzzled him because it was so unlike him to be careful about what he said or did around people. But he found he cared what she thought. That was why he had been so aggressive. He had been trying to get her to back away, maybe hate him, so he wouldn't feel this way. But she hadn't. Instead, she had continued to tend to him.

She suddenly turned away, but not before he saw the look of embarrassment on her face. He instantly realized he had been staring at her the whole time.

I think I might be falling in love with you, he thought, and then chided himself for his thoughts. He could not fall in love with her. That was impossible. She picked up her Bible and opened it, most likely to read to him again, and he became vexed.

See why you cannot allow yourself to fall for her?

She opened her mouth to start reading, and he stood. He would not let her read her scriptures to him again. He shut his eyes for a minute as a wave of nausea hit him. He let the dizziness pass and then looked around for his shirt. He held the wall as he turned to her and asked, "Where is my shirt? The one I was wearing when you found me."

"I burned it."

His eyes widened. "You burned it?"

"It was nothing but rags when we found you."

He sighed, swallowed his pride and asked, "Do you have a men's shirt that I can put on?"

She shook her head. "There are only women and children in this camp."

He looked down at the beige trousers he wore. "But you put these on me."

She looked away again with that mortified look on her face. "I didn't put them on you. Miriam, our leader, did."

If not for his own discomfort, he would have laughed at the look on her face.

She continued without looking directly at him, "Someone in the camp found those trousers amongst their things and gave them to Miriam, who put them on you."

"I need to leave this place right now," he muttered harshly.

She shook her head and then looked at him. "You are not ready to leave. You are too…"

"Don't say weak," he said, glaring at her.

"But it's true. You wouldn't make it past the camp."

He tried to move to the door, but he thought better of it when another wave of dizziness washed over him. He sat down on the sleeping rug and groaned. He looked briefly at her and then shut his eyes, unwilling to keep looking at her beautiful face. Looking at her every day felt like constantly gazing at a delicious meal that he wasn't allowed to eat. It was beginning to drive him crazy.

He groaned again and put his hand on his head. When he felt her sit beside him, his heart lurched, and he opened his eyes and frowned.

"Are you okay?" she asked with a concerned look. "Is your head aching?"

He quickly shifted away from her and then glowered at her when she began to laugh.

"Why are you laughing?" He regarded her in anger.

She covered her mouth for a few seconds, and then she said with mirth, "I'm the one who took a vow of chastity, and yet you are the one shifting away!"

His eyes widened in surprise. "You took a vow of chastity? Why?"

Her smile melted away and a shadow fell over her face. He blinked and regretted asking her the question. It seemed like a sore topic for her. She suddenly stood and started to exit the tent, and he surprised himself when he immediately blurted out, "Please, don't go!"

She turned around, and he was sure the surprise on her face mirrored his. But he genuinely wanted her to stay. In fact, he was almost desperate for her not to leave. He said again, "Please stay."

He held his breath, hoping she would agree, even as he cursed himself for allowing his feelings for her to show this way. For sure, she would now know he had a weak spot for her, and every weakness in a person could be manipulated by another.

For the umpteenth time that day, he asked himself why he couldn't resist the way he felt about her.

She came and sat beside him again, and he exhaled in relief.

*****

Zainah blinked in surprise when Faizan looked earnestly at her and pleaded with her to stay.

Usually, he can't wait for me to leave, she thought. All he did whenever she was in the tent was grumble and be rude and commanding.

She sat beside him again. This time, he did not shift away. As much as she wanted to sit far from him, as her heart was racing at how close she was to him, how aware she was that he was staring at her, she stayed. She picked up her Bible again and began to read from the book of Psalms. After that, she read the story of the prodigal son again. She remembered clearly the day she had first read the story to him. She had told him that God was the father in that story. He had been incredulous, but with all her heart, she longed for him to experience the father's love. A love that never gave up on the sinner, no matter how far gone he seemed.

When she finished reading the story, she opened her mouth to speak, but he said, "You told me the father in this story is God. But that is impossible."

She prayed silently, asking God to give her the right words to say, and then she answered, "God's love is…"

"Enough of that for now!" he commanded suddenly, startling her. "Tell me about yourself." He looked into her eyes, and once again the look of desire in his partly scared her and partly drew her in. She trembled and then told herself to stay calm. She asked him, "What do you want to know?"

"Everything," he said.

"I think you already know my name is Zainah," she smiled at him. "Will you tell me yours?"

For a long moment, he didn't answer, and then he said, "Faizan."

She repeated his name, "Faizan. Well, . . . I was born into a big family in a village in Mali. I am my mother's first child, but the fifth in the family. My father was wealthy and I lacked nothing." She looked up as she remembered her family again, and the familiar pain wrapped itself around her heart. "I was very happy there and didn't have a care in the world. When I was about eighteen, some foreign missionaries came to our village. They preached the gospel to a few of us before everyone in the village realized who they were, and what their mission was, and kicked them out. But by then, I had come to Christ through their message."

His face instantly contorted, but she went on.

"I grew rapidly in my faith as I secretly read the Bible the missionaries had given me. I tried to hide my new faith from my family, but one day, one of my brothers caught me reading it and told my father. He asked if I was a Christian and I timidly admitted that I was."

Faizan looked away from her, but not before she saw the anger on his face. Knowing fully that he was a Muslim and what she was saying might offend him, she bit her lip and slowly continued.

"He asked me to renounce my faith and come back to Islam but I refused." She exhaled as she remembered the persecution that followed that time.

"Every day, I was brought before him and asked if I was ready to renounce my faith and every day, I refused to. They locked me up in my room and no one gave me food to eat. Nobody spoke to me, not even my own mother. My loving family became completely different. They became total strangers who hated me for my beliefs."

For a short moment, she stopped speaking. She shut her eyes as she clearly remembered the day her family had finally thrown her out of the house, and then she continued. "They didn't even care that I had no place to go," she said. "They just wanted me gone. Thankfully, there was another Christian convert who lived near us. She told me about this place. She wanted to leave our village because of the persecution she was facing and asked me to come with her. I stayed in her house for a day until Miriam came to our village at night with a truck. We left that night and found a plane at the edge of our village that flew us here. That was how I came here. Since then, I have dedicated my life wholly to God. He saved me, and therefore I want to live for only Him all the days of my life."

She was surprised when Faizan spoke. "Your family was right to do what they did. I would have…" he suddenly stopped speaking and looked away again, but the tone of his voice chilled her. Uneasy, she changed the subject and asked him about his childhood.

At first, she thought he wasn't going to tell her anything, as he didn't speak for a full minute. And then he said, "I remember the day my birth mother died. I was about five and I found her on the floor, unmoving. I tried to wake her up, but she wouldn't get up and so I began to cry. That's my most vivid memory of her."

Zainah's heart hurt at the sadness in his voice and the look in his eyes.

He continued, "I was taken away to live with some strangers. Those strangers, a man and a woman, soon adopted me, and I came to know them as my father and mother." He looked up at the ceiling thoughtfully. "My mother was a good woman. I loved her very much because she loved me with all her heart. My father, however, was..." Faizan sighed, "Let's just say he was not a good father. He didn't care much for me. As I grew up, I came to know that were it not for my mother, I would not have been adopted. My father didn't really want me, but my mother did, and so he gave in."

Faizan's voice was so filled with pain that Zainah felt an overwhelming urge to take his hands in hers. She stifled the feeling, however, and listened to him as he continued to speak.

"They died when I was twelve."

She gasped and then, despite herself, touched his hand. "I'm sorry."

He looked at her hand on his and she withdrew it. He went on. "A man," he looked into the distance, "kind and wise, took me as his and brought me up after that. He is dead now, but he taught me many things and I owe a great deal to him."

This time she felt the desire to hold him and comfort him, but she held herself in check. She couldn't even imagine what he would do if she gave in to her desire. She put her hands behind her so she wouldn't give in to the urge to touch him again.

She looked at him and, seeing how sad his eyes looked, her heart went out to him. "Maybe that explains your constant anger," she said softly as she tried to hold back the tears in her eyes.

He didn't say anything, only continued to gaze into the distance.

She suddenly couldn't hold back again and took his hand to comfort him. She gasped in surprise when he fell into her arms and wrapped his arms around her.

For several moments, she couldn't breathe or speak. Her heart thudded as she held him. Finally, he pushed away slightly and looked into her eyes. He lifted her chin with his fingers and his eyes searched hers.

Her pulse raced as he leaned in.

He is going to kiss me, she thought with a mixture of panic and desire. And then she stood and hurried out of the tent.

Outside the tent, she shut her eyes and leaned on the tent pillar to steady herself. Tears ran down her cheeks. Tears of fear and regret. She had longed to kiss him, and yet she'd known she shouldn't. She took a deep breath and then prayed, "Lord, I can't keep doing this. I'm falling harder for him every day and I know he isn't a Christian. And he is an angry man."

She walked away from the tent quickly, assuring herself that she was never going to go back there again. Not until Faizan was ready to leave.

She would ask the other women to help her take care of him until he was well enough to go.

Let someone else share the gospel with him from now, she said to herself. I am not strong enough to without becoming emotionally attached.

*****

Lauren sat down on the couch when they got back from Richie's anger management class. Richie looked sullen. The instructor had wanted to know about his progress, but rather than ask him, the man had asked her. Her silence had spoken volumes, and the instructor had immediately known that Richie wasn't doing well. He'd asked Richie why he didn't put the techniques he'd been taught to use into play, and Richie had insisted he had. The instructor had turned to Lauren and said, "The look on your wife's face tells a different story."

After the man had scolded Richie, he reiterated the techniques he'd taught the class to use to control their anger. Richie had been sulking since then. Lauren knew what was coming now. He would take his anger out on her.

He looked down at her with scorn and said, "You tried to make me look bad again today."

Without thinking, she blurted out, "I didn't! You made yourself look bad!"

He glowered at her. "You could have told the instructor that I was doing well; instead you stood looking at him like a dumb imbecile."

Rage burned in her stomach, but she held it in check. She wasn't like him, a fool who was not able to control his emotions. She narrowed her eyes and said to him, "What did you expect me to say? That you've been treating me well? That you haven't hit me since I came back to you? That would all be a lie and you know it."

"I expected you to support your husband. That's why you were there!"

"No, you wanted me to lie for you. You've been hitting me since I came back here, but I didn't even say anything about it. Who knows what the instructor would have done if I'd told him the extent of your brutish behavior toward me."

Richie glared at her. "I thought you would be a supportive wife, but you're just useless."

She nodded. "I am a useless wife; that's why you should just let me go."

He laughed humorlessly and stood again. "No! Your place is by my side."

She sighed loudly and spoke with a boldness she didn't know she had. "This marriage isn't working and you know it! I can't do this anymore."

He snarled at her. "I said you are staying here with me!" He sighed and then bent down and said softly, "Listen, Lauren. If you just do what I ask you every time, we won't have to keep fighting."

"That is your idea of a good marriage?" she spat out. "One party does what the other wants every single time? What about what I want?"

He looked taken aback. "Haven't I tried to be a good husband? I've taken you out multiple times, brought you breakfast in bed, given you flowers, and loved you like every woman wants to be loved."

She looked him in the eye and countered, "And you have also slapped, pushed, and ridiculed me continuously. Most of all, you've kept me captive here."

He blinked. "But you don't really want to leave me, do you?"

"Yes... yes, I do. I've had enough!"

His eyes flashed. "We talked about having a baby..."

"You did! I told you I wasn't ready."

She gasped when he suddenly grabbed her hair, and then his hand immediately loosened and he smoothed it down gently. "I'm sorry."

"It's what you say every time, but it doesn't stop you from hurting me moments after you do."

He ran his fingers through his hair and shook his head. "I am really trying. I don't know what comes over me sometimes." He looked at her again. "Sometimes, you make me so angry..."

"Here you go, blaming me again for your anger issues."

He pressed his forehead against hers and said, "Maybe if we have a baby now, all the anger will stop."

She moved her head away. "No, it won't!" She curled up on the couch and pursed her lips. "I'm tired, Richie. Can we talk about all this some other time?"

He straightened and looked at her for a full minute. She shut her eyes and ignored him, hoping he would go away. When she opened them, she found he had left. She breathed a sigh of relief and for the first time in years, prayed that God would help her find a way out of this house and her troubled marriage.

TEN

The midday sun was blazing hot in the sky when Sadiq stationed himself beside Ahmed and picked up his binoculars. His eyes darted from one end of the small camp of women to the other. The women were going about, doing their various chores. Different tiny tents were scattered around the camp. He could see a few of the women praying in a tent. As far as he could see, there were no guards there or even a single man. The women looked docile enough, easy prey for him.

He almost felt disappointed. He liked a good challenge, and this was certainly no challenge.

As he continued to gaze at the camp, however, his view of the situation changed. Hassan had told him to kill everyone in the camp, but many of these women were beautiful. He didn't have to kill them. He could singularly round them up and take them to their own camp. Hassan would be pleased when he saw them. Those that survived the journey would become wives or concubines for the men there.

He told Ahmed his plan, but the small man only shrugged.

"I'll have to find our remaining surviving man… assuming he is still alive," he said to Ahmed. "If he is, he would probably be tied up somewhere. I'll have to capture one of the women and get her to take me to where our man is being kept."

He lifted his binoculars to his eyes and gazed at the women's camp again, and then his breath suddenly caught in his throat. A woman was carrying a tray of food, probably on her way to one of the tents. She was dusky and beautiful and had an elegant poise about her that he had never seen before.

His heart raced with lust, and he knew immediately that he had to have her. When he carried the women to the camp, he would reserve her specifically for himself.

He looked at Ahmed and decided the small man would have to wait there. Ahmed was not a fighter. He would only be a liability if he took him along to the camp.

"Wait here," Sadiq said, standing up. I'll be back with the women and hopefully with our man alive."

"Can we get all of them into the truck?" Ahmed asked.

"We will get as many as we can in. The rest of them will make the journey on foot."

Ahmed raised his brows but didn't say anything more.

Sadiq turned to watch the camp again and noted that the beautiful dark woman was nearing a tent, probably her destination, with her tray of food. He slung his rifle over his shoulder and hurried toward the tent to apprehend her.

*****

Zainah carried the tray of food slowly to her tent while praying and asking God to help her. She didn't want to go and had vowed to stay away from Faizan until he'd left the tent. But she had no choice that day. Everyone was busy with one chore or another, and since it had originally been her duty to serve his food, she had to do it.

She thinned her lips as she neared the tent. Her attraction to him scared her. When they had hugged the other day, she wanted to stay in his arms forever. What was worse, though, was his attraction to her. It unnerved her. He'd stared at her on that day as though he'd wanted to devour her. Who knew what he would do today? What she would let him do?

She paused in front of her tent and took a deep breath. "Lord, I can't do this," she cried. "I don't want to see him again."

She began to step into the tent and then gasped in fear when a rough hand suddenly grabbed her from behind. The plates of food clattered to the ground. She began to scream just as a hand covered her mouth and another grasped her wrists. She tried to free herself from her attacker's grasp, but she couldn't.

For a brief moment, she wondered if it was Faizan, but immediately discarded the thought. This man smelled different, and she knew intuitively that, in spite of Faizan's cruel words to her in the past, he would never hurt her like this. Not now. Plus, he was still too weak.

Again, she tried to scream, but the attacker tightened his hold on her. Her heart began to beat wildly with fear as he began to drag her away with him.

She prayed desperately, Lord, please help me. Please!

And then she heard Faizan's voice thunder, "Leave her alone, Sadiq!"

The man's hand immediately fell from her mouth, but he still held her hands firmly.

She looked at Faizan. He was leaning on the wall, looking past her with blazing eyes. She immediately became worried for him. He still looked weak. This Sadiq's hand felt huge and something that felt like the muzzle of a gun poked her back. He could hurt Faizan if he wasn't careful. She opened her mouth to tell Faizan to take caution, but the man called Sadiq clamped her mouth shut again.

Faizan roared, "I told you to let her go!"

Sadiq said, "Faizan, Hassan gave me clear instructions to..."

Faizan's eyes flashed with rage. "Is Hassan your leader... or am I? Now, I gave you an order, Sadiq. Let her go immediately!"

Zainah's eyes widened in horror. No... it can't be. Faizan knows this Sadiq! He's the leader of some dangerous group that the man belongs to!

Sadiq loosened his grip on her, and she backed away.

"Go, Zainah!" Faizan shouted. "Now!"

She turned around and began to run, and then her stomach flipped and terror overwhelmed her heart as she heard a loud bang—the unmistakable sound of a gunshot. She screamed. That evil man had shot Faizan! Her vision became blurry and dread overtook her.

*****

Pandemonium erupted in the camp as loud screams broke out everywhere. Faizan frowned, listening to the shouts and dozens of feet running this way and that. He glared at Sadiq in anger. Part of him wanted to go and check on Zainah to make sure she was fine, but he knew that would not be the right decision to take at that moment.

He roared at Sadiq, who had the gun pointed at him, "What do you think you're doing, shooting at me?"

Sadiq shook his head. "You left me with no choice, Faizan. You are acting suspiciously. Our group's tenet is to kill or enslave every single Christian we can lay our hands on, yet you were trying to protect that one."

Faizan raised a brow at him. "And so, if you're going to kill me, why didn't you just do it?"

"I didn't want to kill you. I was just confused because you told me to let that woman go… even though she is a Christian." He gave Faizan an accusatory stare.

Faizan began to calculate in his mind what he could do. Sadiq was a skilled killer, but he was unlikely to just shoot him since he was still the leader of their group. Nevertheless, Sadiq could do so if he didn't proceed with caution. Faizan nodded. "It is not your place to tell me that, Sadiq. I know what our tenet is. I had a plan before you came here and ruined it all," Faizan said.

Sadiq looked at him curiously. His expression seemed partly suspicious and partly relieved. He finally said, "What are your plans? My order was to kill everyone here, but I think it will be a waste with so many beautiful women. I wanted to take them all back to our camp as concubines for the men." He gave Faizan a lascivious grin. "That dark one that I was holding is mine."

Faizan suddenly felt his whole body tremble with rage. He wanted to jump Sadiq, seize his gun, and shoot him right there. In normal times, he could have. Even though Sadiq was a deadly killer, Faizan himself was also trained in the same way and could take Sadiq easily. But now, he was too weak to do that. He had to find another way to overpower the man.

He smiled at Sadiq, a smile he hoped appeared conspiratorial. "My plan was almost the same. I have been recuperating and haven't had enough energy to carry it out. But now that you're here, we could do it together. You should have first asked me what my plan was instead of trying to shoot me."

Sadiq looked apologetic. "I'm sorry." He lowered his gun. "Eh… can I have that woman, then?"

Faizan struggled to control his rage. "Of course. I'm finished with her." He surreptitiously studied the man. He was at ease now with his gun at his side, his expression full of lust. This was the time to act. "So, tell me what exactly your plan is, Sadiq. And how can I help?"

Sadiq nodded. "I accede to you, Faizan. I was thinking we could…"

Faizan suddenly jumped him as adrenaline pulsed through his body, strengthening him for an instant. He wrestled the gun out of Sadiq's hand before the man could realize what was happening and then leveled the weapon at him.

"What is this, Faizan?" Sadiq asked, his face a mask of confusion.

Faizan answered coldly, "You won't be capturing anyone today, Sadiq!"

"What are you doing?" Sadiq asked, his eyes wide.

"You need to leave now, or I will shoot you."

"You have to be bluffing. Why would you take their side over mine?"

Faizan cocked the gun and shot the ground near Sadiq. It made a loud boom, but only elicited a blink from the assassin.

Faizan ordered again, "Leave now, Sadiq! The people here are not to be harmed."

"Says who?" Sadiq asked incredulously.

"I say so. In case you don't remember, I'm still the leader of Al-Muharib."

"And as the leader, you should know better," Sadiq said. "This isn't…"

"How dare you question my judgment!" Faizan glared at him with the gun still pointed. "I'm going to count to five. If you are still here by then, I will shoot you. I promise."

Sadiq frowned and did not move. He said, "You are actually going to shoot me to protect a group of infidels."

Faizan began counting. "One… two… three…" He leveled the gun at Sadiq's chest. "Four…"

Sadiq nodded and said, "I'll go." He began to back away and then snarled at Faizan. "Know that this isn't over. You have betrayed the brotherhood, and therefore you have become our enemy. Know that I will return very soon… with an army."

*****

Zainah walked slowly toward Faizan. He still had the gun in his hand, pointed into the distance. His eyes looked weary.

He suddenly slid to the ground with a groan, and Zainah rushed to him. She stooped, put her arms around him and tried to lift him up.

He shook his head and said to her, "Leave me. I'll find a way to stand up. Everyone in the camp needs to move right now. Sadiq will be back again, this time with more men."

Zainah's heart beat with dread as she studied Faizan's eyes. What kind of man had she been harboring in her tent all this time? He was clearly part of some deadly group. Could she trust him now?

As she stared into his eyes, she found the answer she was looking for, and it took her breath away. He was looking at her with such affection and concern, she knew for her sake he would not allow the entire camp to come to harm.

She bit her lips and nodded. "We have another safe haven some distance away from here. I believe it is also untraceable."

"Nowhere is untraceable for our group," he said to her. He muttered, "Hassan must have hired Ahmed to track this place." He frowned, worry clouding his features.

"I think whoever that Ahmed is was able to trace us because of the plane crash." She stood. "I will gather the entire camp together so we can move to the safe haven now."

He nodded. "I'll stay here to divert them. It's me they really want."

Zainah shook her head vigorously. "We can't leave you here. You're coming with us."

"No, I can't!" he said gruffly. "I will bring harm to everyone if I do." He looked at her with soft eyes and said, "Go and gather everyone now and go to the safe haven." He took her hand. "Thank you for everything."

Zainah looked at him as he sat on the ground, his back against the tent, his handsome face twisted in pain. She knew it was no use arguing with him and there was no time, either.

She nodded and left him there, her heart racing. Immediately, she went to find Miriam and told her what Faizan had said. "We need to gather everyone and leave right away," she said.

Miriam had a grim expression on her face. "I'll get to it." She called two of the women who were near her tent and told them to spread the word that everyone should start packing. "We will leave in about an hour," Miriam said.

Zainah nodded and went to find Leila. Her best friend was in the prayer tent with some other women and children. Their faces were full of fear. Leila called out to her, "What were those loud noises we heard in the camp, Zainah? Do you know?"

Zainah quickly narrated what had happened and their plan to evacuate immediately. "I need your help," Zainah said to her after she'd finished talking. She took Leila's hand and began to run.

"What is it, Zainah?"

Zainah didn't answer until they'd reached the front of her tent. Faizan was still sitting there, his head against the tent pillar, his eyes shut.

"Please help me lift him and take him to one of the camels," she said to Leila. "He is too weak to walk on his own."

Zainah walked up to Faizan with Leila and started to lift him up. Zainah put one of his hands on her shoulders and Leila, the other. He groaned and opened his eyes. When he saw her, he blinked and then said groggily, "What are you doing? I told you to leave me here."

Zainah looked him in the eye and said, "There is no way I am ever going to leave you here, Faizan. You are coming with us whether you like it or not."

He groaned again and shut his eyes.

They took deep breaths as they labored to drag him to the camel. At last, they got to the back of the camp where there were half a dozen camels tied to a tent. Other women in the camp were already beginning to load bags and foodstuffs onto the camels' backs. Zainah and Leila heaved Faizan onto the camel's back, thankfully with some of his help, and secured him firmly. Two other people, most likely children, would ride with him on the camel.

An hour later, just as Miriam had said, everyone and everything they had to carry had been loaded and gathered around the camels. They left immediately, with most of the women carrying their items on their heads or backs. Zainah walked beside the camel where Faizan sat hunched over and didn't leave his side until they'd gotten to the other camp safely.

*****

For some time, Lauren had been wondering about Richie's so-called vacation. It was already weeks in. She'd known him as a workaholic, but suddenly he'd taken weeks off work and never said anything about his job. Even when she asked him if he was still being considered for the promotion he'd wanted for years, he didn't answer.

She couldn't contain her suspicions any longer and decided to call his workplace. One day, after they'd returned from his anger management class, he went upstairs and she remained in the living room. She brought out her cell phone from her purse and called the number he'd given her for his office in case of emergencies. When a female voice came on the line, she asked for her husband, Richard Patterson. She told the woman she'd not seen him for some time and decided to call his office.

The woman asked her to hold. Minutes later, she was transferred to someone else, a man who told her Richie no longer worked there. He had been fired months before.

Her eyes widened in surprise, and then she thanked the man and ended the call.

She paced the living room. So Richie had been lying to her all this time. He wasn't on vacation. He'd been fired. She held her head with her hands and laughed bitterly.

That meant he was never going back to work and this twenty-four-hour surveillance would continue indefinitely. She shut her eyes as a wave of dizziness ran through her. They had probably been living off his savings since she'd come back. With both of them unemployed, it would not be long before they began to lack basic necessities. Maybe she could get a job. In that way, she could kill two birds with one stone. First, they would have some money to buy the basic things they needed, and she would have something that would give her life purpose.

The more she thought about it, the more she wanted to get a job. Maybe she would not have to leave Richie if he let her get a job. She would not have to be in close proximity to him all day long, and then they wouldn't get into fights where he ended up hitting her.

She had been an elementary school teacher when she'd married Richie. He had insisted that he could provide everything they both needed and that she didn't have to work. She hadn't argued with him then, as the prospect of not having to work had been very appealing to her. She'd been glad she was married to a guy who wanted to provide for her. Now she knew he had insisted she stop working, not because he was such a great provider, but because of his desire to control her and everything she did.

She had enjoyed her job as an elementary school teacher. She could find a teaching job again. Her excitement and anxiety increased as she thought about working again. It would be great to find a teaching job, but first, she had to confront Richie about his work status and tell him she needed to get a job. She wasn't looking forward to that.

Knowing she couldn't postpone it any longer, she stood up and went upstairs. At the door of their bedroom, she paused and exhaled to try to get rid of her pent-up anxiety and then entered. Richie was sitting on the bed, watching a game of football. He glanced at her as she walked up to him and then turned back to his game.

"Richie, can I speak with you? It will only take a minute."

He turned to her again, sighed loudly to clearly show her that she was disturbing him and then paused the DVR. "What is it, Lauren?" he asked impatiently.

"Umm…" her heart raced as she considered the best way to talk to him about his job. "How come your vacation isn't over, Richie? I know how much you like your job and it's weird that you took this much time off from it."

He looked at her as if she had completely lost it and then said, "Are you trying to accuse me of something? Because you can just go ahead and say it." He stared at her, his eyes daring her to say what was on her mind.

He already knows I suspect he was fired from his job.

She decided to take the peaceful route and said, "I was just remembering how it felt to have a job. You remember I was a teacher when we got married. I think I want to get a teaching job again, Richie. Besides, the extra income would be good for both of us."

He eyed her. "You don't have to get a job. I told you when we got married that I would provide for both of us and the children we have in the future. I still mean it."

She stared at him. She wanted to tell him she knew he had been laid off and that it was imperative she got a job until he could find another one, but she decided against it. Instead, she said, "I know you can provide for me, but I want to work. I like the feeling of working and getting paid for a job well done. Besides that, I enjoyed teaching kids…"

"You enjoy teaching other people's children

instead of your own!" His eyes flashed with anger. "How will we ever have kids of our own if you are out teaching other people's?"

She sighed wearily. "We've talked about this before. I'm just not ready yet to have kids."

He looked away from her and picked up the TV remote control. "Then this conversation is over," he said. "You aren't going to get a job. I will provide for us, just like I promised." He played the DVR and continued to watch his game. She started to protest, but he raised the volume and drowned out her voice.

She glared at him for a long moment and then left the bedroom. There was no reasoning with him. His mind was already made up. Still, she wanted to work. She had to find a way to make that happen while she also figured out if she really wanted to leave him permanently or stay.

ELEVEN

Audrey stood as the consultant put a wedding dress on her. She hadn't tried any wedding dresses since the wedding planning had begun. That day, she'd come to Satin Dreams with Sienna and Trisha to start her wedding dress shopping, and she felt nervous but excited to try on dresses. Even though Trisha and Sienna had told her she might not, she was hoping, with their help, to find the perfect dress that day.

She shut her eyes as the consultant smiled and turned her around so she could look at herself in the mirror. She took a deep breath. Fingers crossed, she thought. Opening her eyes, she regarded herself in the mirror. The simple fitted satin dress was her pick. She had promised Sienna and Trisha that she would try on theirs if this one wasn't right for her.

The dress was okay, but she was sure Trisha and Sienna would not approve of it. They probably wanted her in an expensive designer gown. As if they didn't understand her simple tastes by now.

"What do you think?" the consultant asked her.

"Umm… I like it, but I first want to show my sisters and see what they say. I have to get their approval on the dress I wear for my wedding," she grumbled, but in truth, she was relieved her sisters were here to help her with the shopping. She wasn't very good at picking the best dresses. Trisha and Sienna would help her find the perfect wedding dress, one that would cause Ken's jaw to drop on their special day. She couldn't wait.

She stepped out of the dressing room and walked into the private reception room where Sienna and Trisha were waiting.

She stood in front of them and twirled. "So, what do you think about this one? Is this my wedding dress?"

Trisha shook her head. "It's too simple, Audrey. I know you like simple dresses but it's your wedding day. You're only going to have one." She paused and Audrey gave her a sympathetic smile. "Well… as long as you marry the right guy. And I know you are going to marry the right guy. Unlike Stan, Ken is a gem."

Sienna stood and came to feel the dress's fabric. "It does look nice on you," Sienna said in her usual encouraging way. "But I agree with Trisha. It's way too simple."

"So this is not the one," Audrey said.

"Definitely not!" Trisha replied.

"'Kay, then." The consultant came and led Audrey back to the dressing room to try on Trisha's pick.

Audrey put on the next dress and the consultant helped her with the bustier. She exhaled after the lady finished and then turned around. She stared at herself in the mirror and then shook her head. "This one is definitely a 'heck no'! What was Trisha thinking when she picked this dress for me?" She looked at the strapless, cleavage-baring, lingerie-inspired dress. The lacy bodice was transparent and too tight. She groaned. What will I do with Trisha?

"Are you going to come out and show your sisters the dress?" the consultant asked her.

She sighed and considered the question. She would rather not, but Trisha had to see this on her. She needed to understand why her sister had chosen this dress.

"I'll go show them," she answered.

She stepped out again and walked to the room where Trisha and Sienna were waiting. She shook her head as she entered the room. "What were you thinking, girl?" she looked down at Trisha. "Look at this. Why did you think I would ever want to wear this, Trisha?"

Sienna giggled. "It looks like some of the lingerie I wore during my modeling days."

Trisha shrugged. "I happen to like it, Audrey. But I guess it is a bit more revealing than I thought."

"A bit?" Audrey chuckled.

"Okay… lots more, but it does look great on you."

Sienna gave her a wink and a teasing smile. "Maybe you could buy it for your wedding night and…"

"Stop, Sienna!" Audrey waved a finger at her and laughed. "Why are you always going on about that?"

"'Cause she's a newlywed," Trisha said and sighed. "I'm a little jealous." She looked at Sienna. "It's not easy being divorced. You get used to having a constant companion for years and then suddenly you have no one. Sometimes I feel lonely… but I'm still grateful to the Lord. I have baby Ruby to keep me company."

"When will you be ready to start dating again?" Audrey asked, thinking about Frank.

"Stop it, Audrey! Stop asking me that question. I know where it's going. You want me to date Frank." She gave Audrey a weary look. "I'm just not ready to date anyone now. It's too soon. And I don't know that I will want to date Frank even if I was."

"Why not?" Audrey asked.

"Just 'cause!" The dismissive look on her face told Audrey she was through with the topic.

Audrey sighed and said, "Well, no to this dress as well." She smiled at her sisters before exiting the room to go to the changing room again.

As the consultant put her in the wedding dress Sienna had picked for her, Audrey held her breath. Lord, please let this be the one, she prayed silently.

She turned to look at the mirror after the consultant had zipped up the dress. The gown was a full lace mermaid vintage dress. She smiled as she turned this way and that. The dress looked nice on her. It was simple but elegant at the same time. It had just the right amount of crystals. She liked it. The only problem was that she didn't feel the spark she thought she would when she found her dress. She stared at the gown in confusion and then decided to immediately show it to Trisha and Sienna. Perhaps they would keep her focused and help her see that this was her dress.

She came out again and stood before her sisters. "What do you guys think? I really like it but there is just something missing… I don't know what it is."

"You look lovely, Audrey," Trisha said, "but if you aren't feeling this dress the way you should, then it isn't it."

Sienna nodded. "It looks great… but I do agree, even though I was the one who picked it out for you. There's something missing."

Audrey sighed. "Great. What do I do now?"

Sienna suggested, "Let's go home and talk about it. You've worn different styles and still haven't found the right dress. We will come back again when we can decide on what style would be best for you."

Audrey went and changed out of the dress, feeling slightly disappointed that she hadn't found the perfect one that day. They trooped out of the store and decided to reconvene at Audrey's before the end of the week.

"Don't worry, Audrey," Sienna said. "You will find the right dress soon, the way you have found the right guy."

Audrey nodded. "I hope so. Talking about the right guy, I have to call Ken today."

They went in different directions—Audrey to her house, Trisha to hers. Sienna took a cab back to the Bible school. Audrey took a deep breath as she got to the house. Hopefully, she would find 'the dress' soon. But even if she didn't, she wouldn't let it mar her wedding day because she would be marrying her best friend and the love of her life.

*****

"Lauren, our marriage counseling session is in an hour!" Richie exclaimed as he came into the bedroom. Lauren was lying on the bed, pretending to still be asleep. "How come you're still in bed, in your pajamas?"

Lauren grumbled and turned over. She had told Richie she wasn't going to go back to that marriage counselor again when he'd told her about their appointment that day. He had said nothing then and she'd thought she was off the hook. Now she knew he'd just ignored her.

He called out again, "Lauren, stand up!"

She didn't answer. A sudden sharp slap on her back caused her to spring up. She touched her back, wincing in pain. "You hit me again, Richie," she glared at him.

"And I will do it again if you don't start to get dressed right now! We'll be late for our counseling appointment today if we don't get moving now."

An intense anger suddenly came over her, and she faced off with him. "I am not going! I told you I didn't want to go when you brought it up yesterday, and I haven't changed my mind!"

His eyes blazed with anger as he spat out, "You will do exactly as I say…!"

"No, I won't!"

His face grew red, and then he slapped her so hard she fell to the ground.

She held her cheek in pain but refused to cry. This was the third time he had slapped her since she'd returned to him. The first time, her cheeks had reddened and the pain did not leave for days. The bruise took longer. This time, from the pain she felt, she was sure it was going to bruise again. She looked up at him, but instead of anger, she felt defiant. She laughed bitterly. "I'm sure my cheek is going to be badly bruised. Maybe I should go with you to that stupid counselor's office and show him what you've just done to me. Perhaps that will get him to drop his weird chauvinistic views… or maybe not."

Richie gave her a dirty look. "You made me do it."

She laughed again. "Of course I did. I'm to blame for all your angry outbursts. Has it ever occurred to you that you make me very angry too, and yet I never hit you?"

He looked at her with an expression on his face she couldn't decipher and then turned around and left the room.

She felt a little triumphant at having gotten herself out of going to his counseling appointment. But she knew it was a temporary victory. He would be back a day or two later with even worse demands, and maybe, having regrouped, even angrier. She remembered her time with the Gibsons and what they were encouraged to do every time they were in a bind. Diane would always say, "Take it to the Lord in prayer." Lauren smiled sadly. She never did because she didn't want to have anything to do with the Lord or prayer. But, now, she felt tempted to do exactly that—pray.

She gave in. "God," she whispered, "I know you are there… but I just don't know that you hear me. If you do, please give me a way out of this mess I'm in." She sighed after she'd said the prayer and lay back on the bed. She was going to sleep in today.

An intense desire to call Diane suddenly took hold of her and she sat up. She hadn't spoken to the woman since she'd left Rosefield. What would

Diane say to her? She would definitely be disappointed that she'd gone back to Richie. It was the painful feeling that she'd disappointed the woman who had been so kind to her that Lauren had been trying to avoid. But she didn't want to put off calling her any longer.

She picked up her cell phone from beside her and searched for Diane's name and number. When she found it, she called Diane and waited as the phone rang.

Diane's voice came on the line and Lauren's heart thudded. She said, "Diane, this is Lauren Patterson."

Diane chuckled. "I know, honey! I have your number."

All Lauren could say was, "Oh!"

"How are you, Lauren? We miss having you at our home. Are you well?"

Lauren didn't answer for some seconds while she wondered what to tell Diane. She finally decided neither to lie nor tell her the full truth. She said, "I miss you guys too. I guess I called to thank you for everything you did for me when I was at your house. I've been feeling really crummy about not telling you and Paul I was leaving. You both were so kind to me, taking me in and treating me like your daughter. I just want to say thank you."

Dianne laughed. "That's okay, darling. Remember, though, that we did it all because Jesus asked us to. We always want to be his hands of love."

Lauren smiled. It was what the couple always said. She missed them so much. She said, "Well... again, thank you."

"You are welcome, dear. And I hope you know

you can call me anytime and talk to me about whatever problems you might have."

Lauren said with a voice choked with emotion, "I will, Diane. And I hope to visit again one day."

Diane replied, "You are welcome anytime. And know that Paul and I will be praying for you every day."

The call ended, and Lauren sighed sadly as she ran through her mind what Diane had just said to her. Diane had reminded her she could talk to her about any problems she had. Ken had told her something similar. Why couldn't she just tell them what was going on with her and Richie?

Well, I know why I can't tell Ken. He might appear on my doorstep with a loaded gun and shoot Richie.

As for Diane, she wanted the woman to think well of her. Telling her she'd chosen to stay with Richie in spite of all his abuse would be like a slap to the woman's face. Diane had taught her over the months to resist every kind of abuse, and yet she had walked right into it with her eyes wide open.

Now, she felt trapped. Hopefully, one day soon, she would not only find a way to leave Richie, but have the strength to do so.

*****

Faizan looked around him. He was in the tent at the safe haven. In spite of his protests, Zainah and her friend, Leila, had brought him here. It was similar to the old tent at the old camp. The only difference was that it was smaller and had fewer furnishings.

He couldn't stop thinking about his encounter

with Sadiq the day before. The assassin had been sent to destroy every single person in the camp. Faizan understood the ideology behind the decision and had totally believed it. But when he'd come face to face with the decision to do it or even allow it to happen, he just couldn't. Something in him rebelled at the idea of killing so many innocent people, especially people who had been so kind to him, just because they believed differently from him. Most of all, he had gone crazy when Sadiq had set his lustful eyes on Zainah.

I'm in love with her, he admitted to himself. The thought of her getting hurt in any way had made him sick to his stomach.

His mind focused on Zainah. He loved everything about her—her beauty, her poise, her kindness, the feel of her hands on his skin when she tended to his wounds, the sound of her voice as she talked or read to him. Everything.

But he didn't know if it was such a good thing, his love for her. She didn't even know who he really was. She would reject him in a split second if she knew. Besides, she had told him about her vow of chastity, whatever she meant by that. He was pretty sure she wasn't about to break it because of him.

He turned on the sleeping rug he was lying on. If only she wasn't a Christian. If she was a Muslim, maybe they would have a chance.

A small voice whispered in his ear, But it is her faith that makes her who she is, who you have fallen in love with.

He jerked his head up. The voice was so clear. Where had it come from?

He lay his head down again. But it was true. She

had told him time and time again that God's love for her had changed her and that she wanted to love others the way her Jesus loved her.

His emotions roiled as he thought about that. Her faith in God and his were so different. She believed in a God of love, while he believed in a God of wrath. And what had happened the previous day with Sadiq had caused him to question everything he had previously believed. The thought that he would have easily given the order to wipe out the whole camp if he was in Hassan's shoes made him sick. What if Sadiq had succeeded in doing it or had taken the women, even Zainah, as sex slaves for the men in the camp?

He turned again as terror gripped him. Thinking about it was driving him crazy. He could not allow anything bad happen to Zainah, and by extension the whole camp. He didn't know what he would do if she was harmed. He knew one thing, however. He would give his life if need be in order to protect her.

Again, his mind went back to his dilemma. What would he do about his love for her? It was growing every day.

He didn't know the answer to that. The wall separating them was insurmountable. Maybe the best thing would be for him to leave. Then he would no longer have to long for her every day. All the women and children were most likely safe there. He could go back to camp and hand himself over to Hassan. He would tell Hassan not to keep trying to find the women anymore since it was him he really wanted.

He pressed his lips together as he made up his mind. As soon as he was well enough, he would go back. Hassan could do with him as he pleased as long as Zainah and the others here were safe.

*****

Zainah bent down to put a damp cloth on Faizan's forehead. He'd been getting better and stronger every day, but she was scared that the strain of his confrontation with that evil man, plus the stress of travel, would slow his recuperation.

He looked up at her and smiled. "You don't have to look so worried. I'm fine."

Her heart skipped a beat at his smile. He had never smiled at her before. The day before, after they'd arrived at the safe haven—a camp with tents like the first one, but much smaller —she and Leila had taken him to the tent farthest away from the camp's border. She'd been afraid that he had opened one of his wounds, but that had not happened. She was sharing a tent with several women now. Until they could build more tents, it would remain that way.

She sat beside him, folded the damp cloth and put it away. She frowned. The events of the previous day were still deeply troubling to her. She could not forget what he had said to the bad man about being the leader of some violent group. She looked at him again and asked, "I am really curious, Faizan. You knew that man who wanted to kidnap me yesterday, and even said something about being his leader." She ignored the frown he gave her and went on. "I need to know. What is the group you spoke about yesterday… and who are you, really?"

There. She had asked the question that had been bothering her, not just since the day before, but for some time now.

He sighed loudly as he looked at her and then said, "When I tell you, you might hate me."

She searched his eyes. He doesn't even know how I feel about him, she thought. "I won't hate you. I promise."

"You will… but I will tell you anyway. It's better you know the truth about me. I don't want to lie to you." His eyes were soft as he looked at her. "I belong to a group known as Al-Muharib. And you heard rightly. I am the leader of that group. I became the leader not long ago… after the old leader died." He looked down for a few seconds and then looked at her again. "It's a group you would call a terrorist organization."

Zainah sucked in her breath sharply. She was in love with a terrorist?

"That isn't all. Our mission is to kill infidels… like Christians. We were on a mission to blow up some targets in a city I won't tell you for now… when our plane crashed."

Zainah shut her eyes in utter disbelief. She'd been tending to a dangerous terrorist for the last few weeks. She had nursed a man who had been on his way to murder people. The whole camp had been in grave danger due to his presence among them and they had not even known it.

She trembled as she looked at him, and then she heard the Spirit's voice. Would you have let him die if you'd known he was a terrorist?

She blinked. Would I have let him die if I knew who he truly was? She couldn't come up with an answer. She looked at him again. His eyes scrutinized her face. She could see in them acceptance and what she knew was care for her. The deadness she had seen in them when he'd first arrived was mostly gone. Still, she couldn't shake the dread that settled in her heart. He was dangerous, no matter how he now looked at her.

And yet, as she gazed at him, she discovered that her feelings for him had not changed despite what he had just told her.

They stared at each other in silence for a few minutes. At last, Faizan said, "I'll fully understand if you want me to leave right away. I was already planning to."

She asked him, "Where will you go?"

"Back to the Al-Muharib camp," he answered.

She cried out, "You can't go back there! They might kill you. Besides, you aren't well enough to leave the tent." She wondered at what she had just told him. She wanted him to stay… but for utterly selfish reasons. She couldn't bear the thought of not seeing him again, getting to care for him, touching him. However, she had to think about the safety of the camp.

But I don't want him to go back to a place where he might be in danger.

Most importantly, he still hadn't accepted Jesus into his life. He might never have the chance if he left. His eternal soul was in jeopardy.

"I have to go," he said.

"At least stay here until you are well enough," she said to him. Maybe he would come to Christ before he was healed and then he would remain in the camp with them; with her.

He looked intensely at her, his eyes curious and confused. "Are you saying that in spite of what I just told you, you still want me to stay here?"

She nodded.

He scrunched up his face and for a brief moment, she thought he was about to cry. He smiled and then said, "I will stay. I'll try to protect everyone here. With my life if I have to." He took her hand and jolts of electricity shot up her arm. "But, when I get well, Zainah, at some point I will have to leave… Unless…"

He didn't complete his sentence, but from the look in his eyes, she guessed what he was saying. Her face and body grew hot. He wanted her.

For a few seconds, she basked in that thought, and then she quickly came to her senses. She couldn't be with him. They couldn't be together. He didn't believe in her savior. And even if he gave his heart to the Lord today, she still had her vow of chastity. They were doomed to be apart.

She stood up slowly and exited the tent. When she was outside, she ran as far away from the tent as she could so she would not be tempted to forget about everything and give in to what he wanted.

TWELVE

Faizan kept thinking about his conversation with Zainah long after she'd left his tent. He had thought she would ask him to leave the camp immediately after she'd found out who he really was, but she hadn't. Instead, she had extended to him an unexpected kindness in addition to the kindness she'd already shown him. He marveled at that. It brought up a lot of questions. Those questions had haunted him for some time now, but with this new kindness she'd shown him, the questions demanded instant answers.

Was his way right or was hers? Was he really pleasing God by living as he had for such a long time, or was love, the kind she demonstrated, God's true path?

He tossed and turned as night came and he couldn't sleep. Finally, he knew he had to ask the only one who knew the answers to his questions.

He lifted a silent prayer to God, asking for a clear sign to know if her way, her belief in Jesus, was the right way. "You know I want to please you," he prayed. "If Zainah is right and I am wrong, please show me."

After he had prayed, he looked up at the ceiling and waited… and then he scolded himself. Maybe his prayer had been foolish. And why was he questioning everything he knew?

But he knew in order to discover the truth and clear his confusion, he had to find answers from God.

"You have to be patient," he said to himself.

His thoughts again turned to Zainah. If only he could tell her the truth of how he felt about her, just as he had told her about who he really was. But he was afraid she would reject him. Maybe that was one of his major weaknesses. The fear of rejection. It was why he had striven so hard to fit in Al-Muharib and prove to all that he was as devout as they were.

Just tell her how you feel. If she rejects you, so what? At least you did your best, he thought.

Angrily he spat out, "It is not if she will reject me, it's when. And that is exactly why I won't tell her anything."

He sighed. Why would she want to have anything to do with him after she knew the truth about him? It was one thing to show him kindness as a fellow human being and another to want to have an intimate relationship with him. Just as he'd decided earlier, the only solution would be to leave here as soon as he got better. No matter what Zainah had said.

He turned around again and tried to force himself to go to sleep. Still, sleep eluded him.

*****

Audrey lay on her back on her living room couch as she waited for Trisha and Sienna to arrive. Already, she was going stir-crazy. She had immensely enjoyed her vacation so far, but she wanted to go back to work.

After she had received news about her father's inheritance, she'd contemplated leaving the force. She had financial freedom now and didn't need to keep working a nine-to-five. But she had decided two weeks into her vacation that she liked working and she still loved working as a policewoman. She missed her job. Thankfully, the wedding was coming up soon. After her wedding day, she would start working again.

She and Ken had decided on where they would live. As police chief, she didn't have to spend every day at the station. She would spend some of her days in Miami and some in Rosefield. Ken would also come with her to Rosefield on weekends and whenever he was free to. That way, neither of them would feel like they had given up the job they loved.

The doorbell rang and she sat up. She went to open the door and Trisha came in, carrying Ruby. Audrey smiled at her in greeting and cooed at the baby. She lifted Ruby out of Trisha's arms and carried her to the sofa.

"You grow bigger and bigger every single day," she said to the baby and kissed her soft cheeks. Ruby smiled at her as though she knew Audrey was her aunty.

"She smiled at me." Audrey lifted her eyes to Trisha and beamed. "I'm her favorite aunty."

"Don't let Sienna hear you say that," Trisha chuckled.

Audrey laughed and then said, "Talking about Sienna, what time did she say she would be here?"

Trisha glanced at the clock on the wall. "Umm… any moment now… I think."

"Great, because we still have to go for the cake tasting after we go to Satin Dreams." Audrey sighed worriedly. "Hopefully, I will find a wedding dress today. If not, maybe I will just wear one of my old dresses."

Trisha smiled widely. "And knowing you, I'm pretty sure you will do that."

The doorbell rang again, and Trisha held up her hand. "Must be Sienna. Let me go and get it."

When she went, Audrey looked down at baby Ruby again. She couldn't wait to have a child with Ken. From the love she had for her niece, she couldn't imagine how she would feel when she had her own child. All she knew was that she would love her unconditionally and fully. She and Ken would.

Sienna came in with her eyes sparkling. "Is that my little niece? I call dibs!"

Audrey cuddled Ruby closer to her bosom. "You can't call dibs, Sienna. I already did before you got here."

Trisha laughed. "Both of you should hurry and have kids of your own so I don't have to hear this argument any longer."

Sienna's expression suddenly turned somber and Audrey frowned at her. "What is it?"

Trisha put her hand around her shoulder as she

sat on the sofa. "Are you worried you won't have a baby? You just got married, Sienna. Give it time. You will be pregnant in no time."

"I hope so," Sienna said. "I'm just a little worried about something else, that's all."

Audrey frowned. Sienna didn't look a little worried. She seemed quite troubled.

Fear entered Audrey's heart. I hope her anxiety and panic attacks haven't returned. The attacks nearly took her life last year.

Trisha said, "You look really worried, Sienna. What is it?"

Sienna smiled. "It's nothing serious, really." She beamed. "Enough about me. Audrey, when are we leaving for Satin Dreams?"

"We should leave now. I just hope I find a..." She suddenly thought about something and gasped and sat up. She looked down at the baby to make sure her sudden movement had not disturbed her. She breathed a sigh of relief when she saw Ruby had fallen asleep.

Sienna blinked rapidly. "What is it?"

Trisha leaned forward. "What is on your mind, Audrey?"

Audrey beamed and looked from Sienna to Trisha. "I think I know where I can find the perfect wedding dress."

Trisha's eyes widened. "Where, Audrey? Do you want to go to another bridal store outside Rosefield?"

Sienna leaned forward and stared at her quizzically. "Well... tell us, Audrey."

Audrey smiled at her sisters. "I'll need both your permission before I can get the dress."

Sienna put her hand on her chest and tilted her head. "You need my permission before you get your wedding dress? Wow! I'm really curious now."

"Out with it!" Trisha ordered.

Audrey held out her hand. "Okay, okay! The wedding dress is in this house. You guys will have to come and see it." She stood and gently laid Ruby down on the sofa. She surrounded her with pillows so she wouldn't fall.

"You bought a wedding dress already… without us?" Trisha asked.

"No. Just come along."

Audrey began to head to her parents' old bedroom. Trisha and Sienna followed her. She stopped in front of the room, opened the door, and entered. The musty smell immediately hit her. She hardly ever came in here. It reminded her way too much of their late parents. From the matching flowery bedsheets and curtains that their mother had loved but dad had hated, to the large ornate armoire, everything was still in the same spot as the day their parents had died.

She opened the armoire and began to search diligently until she found what she was looking for. She pulled the dress out and held it out to her sisters. "This dress," she said.

Trisha and Sienna gave a collected gasp and chorused. "Mom's dress!"

Audrey nodded. She inspected the dress again. It was a beautiful, short-sleeved, lacy dress with no embellishments except for a thin gold belt. She hadn't seen it in over five years. The last time she had was just after their parents had died. She had taken it out and cried her eyes out. Now she smiled and said, "See why I need your permission?"

"You want to wear Mom's old-fashioned dress," Trisha said, a look of surprise on her face.

"Yes! I know now that it is what I really want. But if you want it, Trisha, then I won't fight you for it."

Sienna had tears in her eyes. She fingered the dress and said, "I think it would be amazing if you wore it on your wedding day."

"Thanks, Sienna," Audrey said, smiling. She turned to Trisha. "What do you say?"

Trisha didn't speak for a long moment, and then she said, "I also think it's a beautiful gesture. I certainly don't want it. If I ever get married again, I will be in a new dress." Her eyes regarded their mom's wedding gown. "It is very pretty, though. Maybe you could have it retailored so that it's more modern. Or would you prefer to wear it as is?"

"I'll wear it as is," Audrey answered. "The simple style suits my tastes. I'll just have it laundered and if it needs to be fitted to my size, I'll do that."

Trisha clapped suddenly. "Well, I think we've found the perfect wedding dress!"

Sienna nodded. "Your day will be very special, Audrey."

Audrey smiled and then sighed sadly. The only thing that would have made it even more special was if they had found their brother so he could be at the wedding.

*****

"Zainah, you are in love with him!" Leila exclaimed as they both sat in the tent they shared with two other women.

The women looked up at them from the other end of the tent, and Zainah shushed her.

"Do you want everyone here to hear you?" Zainah scolded.

Leila whispered. "It's true, isn't it? You are in love with him. From the look on your face when I mentioned it now, I'll say you have been in love with him for some time."

Zainah sighed and then nodded. "Okay… I'll admit that. I do love him very much, but I don't want to."

Leila nodded. "I understand. He isn't a Christian."

"Yes. And I don't even know if he feels the same way."

"From the way he looks at you every time I see you both together, I'll say he does."

Zainah shook her head. "I know he likes me. He is attracted to me, but I don't know that he loves me… or that he is even capable of it."

Leila frowned. "What do you mean?"

Zainah wondered if she should confide in her friend about what Faizan had told her. But how would she say it? I'm in love with a terrorist. Leila would disown her for sure. Besides, it wasn't her place to share what he'd told her in confidence. In fact, it would be wrong.

She said instead, "All that doesn't matter, anyway. He isn't a believer and we can never be together."

"What if he becomes one?"

Zainah asked, exasperatedly, "When will that be?" She sighed. Clearly, she'd become exhausted with reading the Bible and praying every day for him to come to Christ. Her motives had to remain right. She couldn't be praying for him to give his heart to Jesus so that they could be together rather than for the sake of his soul.

She remembered the scripture that said Christians were not to be weary in well doing, and then held the scripture close to her heart.

She told Leila her thoughts, and Leila smiled. "That is indeed a dilemma. But the Lord will help you."

Zainah decided to tell Leila about the dream she'd had about a month before where she had seen the blurry image of a man she was presumably meant to marry. She still didn't know if the dream was from God, but she knew she was meant to stay single forever. However, she didn't tell Leila that. She said instead, "I had a strange dream some months ago."

"What dream?" Leila asked.

Zainah told her about the dream.

Leila looked up with a thoughtful expression on her face. "You said you didn't see the man's face and you are not sure the dream is from the Lord?"

"Yes."

"What if the dream is truly from God and the man is Faizan? After all, how many men do you see around here? It will take a miracle for any of us to meet any man now and get married. And it actually took a miracle for Faizan to come here." She smiled with an excited look on her face. "I think Faizan is the man of your dreams."

Zainah shrugged, unconvinced. Leila thought Faizan was just a non-believer who God would save easily and then they could live happily ever after. But the truth was that he was a terrorist. A hardened sinner. He had never indicated he wanted anything to do with her faith. He had only shown contempt for what she held dear.

She looked at Leila's face and decided not to share her thoughts. It would be useless. Leila was a hopeless romantic.

Zainah smiled at her dear friend. "I hope the Lord works a miracle for you, Leila. You have so much love to give. It would be lovely to see you married to a worthy man."

Leila gave a long, wistful sigh, and for a short moment her face turned sad. And then she brightened up. "There are many women here who also long to be wives and mothers one day. Perhaps this miracle the Lord has worked for you is a start to more miracles that he will perform."

Zainah resisted the urge to groan and said nothing.

*****

Faizan shut his eyes and relished Zainah's voice as she read to him from the Bible. From time to time, he opened his eyes and surreptitiously studied her beautiful face. He ached for her every day, but he knew there was no point in expressing his feelings for her. Especially as he didn't have the same faith as she did.

He listened again to what she was reading. Something about a deer panting for water. "So my soul pants after you, oh Lord."

His heart suddenly grew troubled as he realized that the writer of the scripture she was reading was talking about God. He had never realized that a person could love and yearn for God so much that he would thirst for Him like a deer thirsts for water. What kind of God elicited such a declaration of love and longing?

He looked again at Zainah's earnest face as she read. It was definitely the kind of God she had spoken and read to him about since he'd met her. The kind of God she worshipped.

Suddenly, a sob rose up in him as he discovered he wanted to know that kind of God. He wanted to worship a lover like the God she read about. Not the kind of God he had served for such a long time. A God who loved to kill.

She looked at him and he quickly looked away so she would not see the excruciating pain of longing and confusion on his face. His emotions were a mess. He had never been one to entertain soft emotions like this. But now he was in a circle of yearning. Yearning for a woman he could never have and a God who he didn't understand or think would want him.

"What is it, Faizan?" she asked him.

He said gruffly, without looking at her, "Nothing. I'm just tired."

"Should I leave?" she asked.

He quickly turned to her. As much as her presence was driving him crazy, as he couldn't do anything about his love for her, it was also soothing. Plus, he wanted to listen to her voice all day long and to look at her pretty face when he wanted to. "Please don't go," he said. He gingerly took her hand. When she didn't pull it away, he sighed with relief. Her hand felt soft and delicate in his, and his heart thumped as he held it. He felt tempted to caress it, but he didn't want her to pull it away and so he suppressed the urge.

She smiled shyly at him. "Do you want me to go on reading?" she asked.

The hope in her voice pierced his heart and he nodded. He was in trouble now because he knew if she asked him to jump off a cliff for her, he would.

She continued to read the Bible, and he continued to listen. But after a minute she stopped reading.

He looked up at her and noticed she was looking at their joined hands. And then he realized that he had been absent-mindedly caressing the back of her hand with his thumb. He cursed himself as he waited for her to withdraw her hand. When she didn't after a minute, he looked quizzically at her.

For a long moment, his heart pounded violently as they stared at each other. Finally, he pulled her hand to his lips and kissed it.

She gasped and her eyes grew wide.

He decided that this might be his only chance to kiss her. He wasn't sure what she would do, but he tentatively leaned forward and tilted her chin up.

Her eyes scrutinized his, and he could see in them a mixture of fear and desire. The desire he saw in her eyes lit a raging fire in him and he couldn't hold back any more. He took her face in his hands and leaned in to kiss her.

But just before their lips touched, she moaned and then pulled away.

He instantly felt the pain of rejection and unmet desire and groaned.

She stood up, looked at him for a few seconds

and then hurried out of the tent.

For almost an hour, he sat staring at the entrance to the tent, hoping she would return. When she didn't, he lay back down and shut his eyes. He couldn't stand all this anymore. The next day, he would have to leave this place. It would kill him to never see her again, but it would be better than the torture of constantly seeing her but knowing she didn't want him.

THIRTEEN

Faizan felt himself being pulled down into a fiery pit, and he began to scream. He could hear other people's screams as well, mingled with his. The lower he descended into the pit, the hotter it became. Soon, he began to clearly see the sweltering flames and then people burning up in them.

He screamed louder at the excruciating pain that went through him as his feet touched the fire, and then he felt himself being pulled up by an invisible hand. He ascended farther and farther away from the flames, but he could not see the person pulling him out. Finally, he landed on something that felt like soft grass. He looked down at his feet and saw that he was indeed standing on lush green. When he looked around him, he discovered he was in the tent at the new camp but also in another place; a strange, beautiful place with a profusion of flowers in vivid colors he had never seen before.

He felt amazed, not only by his surroundings, but especially by the fact that he was in two places at the same time.

He kept walking through the field of grass. All around him were flowers. He soon began to hear music that sounded angelic and otherworldly. It felt like it was coming from the flowers. When he put his ear to what looked a little like a red rose but more beautiful than any rose he had ever seen, he gasped. The sweet music he was hearing was indeed coming from the flowers.

He kept listening, and then he looked up and for the first time noticed how blue and bright the sky was. He felt a peace he had never known before as he walked through the field, and then suddenly a bright light began to come toward him and he blinked. The closer the light came, the more intense it became, until he couldn't see anything anymore.

And then the light engulfed him. He felt as though the light was more a personality than just a bright light. Then it began to enter into him, and for a few seconds it felt painful. But then, it turned to the sweetest sensation he had ever felt.

He cried out with joy and ecstasy, and then he grew curious. He asked, "What is this light?"

He jerked when a clear, loud voice said, "Not what, but who!"

He corrected himself and asked again, "Who is this light?"

And then he heard a booming voice say, "I am the light of the world. He that follows me shall not walk in darkness but shall have the light of life."

"I want that light!" he screamed. "I want you!"

He cried out in pleasure as a shaft of light pierced through his chest. It seemed to go to the depths of his soul. And then he suddenly opened his eyes and found he was on the sleeping rug in the tent.

He sat up and shook his head. The dream had felt so real. He wasn't even sure it was a dream. He took a deep breath and then felt a deep hunger settle in him. Not hunger for food, but a hunger that seemed to come from his dream. A hunger to know that light that had felt so wonderful.

He suddenly remembered once when Zainah had read a scripture to him and then realized it was the same scripture the voice from the light in his dream had uttered. He had thought he wasn't paying attention at the time she'd read those words to him, but apparently, they had found a way into his soul.

He didn't know if the dream was real or what it meant, but he knew if there was any truth to what he had experienced there, about the words that Zainah had read to him, he wanted it. No, he wanted Him—the personality that was the light. He knew it was the Jesus that Zainah had been telling him about.

He couldn't wait any longer. That light had taken away every terror he had felt while descending into the pit of fire. He had to tell Zainah about his dream, get her to read those words in the Bible to him again, and explain exactly how he could receive the light.

He stood up and went out of the tent. It was the first time since he'd arrived that he had gone outside. The sun was just rising, casting a delicate glow on the camp.

How do I find Zainah? he thought.

He didn't know what tent she was in, and he didn't want to disturb the other sleeping women. But he had to speak to her now. His desperation to get the answers to his questions grew. He paused in front of his tent and looked up to the sky. "Please help me find her," he said. He wasn't sure who he was praying to, but he guessed it was to the God that she served.

His eyes widened in astonishment when he heard her voice behind him.

"How come you're out here at this time, Faizan?"

He turned and beamed at her. She had a clay pot in her hand, probably on her way to get water from the well. "I came out to look for you," he answered.

Her brows lifted. "For me?" She studied him and said with concern in her voice, "Are you okay?"

He nodded. "I need to tell you something." He looked back at his tent. "Will you come in with me so we can talk?"

She didn't answer for a few seconds as her eyes searched his face, and then she nodded. She followed him into the tent but didn't sit beside him as usual. Instead, after he had taken his seat on the sleeping rug, she picked up one of the pillows on the rug and sat on it, facing him.

He began, "I had a strange dream just now." He narrated the entire dream to her while she listened silently, with eyes as round as saucers. After he'd finished, he asked, "Will you read that scripture to me again?" He looked up and then realized she didn't have her Bible with her.

He wanted to mention it, but the tears in her eyes stopped him.

She wiped her tears as they fell down her face. "I'm sorry. I'm overwhelmed, but with joy. Of course I will. I know that scripture by heart." She spoke the scripture word by word, just like he had heard it in his dream. She sniffled again and said, "You want the light that you saw? You know that is Jesus?"

He nodded. "I do."

She let out a sob and he blinked. "What is it?" he asked.

"I'm so happy." She shook her head and said, "Okay, will you close your eyes and pray with me? We will ask the Lord Jesus to come into your heart and make you His."

He nodded earnestly. "That is what I want!"

She began to pray, and he said the words after her. As he did, asking Jesus to come into his heart and fill him with His Spirit, he began to feel bolts of electricity go through him. The feeling was pleasurable, like he'd had in his dream. This time, though, he felt like the power surging through him was burning up everything in him that was wrong.

And then he began to feel an intense love in combination with the powerful force enveloping and surging through him.

He trembled as the intense power and love continued to go through him and tears fell down his cheeks. He couldn't remember the last time he had cried, but he couldn't stop crying now. The feeling was so intense that he rose and then fell on his knees. For a long time, he stayed in the kneeling position, embracing and basking in everything he felt. And then it suddenly stopped and he collapsed to the floor, exhausted but full of joy.

He felt a hand on his shoulder and looked up. Zainah was kneeling beside him, a huge smile on her face. He sat up and took her hand, laughing loudly. "I have what you have!" he said. He wasn't even sure he was making any sense but he had to proclaim it. He couldn't hold back.

He kissed her cheeks and beamed. "Thank you."

She smiled widely, her cheeks stained with tears and burning where his lips had touched them. "You belong to the Lord now."

He nodded vigorously, thrilled beyond words. The only regret he had now was that he had wasted his life for years. He would have done this a long time ago if only he had known the truth. He told her what was on his mind.

"The important thing is that you have Christ in your heart now. You are a brand-new person in Him."

He nodded again, lifted his hands to the sky, and yelled, "That I am!"

*****

Hassan looked through the binoculars Ahmed had given him and sighed. The camp did look empty. Still, they could never be sure. Faizan was there. Maybe he had even set a trap for them knowing they would return to the women's camp. That was why he had brought a few other men here. Faizan was a cunning and skilled fighter. That was why he had been made leader of their group.

Hassan had been stunned when Sadiq had come back with the news that Faizan had turned. It had taken him days of soul searching to decide that they needed to hunt Faizan down and kill him, along with the women he was trying to protect. It was why he had decided to go along this time. He had to see for himself. Plus, Sadiq had failed to carry out his mission. Hassan believed in the saying, "If you want something done, you have to do it yourself."

They began to head silently to the camp. It was early morning but bright enough for them to see.

Hassan pointed to one of his men and made a signal for him to station himself near the entrance of the camp. His other men had surrounded the camp. No one would escape. His instructions were for them to capture all the women. Anyone who resisted would be killed on the spot. As for Faizan, they would take him back to camp, dead or alive. Hassan had his doubts that Faizan and the women were still there, but he wanted to leave no stone unturned.

He looked at Sadiq, who was on his left side, and Ahmed, the tracker, on his right. "Since you both bungled the mission, I sent you here to do and you decided to announce our return, I doubt anyone is still here, waiting to be attacked." He shook his head. Still, he had decided they would come. If Faizan and the women had already left, they would probably have left some clues as to their where-abouts.

He indicated for the man at the entrance of the camp to enter. As soon as the man did, pointing his gun, they all stormed the camp. Hassan went from one tent to the other, his gun raised. All the tents were empty. He thoroughly searched every tent he entered, looking for clues. He was enraged when he found none.

These people were definitely skilled in the art of evasion. Faizan must have also helped them. There were no signs that anyone had lived there for the past year.

He sighed deeply and turned to Ahmed. "Can you track them down?"

Ahmed nodded. "I think I can. However, it will take time."

Hassan said, "That's fine. Take all the time you need as long as you find them." He looked at Sadiq, who was staring grimly at the tents with a faraway look on his face. "Sadiq, for stealth's sake, you will go with Ahmed and track down the place where those women and Faizan are. When you do, send word immediately. I and the other men will come and help you. This time, none of those women or Faizan will escape our hands."

Sadiq nodded.

Hassan watched as Sadiq and Ahmed left to carry out his instructions. Hopefully they would quickly find out where those Christians were hiding. And then he would enjoy meting out to them the punishment they deserved.

FOURTEEN

Audrey laughed as she entered her house with Ken. He had arrived in Rosefield the day before to choose the wedding venue with her. That day, they had seen several venues and finally decided on one. "That man wanted us to book a hall that seats only twenty people for our almost hundred guests," she said, shaking her head.

Ken chuckled. "I guess our remaining eighty guests are supposed to sit outside." He sat down on the couch and sighed with a contented look on his face. Patting the space beside him, he smiled up at her. "Come sit," he said.

Audrey came, sat beside him, and put her legs up on the couch. When he reached out and placed his arm around her, she snuggled up to him.

"How many more things do we still have to do before the wedding?" he asked.

"Very few now, thank God."

"I wish I was here in Rosefield so I could help with the wedding planning," he said, and kissed the top of her head.

"I wish you were too, but Trisha and Sienna have been great. I don't know what I would have done without them."

"I'm glad they are here to help," he said. He smiled at her as she looked up at him. "Most of all, I'm glad we'll soon be married." He leaned down and kissed her lips softly. When he started to pull away, she pulled down his head and kissed him again.

He wrapped his arms tightly around her as they kissed. Soon they were lying on the couch, wrapped up in each other's arms, kissing passionately. She heard the now familiar alarm bells going off in her ears and pulled back for a brief moment. She said to him, "Ken, we should stop."

He shook his head, his eyes glazed with desire. He said huskily, "We are just kissing. Nothing more." He pulled her down again and kissed her until she forgot everything except the feel of his lips on hers. She started to unbutton his shirt, and then he sucked in his breath loudly. He pulled away and sat up.

She bit her lip and sat up beside him. "I'm sorry."

"No," he said, turning to her. "It's not your fault. I should have listened when you said we should stop."

She breathed a sigh of relief. "Thank God you pulled away when you did, Ken. 'Cause I wasn't thinking just now. I would have gone all the way if you hadn't."

He looked at her and then stood and went to sit on the other sofa facing her. "This keeps happening every single time we're alone. Maybe we should start meeting in public places. Unfortunately, Bryan and Sienna aren't here to chaperone us."

Audrey shook her head. "When they were, they

were not very good chaperones, remember?"

He laughed. "Well… that's true. But seriously, I think we should start meeting in public places until after the wedding."

Audrey sighed. As much as she didn't like the idea at all, it sounded wise. And they really had no choice now. She nodded. "I think you're right." She smiled sadly at him. "I'll miss our private kisses, though."

He raised his brows. "Those private kisses are the reason why we should not be alone like this anymore. They always end up almost getting us into trouble… just like now."

Audrey sighed again. "And here I was thinking about showing you my new bedroom décor."

Ken shook his head and laughed out loud. "It's not funny, Audrey. Stop it!"

She laughed with him. "Okay. This is serious, though. Should we go out now?"

"Yes, I think that's a good idea."

She stood. "'Kay, then! Let me get my…" She frowned as the doorbell rang. "I wonder who it is. I'm not expecting anyone today." She went and opened the door and then grinned. Sienna and Bryan were there, smiling at her.

"Guys, I didn't know you two were coming to Rosefield today."

Sienna said, "We remembered what you said about needing us to chaperone you when we were in Spain. And since I knew that Ken was going to be around this weekend, I asked Bryan to come to Rosefield with me and spend the weekend with you guys."

"Aww, that's really sweet of you," Audrey said

to both of them. She hugged them and opened the door wide so they could enter.

Ken got up to hug them. He said humorously, "You guys are the worst chaperones, though. We're better off taking our chances alone than with both of you."

Bryan put on a feigned hurt look and said, "You've wounded me deeply, Ken. In my opinion, we are the best chaperones you could ever find."

"Right," Audrey said. "Where were both of you just a minute ago when we almost…?" She immediately stopped speaking as she realized she'd said way too much. As usual, she had blurted out what was on her mind without thinking.

For a brief moment, there was an awkward silence in the room, and then Ken chuckled.

Soon they were all laughing. After a while, when they had calmed down, Bryan looked at Ken and then at Audrey and said, "I know it's hard now, but you have God's abundant grace. You have to trust that His grace will keep you until your wedding day."

"We decided to start meeting in public spaces until after the wedding," Audrey said.

Bryan nodded. "I guess that's wise. If you're struggling to stay pure, setting up boundaries is a good idea." He wrapped his hand around Sienna's waist. "We'll be around this weekend though. So, you guys can meet here for now."

"We were planning to go out… maybe to dinner," Ken said. "Would you guys like to come?"

Sienna looked at Bryan, and Audrey saw him wink at her. "Umm… no," Sienna said, shifting her body closer to her husband. "I think we will stay in today. You guys go and have fun."

Bryan nodded. "Yeah. You both can go. My wife and I have stuff we need to do for now." He gave Sienna a look he must have thought was discreet, but Audrey caught it and sighed wearily.

Ken laughed and shook his head at them. "Audrey and I know what that 'stuff you need to do' is. Like I said earlier, you two are the worst chaperones in the world."

Sienna and Bryan laughed. "Okay," Sienna said. "Maybe we can go with you guys. But do you blame us? We are trying really hard to make a baby."

"You two are impossible," Audrey chuckled and shook her head. "Come on, Ken. Let's leave the newlyweds alone." She picked up her jacket from the sofa and took Ken's hand. When they got outside, they both laughed. She smiled as she looked up at Ken and said, "Hopefully they will be through with the 'stuff they need to do' before we get back."

*****

Faizan listened as Zainah read the Bible to him. He thought it ironic that just three days before while she'd read this same passage to him, he had been frowning, not particularly interested in hearing what she had to say. Now he listened closely, not wanting to miss anything.

Since he had given his heart to Christ two days prior, Zainah had been coming to do what she called 'fellowship' with him. She had read the Bible about three times daily to him, but he couldn't get enough. He wanted to sup up as much of God's word as he could.

She looked up as he asked her to explain a particular verse she had just read. She nodded, looked down at the Bible, and read the verse again. "If ye then, being evil, know how to give good gifts unto your children, how much more shall your father which is in heaven give good things to them that ask Him?"

Faizan asked, "Is this verse symbolic or does Jesus really mean it when he says God will give good gifts to us when we ask?"

Zainah answered, "He really meant it. The Lord always says what He means. It is just us who usually don't believe His words."

He smiled at her. "And do you believe that God will give you what you ask for?"

She looked up thoughtfully. "That's a good question. Sometimes I do and sometimes I don't. It depends on a lot of things. But my unbelief does not change God's word." She cocked her head, smiled, and asked curiously, "Is there anything you want God to give you? We could pray about it together. You heard the words I just read. The Lord is willing to give good gifts to all His children who ask."

He stared at her for a long moment. How would she react if I told her what gift I wanted to ask God for? he thought. In spite of his uncertainty about her reaction, he smiled and said softly, "I want you, Zainah. I want to ask the Lord for your heart."

She gasped and her eyes grew round.

She didn't speak for a long moment, and he sat gazing at her. His heart raced, wondering what she would say when she finally spoke.

At last, he grew tired of waiting for her to say something and decided it was time he told her how he really felt about her. If she didn't feel the same way, then so be it. At least, he would have spoken his truth. He stared into her eyes and said, "I love you, Zainah. I love you with everything in me. You don't have to say anything right now, but I just wanted to let you know how I felt about you."

She turned away, but not before he saw the tears that shimmered in her eyes.

His pulse raced. All he wanted to do now was take her in his arms and wipe her tears away. But he knew he shouldn't. She wouldn't like that. Again, he waited for her to speak while he held his breath.

Finally, she said, "Faizan, you just gave your heart to Christ. I think we should take one step at a time. Concentrate on growing in the Lord and…" She bit her lip and he blinked.

"What is it, Zainah?"

"It's nothing." She smiled and rose. "We will continue tomorrow."

He shook his head. "You don't have to leave, Zainah," he said to her. Even though his heart hurt at her reaction to his declaration of love, he didn't want her to leave. "I won't speak any more about my feelings for you if it makes you uncomfortable."

Zainah sat down again and looked at him. "Are you angry with me?"

He blinked in surprise. "Why would I be angry with you?"

"Umm… you get angry easily, Faizan. I'm just afraid you might be angry with me because I didn't give you the answer you want."

He looked away from her. He did get angry easily. The strange thing was that his quick temper had served him well in the past. He had learned to use it as a weapon and it had protected him a lot of times. He said to her, "You are right. I am very sure I would have been very angry about two weeks ago if you had rejected me. But I don't feel angry now. Just sad..."

"Faizan, I didn't mean..."

"It's okay, Zainah. I didn't tell you how I felt to make you feel guilty. I just wanted to tell you where I think all the anger came from." He looked up thoughtfully, remembering his childhood. Not the one with his adopted parents, but with his birth mother.

"I've told you I was very young when my mother died and that I can recall the day clearly. But I didn't tell you I also remember being given a locket. Inside was a picture of her and a man who she told me was my father." He looked at Zainah again. "I had never seen him before in real life, but she had shown me the picture several times. Before she died, she showed it to me again and asked me not to forget her or my father. It was as if she knew she would not make it to the end of the day."

Zainah touched his hand briefly.

He sighed sadly and continued. "When she died, even though I was only five, I vowed I would find my father one day. However, after my parents adopted me, that vow quickly changed to wanting my adopted father to love me, the way my mother did. I craved for that and I tried my best to be good and to win his love. But I never did. He didn't care a bit about me. I soon realized he never would, and that left a deep hole in my heart and caused me to be very angry. I was angry first with him, and then with the world."

Zainah looked up at him. "I'm so sorry, Faizan."

He shrugged. "When Mustafa took me to my former group after my parents died, I found out that my quick temper was actually looked upon as a good thing. Soon, the anger became a part of my personality. But all of it, I think, arose from not having a real father who loved me."

Zainah smiled at him. "Now you do. Your heavenly Father loves you very much."

He nodded. "That was the first thing that drew me in as you read the Bible to me every day. I wanted a loving heavenly Father." When Zainah took his hand, his eyes widened in surprise and he sat very still, afraid she would withdraw hers if he even moved.

"Starting from today, we will learn as much as we can about the Father in heaven and how much He loves us, His children. Would you like that?"

He nodded. "Very much!"

FIFTEEN

Zainah patted the head of one of the little children playing around the camp and then entered the tent she shared with Leila and a few other women. She found Leila in a corner of the tent, searching for something. Apart from Leila, no one else was around.

She went and put her hand on her friend's shoulder. "What are you looking for?"

Leila was going through her basket of clothes and some of them were on the floor. "Just my red scarf. Fatima lost hers and I promised to give her that one of mine."

Zainah said, "I wanted to talk to you about something... but I will come back later."

Leila shook her head. "No, I'll look for it some other time." She turned to Zainah. "What do you want to speak to me about?"

"It's about Faizan. He told me he loves me." Zainah's heart pounded as she recalled their conversation the day before.

Leila's eyes grew as round as saucers. "What? He did?"

"He told me he wanted to be with me."

"When? Wow! That's great, Zainah! I'm so happy for you. Now that he is a Christian, you…"

"I didn't give my consent, Leila. I told him he needed to concentrate on growing in the Lord for now."

Leila shook her head, her eyes filled with questions. "I don't understand. You have told me that you are in love with him and he loves you. He is a Christian now, so why did you reject him? Please help me understand."

Zainah sighed and then sat down on her sleeping rug. Leila sat next to her and stared at her. "I didn't tell you about my vow of chastity," Zainah said to Leila.

"Your what?"

"I made a vow of chastity… to the Lord. I had always wanted a family of my own, a husband and children. After I became a Christian, it was all I prayed for; that one day soon, I would meet my Prince Charming who would sweep me off my feet and we would have a dozen children." She chuckled as she remembered her naiveté.

"But I soon began to find out that the desire to be married was consuming me even though I was only eighteen. I guess it was because the women in my family got married and started having children really young. But the desire to get married had become sort of a god to me. A month before I came here, I told the Lord that I would not make marriage a god anymore. I told him he would be my only husband and I would never get married or have any children… to honor him. When I got here and found out there were no men, I knew God had taken me up on my vow."

Leila stared quizzically at her. "So, you are telling me you made a vow to the Lord never to get married?"

"Yes, and I cannot break my vow. So, you see my dilemma. I love Faizan with all my heart, but I have to keep my promise to God."

"But what of the dream you told me about? You said you were shown a man and told he was your husband."

"I think I had that dream because of my desire to be married."

Leila shook her head. "I actually think it was from the Lord. It's a pity you didn't see the man's face in the dream. It probably would have been Faizan's."

"It wouldn't have been. I didn't know Faizan when I had the dream."

"But God did and showed him to you."

Zainah sighed wearily. They were going round and round in circles and it wasn't helpful. "I'm just really confused right now, especially as Faizan has become a Christian. With everything in me, I yearn to tell him I want to be with him… but I can't do that."

Leila put her hand on Zainah's shoulder. "The only thing I can tell you right now is to pray about it. Tell the Lord everything. He will let you know what to do."

Zainah nodded. "I guess you are right. I just didn't want to do that because I would be essentially asking God if I can break a promise I made to him. That just doesn't seem right to me."

"You are not asking if you can break your vow,

but what to do about it and about your feelings for Faizan."

"I'll start praying right away." She smiled at Leila. "Please pray for me to hear God's voice clearly so I can follow His will and not mine."

"I will," Leila said.

*****

Zainah closed the Bible after she had finished praying and stood to leave Faizan's tent. Since he had told her two days before about his feelings for her, he hadn't brought it up again. She had read the Bible and prayed with him, and he had kept his word and not mentioned it at all. Even though she could still read his feelings for her in his eyes, she was grateful he had said nothing else about it. Nothing would come of his rehashing his feelings for her, or she confessing hers to him.

She was almost outside the tent when he said, "Zainah, can I speak to you about something?"

Her heart immediately skipped a beat. She prayed silently that he wasn't about to tell her he loved her again, or worse, ask her to give him a chance. She turned around, "What do you want to speak to me about, Faizan?"

Faizan gave her a small smile. "Umm... will you please sit?"

She came back and sat across from him.

He said, "I told you yesterday that my mother gave me a locket with her picture and my birth father's in it. Would you like to see it?"

Zainah nodded eagerly. She definitely wanted to see the picture, to know where he had gotten his features from, his sparkling hazel eyes.

He put his hand into his shirt and brought out a chain with a heart locket. It was the chain she'd noticed when he had been rescued from the plane wreck. He never took it off.

He removed the locket, opened it, and then handed it to her.

She stared at the picture in it. The beautiful woman in the picture had raven dark hair and lush lips. She could see where Faizan had gotten his dark hair and eyebrows from. But it was the man in the picture that stole her attention. Apart from their different coloring, the resemblance was uncanny. She looked up and said to him, "You look exactly like your father, Faizan."

"Do you think so?" He sounded partly pleased and partly troubled.

She nodded. "Yes." An idea came to her and she wondered whether to tell him about it. She instantly decided to and said, "Why don't you try to reconnect with your birth father? He might still be alive."

The sudden change in Faizan's demeanor and expression startled her. He turned away with an angry look.

She said to him, "You don't want to be reconnected to your father even though he is probably the only family you have now? Why?"

"Why should I try to find someone who abandoned my mother and I as a child?"

"I know what he did was wrong, but maybe he had a good reason for doing so. Even if he didn't, you need to forgive him, Faizan. It's what the Lord Jesus would want you to do."

He turned to her again and said roughly, "I can't

forgive him. Maybe if he hadn't abandoned my mother and I the way he did, my mother would still be alive."

"You don't know that."

"What I do know is that he didn't care enough to stay. I just don't want to have anything to do with that sort of person."

Zainah sighed. She suddenly felt a tug in her heart, a deep knowing. He needed to forgive his father and reconcile with him. She just knew that was what he was meant to do.

Maybe this was why the Lord still had him here: so she could help him reconcile with his father—his heavenly Father, first of all, and then his earthly father as well. She said to him, "Do you know what the Lord says in the Bible? He says we are to forgive others even as he has forgiven us." She leaned forward. "Think about it, Faizan. Think about everything you have done and how God has forgiven you in spite of it all. He asks that you forgive others as he has forgiven you. Besides, I think connecting with your father will do you a world of good."

Faizan didn't say anything for a few minutes, and she prayed silently that the Lord would touch his heart and give him a desire to forgive his dad.

At last, he sighed loudly and said, "Okay. If the Lord has forgiven me even though I was such a fool, the least I can do is forgive my birth father." He smiled at her. "And I think you are right. Finding my father would probably help with the problems and anger I've had since I was a child." He grinned. "I suddenly feel excited about the prospect. But I don't know where or how to start."

She shook her head. "Umm… the Lord will show

you the way."

He suddenly raised his brows and said loudly, "I think I know what to do."

"What?"

"I know a man who does stuff like that."

"Like what?"

"He finds people." Faizan stood, and she saw he was not unsteady on his feet anymore, nor did he hold on to the tent pillars. He was mostly strong and healed now. He continued, "That man owes me a favor. I'll call him up and ask him to help me find my father. I know my father's first and last name. That should be enough for Khalid to find him."

Zainah lifted her brows and stared at him quizzically. "What sort of favor does he owe you?"

Faizan waved his hand dismissively. "It doesn't matter. Do you have a cell phone, Zainah?"

"No. Nobody here does."

He frowned at her. "Nobody? How do you connect with the outside world?"

"We mostly don't, except to buy the things we need." She sighed. "Okay, Miriam has a cell phone, but it is really difficult to connect to the service provider out here. Sometimes it works, and other times it doesn't." She gazed intently at him, feeling a little uneasy about the guy he said owed him a favor. "Maybe we should pray about it and wait for God to send someone."

"He already has. Khalid." Faizan smiled. "I'll go find Miriam and ask her now. I'll keep trying until I can connect to Khalid." He grinned at her. "I can't wait, Zainah. Thank you for suggesting this to me. I would never have decided to take the initiative if it weren't for you."

His excitement was contagious, and she found herself grinning and feeling as excited as he was.

"Will you come with me and help me through this journey to find my father?" he asked, gazing at her, a solemn expression on his face.

"I would love to," she answered. She stood and went out with him.

As they walked to Miriam's tent, she quietly asked the Lord to grant them favor so they would find Faizan's father, and that the man would want to have a relationship with his son. Because if he didn't, it might break Faizan's heart and send him on a downward spiral.

*****

Zainah carried her pot of water on her shoulder and sighed. Leila was by her side, carrying a big jug also filled with water. Zainah said as they walked back to the tent, "I have been praying, but I still don't know what to do."

"If you still love Faizan even after praying, then maybe that's a sign from the Lord that he's the one." She winked at Zainah. "I think you will get married soon. And thanks for asking. I will be your maid of honor."

Zainah smiled in spite of herself. "It's not funny, Leila. My plan was to spend as little time with him as possible until he left the camp, but I don't want him to go. He asked me to go with him on his quest to find his birth father. So, in addition to the time I already spend with him praying and reading the Bible, I have to spend time helping him with that."

"You're complaining so much, Zainah. I wish I

had your problem. If a handsome man like Faizan who was also a Christian was in love with me and I with him, I wouldn't waste any time marrying him."

"But you didn't take a vow of chastity like I did, did you?"

They reached the camp and dropped their containers of water in the cooking area. They left the cooking tent and made their way to theirs. The desert dust swirled around them and Zainah prayed another sandstorm wasn't on the way. Zainah turned to Leila and said, "Another thing that worries me about Faizan is his past. He had such a dangerous life."

"But you just said it now: it's his past. Let it stay there."

They got to the tent and sat down on Leila's sleeping rug. Aisha was on the other end of the room with her three-year-old daughter, Hadiza. She'd been married to Hadiza's father until the man had found out she was a Christian and thrown her out.

The precious child ran up to them and Zainah lifted her into her lap. Leila pinched the girl's chubby cheeks and said, "Can I have a little bit of your cheeks, please?"

The child said in her baby voice, "Why?"

Leila tickled her and said in a monster's voice, "So I can eat it up!"

The girl laughed and shook her head. "You can't have my cheeks." She struggled out of Zainah's arms and ran away, laughing.

Zainah laughed as she watched the little girl skip out of the tent. Her mother called out, "Don't go far,

Hadiza!"

Leila chuckled and then sobered. "Don't you want to have children someday, Zainah? You know we women have a ticking biological clock. In several years, you won't be able to have children anymore." She sighed deeply and whispered, "Neither will I."

Zainah felt her heart skip a beat at Leila's words and she groaned. She had thought she'd come to terms with the fact that she would never have children. But, apparently, she hadn't. She shut her eyes to try to shut out the pain in her heart and said, "I thought I had made peace with the fact that I will never be a mother. But it seems I haven't."

"You probably had," Leila said. "Until you met a man you want to have children with. Now your heart won't let it go."

Zainah moaned. "I have to go to that man's tent now." She picked up her Bible from the small table near the sleeping rug and got up. "Please pray for me that I don't misbehave and that he doesn't either. The tension in the room when we are together is so tiring."

As she went to Faizan's tent, an idea came to her. Zainah knew Leila was suffering even though she was hiding it well. She was desperate to have a family of her own. Zainah bit her lip. As bad as it might hurt, maybe it was time she did something selfless and tried to get Leila and Faizan together. If not, her dear friend would never meet anyone in this place and have her dream of a husband and children.

Thinking of Faizan with another woman, even though that woman was her best friend, sent shafts of pain through her. But getting them together might be the best thing for all of them. After tonight, she could ask Leila to help with Faizan's private Bible studies and prayer time so he could continue to grow in his walk with God while getting to know Leila better. She would tell her friend she had way too much on her plate and that it was a temporary thing. Maybe Leila could also help him find his father. Leila was a good woman and she was pretty. Faizan would come to love her.

Zainah felt tears pooling in her eyes, but she blinked them back. In due time, Faizan's love for her would fade and he would love Leila instead. She couldn't continue stringing him along knowing she would never be able to be with him. She didn't tell Leila, but after praying about it, she knew that the thought of breaking her vow to God was not something she could ever do.

But how can you give him up? her heart cried out.

She paused in front of the tent as tears fell down her face. It would be pure torture to see him. She loved him so much and yet they couldn't be together.

Lord, please help me, she prayed. She quickly wiped her eyes, composed herself, and then entered his tent.

SIXTEEN

Faizan sat thinking about his phone call to Khalid the day before. The man had promised to do the best he could to find Phil Gardner. By the next day, Khalid would have word for him and let him know what he had found out about his father.

He looked up as Zainah entered the tent. His heart did a flip, and he exhaled to try to calm down. Ever since he'd told her how he felt about her and she'd blown him off, he had oscillated between desperation and despair. The new quest to find his father had alleviated the pain somewhat, but not much. She looked as beautiful as ever. Her hair wasn't covered today. She had braided it. Her brown eyes sparkled as she looked at him. And then he blinked. Her eyes were not sparkling, they were red. She had been crying.

His stomach quivered as he wondered what had made her cry. He frowned with concern and asked, "What's wrong, Zainah?"

"Nothing." She sniffled and looked away. "We will be reading from the book of Acts today." She opened her Bible.

His frown deepened, but he said nothing more. He picked up the small green Bible she had given him and opened it up. He searched until he found the book of Acts.

She started to read from chapter one and then stopped briefly as her voice choked with emotion.

He looked up in alarm and then shut his Bible. He stood and came to sit beside her. "What is it, Zainah? Tell me!"

She shook her head. "It's nothing. Let's get back to our reading."

He took the Bible from her, closed it, and studied her face. "Something is wrong, and I need to know what it is!"

She barked, "I said nothing is wrong with me! Why won't you just leave me alone?"

He winced for just a second, and then he took her hand. "If you think a raised voice is going to get me to back down, then you don't know me well." He looked into her eyes and his breath stopped at the sadness he saw there. "Now, Zainah, tell me what is wrong with you. I won't stop troubling you until you do."

"No!" She jerked her hand away and stood.

He stood, took her hand again and blocked her path. "You aren't leaving this place until you tell me why you've been crying."

"Why do I have to tell you?" she cried, tears pouring down her cheeks.

"Because I love you," he said gruffly. "And I will give my life for you if that would take away your pain and make you happy again."

She covered her mouth as a sob escaped her lips.

She looked up at him and shook her head. "Please, Faizan. I can't!"

"You can't what?"

"I can't tell you."

"Tell me," he insisted. He held both her hands and looked into her eyes. "Please."

She pressed her lips together and then said, "I love you, Faizan. I'm in love with you. Is that what you want to hear?" she began to cry.

He blinked as his emotions roiled with a confusing mixture of elation and misery. His heart soared and then fell again. He looked at her as she cried. She loves me. But why is that such a bad thing that it would elicit such misery?

He lifted her hands to his lips and kissed the back of her left hand and then her right. He looked into her eyes and asked, "If you love me, then why are you so miserable? I love you, too. You already know that."

"I am miserable, Faizan, because in spite of our love for each other, we still can't be together."

He sharply sucked in his breath as pain tore through him. "Why not?" he asked, unable to hide the desperation in his voice.

She sighed loudly and answered, "I told you once that I had made a vow of chastity. I was serious about that. That vow was made to the Lord with no intention of ever breaking it. And that hasn't changed." She smiled sadly at him as tears ran down her cheeks. "I cannot break my vow to God, Faizan. Not even for you."

He shut his eyes against the pain that shot through him. Even after she'd told him to concentrate on his Christian growth, he had harbored a firm hope that she would give him a chance once his faith was stronger. But now, with what she had just told him, he knew they were destined to be apart. Her confession of love only made things worse for him. Now he knew she loved him as well but would never act on how she felt about him. His dream of a future with her shattered completely, and unbearable pain coursed through him; it was a pain worse than the physical one he'd suffered from the plane crash.

He sat on the sleeping rug, his legs unable to carry him any longer.

She stooped before him and said, "I'm sorry, Faizan. I wish things were different."

He looked at her and wiped her tears away with his thumb. "I wish things were different too." He couldn't resist and placed his hand on her cheek. "Why?" He wanted to be strong, but the sense of loss felt terrible. Her eyes searched his, and then he couldn't hold back any more. He drew her close and touched his lips to hers.

She gasped and then sprang up immediately. "I have to go, Faizan. Leila will be reading the Bible with you starting tomorrow." She exited the tent before he could say anything more.

For a long moment, he sat very still, pondering on everything. He wouldn't even get to see her frequently the way he had for the past month. Her friend would now have the Bible studies with him. Zainah might as well have reached into his chest and torn out his heart.

He covered his face with his hands as tears fell down his cheeks.

*****

Faizan stood as Miriam, the aging leader of the camp, entered the tent. She held out a cell phone to him. "You have a call," she said. "A guy named Khalid."

Faizan thanked her and took the phone from her. She left the tent, and he put the cell phone to his ear. "Hello, Khalid!"

"Yes, Faizan, I found out some things about the American, Phil Gardner."

The way Khalid spat out the words, "the American" caused Faizan to cringe. He asked, "Yes, what did you find out?"

"I found out he died years ago with his wife in a car crash."

Faizan shut his eyes and his heart sank to his feet. He pressed his lips together as an overwhelming sadness settled on him.

"Faizan, are you still there?"

"Yes… Ehmm… did you find out anything else?"

"Nothing much except that the man has three daughters. Of course, they are all grown up now."

Faizan couldn't believe this news. "Thank you, Khalid. This is remarkable news. If you find out anything else, please let me know."

Khalid promised he would and the call ended.

Faizan sank down on his sleeping rug, and for half an hour he stared at the empty space in front of him. Anger began to invade his heart at the thought that everyone in his past, everyone he had been related to, had died. First, his birth mother, and then his adopted parents. Then Mustafa had died, and now he'd just found out his birth father had died a long time before.

As if he didn't have enough pain with what Zainah had told him yesterday, this had to compound his misery.

Every hope he'd nurtured for the last few days about finding and finally knowing who his father was evaporated. It was the week of broken dreams. All his hopes and dreams for the future were crashing down around him.

He picked up the embroidered pillow next to him, screamed, and threw it across the tent. He had hoped that Zainah would at least help with his journey to find his father, which would have meant spending some time with her. Now, that wasn't even possible.

He looked around the tent. What was he even still doing there? He was completely whole now. He needed to leave. Obviously, he would not go back to the Al-Muharib camp as he didn't hold to their tenets anymore, but he had to go somewhere. Somewhere far away from here, where he could forget about Zainah.

A few weeks previously, before he had given his heart to Christ, he'd decided to leave, but changed his mind after he'd become a follower of Jesus. Now he had to go. He would leave first thing the following morning. It would tear him to pieces to leave here without saying goodbye to Zainah, but it would be the best thing to do. If not, he would change his mind when he saw her beautiful face again and decide to stay even though they had no future together.

He looked around the tent again. There was no

luggage to carry. He had nothing except the few clothes that had been donated to him here. He would leave those for them. The fewer memories he carried with him out of this place, the better for him.

*****

Faizan looked up that evening as someone entered his tent. He held back a groan when he saw it was Leila, Zainah's friend, holding a Bible in her right hand. She had come to read the Bible with him just as Zainah had said. But somehow, he knew there was more to what Zainah had told him. From the way she had said her friend was taking over from her, he knew she was trying to set them up. That only increased his anger.

Leila sat across from him and said, "Zainah sent me to read the Bible and pray with you. She said she's busy right now."

He looked at her and realized she didn't even know that Zainah was trying to get them together and decided to tell her. He wasn't in the mood for company except Zainah's. But she was probably not going to come anymore.

"I think your friend is trying to get us together," Faizan said, making sure there was no antagonism in his voice. Zainah's decision wasn't this woman's fault, after all.

Leila frowned. "How do you know that? She simply told me she was busy."

"I know people," he said. "Most of all, I know Zainah. I could see it in her eyes when she told me you were going to be taking over the reading of our daily Bible studies."

Leila shook her head. "Wow! And here I was thinking she chose me because I'm a good Bible teacher."

He smiled in spite of himself. She had a good sense of humor. He had wanted to send her on her way, but he shrugged. Since he was leaving the next morning, it didn't matter anyway. "You might as well teach today," he said. "You're already here."

She nodded and opened her Bible. "Zainah told me you two just started a study of the book of Acts. I will continue from where she stopped."

He nodded.

As she read and then taught the Bible, he listened on and off. He couldn't get his mind off Zainah and his intense wish that she was there and the one reading to him. He finally scolded himself. Get a grip, Faizan, and listen to God's word. What does it matter who is reading it?

He forced himself to forget about Zainah so he could focus on what was most important now—growing in his relationship with Christ.

An hour later, just as Leila was rounding up their Bible studies and prayer session, Miriam entered the tent. She had her phone with her.

"You have a call… from the same man who called you earlier today."

Faizan took the phone from her and frowned in surprise. He had not expected to hear from Khalid again. He lifted the phone to his ear just as Miriam and Leila left the tent.

"Khalid," he said.

"Faizan, I found out something else that I think you might want to know."

"Yes, I'm listening," Faizan said curiously.

"Phil Gardner's daughters and their spouses were in Spain a few weeks ago looking for a man called Rafael. From my source, I found out that Rafael is their missing brother. And that brother is you, Faizan."

Faizan shot up as his heart began to race. "What? Phil Gardner's daughters were searching for me?"

"Yes. Apparently their father told them to search out their missing brother."

He shut his eyes and then opened them again. This changes everything.

"Khalid, thank you. I owe you one," he said.

"I thought we were even now?"

"Yes… thank you again."

"There is something else," Khalid said.

Faizan's emotions churned. What else was there that would surpass this news he'd just heard?

"One of your sisters, the oldest one, is getting married in a few weeks. Her one wish is to have you at her wedding. That was why they were searching really hard for you."

Faizan pressed his hand to his forehead. His sisters, his only living relatives, wanted to see him. He suddenly felt an overwhelming urge to be connected to them and immediately knew he would do anything to see them now, to let them know he was their missing brother and he wanted a relationship with them.

"Jes…" he winced inwardly and tried again. "Yarhamuk Allah, Khalid. Thanks again." He sighed in relief. He'd nearly let it slip that he was now a follower of Jesus. If he wasn't a marked man before, that would have surely made him one.

"Khalid, do you know what part of America the Gardner sisters are from?"

"I don't. But I will try to find out and let you know," Khalid promised.

"That would be great. And remember, Khalid, this has to be kept between the two of us. Understood?"

"Of course. You know you can trust me, Faizan."

"I wouldn't have entrusted this to you if I didn't."

After the call ended, he looked up and breathed a prayer of thanks to God. He wouldn't leave this place the next day as he had planned before. He had to keep communicating with Khalid and discover where his sisters lived and where the wedding was going to take place. If they wanted him there, he hoped he would be able to attend. Maybe he would surprise them if he could pull it off.

He smiled. At least he now knew where he was going when he left this place. He would go where his sisters were. Then he could be part of a real family. Not the one that had been full of bloodshed, but a peaceful one, with sisters he hoped would love him.

*****

Hassan held the phone tightly to his ear. "So you think he will want to go to that wedding in America?"

Khalid answered, "From the tone of his voice, I am almost certain of it."

Hassan breathed a sigh of relief. That bumbling Ahmed had still not been able to find out where the women's Christian camp was located. This was a great way to do it. They would have to forget about those women, at least for now, but Faizan was who he really wanted to apprehend anyway.

Hassan laughed without humor. Who would have guessed Faizan was a filthy American? But maybe he should have. There had been something about his appearance that was slightly off. He said to Khalid, "That's good. Once you find out the exact city and location where the wedding will take place, let Faizan know about it and report to me as well."

"I will," Khalid said.

Hassan nodded. "This time, that traitor will not escape our grasp. I'll personally make sure he pays for his treachery with his life."

SEVENTEEN

Faizan stood from the sleeping mat and put on his shirt and a pair of pants. He paused at the door of the tent for a few seconds, thinking about what he wanted to do, and then went out of the tent.

He knew the specific time when the general evening prayers took place because Zainah had told him about it, but he had never joined in. Today, he wanted to for two reasons. The first was that he felt a deep, unfamiliar hunger to fellowship with other Christians, and not just the regular prayer sessions he'd had with Zainah and now with Leila.

Secondly, he wanted to see Zainah and share with her the good news about finding his siblings. Since she would not come to his tent, this was the way he knew to reach her. He could have gone to her tent to find her, but he wasn't sure he would find her there at the specific time he went. Plus, going to find her in her tent might be a little too personal and she might not appreciate that.

He walked on, listening for sounds of people praying. He soon heard a chorus of voices singing and followed the sound to a large tent, where he found the women and a few children. Some were clapping, some swaying to the upbeat music as they sang. There were no instruments, but the sound of their singing was melodious to the ear.

He stood at the back and listened to the beat and the lyrics they sang. They were simple lyrics about the greatness of God. The beat and lyrics were catchy. He picked up the lyrics quickly and sang along.

After the song ended, the middle-aged woman leading the worship started singing a slow song. He stood mesmerized as everyone closed their eyes and lifted their hands in the air. He did the same and joined in the worship.

It seemed like an eternity as he was lost in the presence of God, and then he heard a familiar voice that pulled him out of his ecstasy. His heart skipped a beat as he opened his eyes and saw Zainah in front of the small crowd. She had her Bible open in her hands and she began to read aloud from it. He watched her for a minute, not even hearing what she was saying. His heart drummed as he listened to the familiar lilt of her voice as she read. He missed her voice, the way she read the Bible to him and their prayer time together. He missed her.

She suddenly looked his way, and for a few seconds she stopped reading. Her face contorted and he held his breath. And then she looked down at her Bible and with a quivering voice, continued.

He tried to focus on the words she was reading, but his mind kept straying to their brief kiss days before. It was the last time he had seen her.

She shut her Bible and began to lead the prayers.

Everyone soon joined in the prayers and he forced himself to pray with them. At last, his mind focused on the Lord again, and he lifted his voice, asking God for help and guidance as he made the trip to meet his sisters.

Again, Zainah's voice cut into his concentration as she rounded up the prayers.

After the evening prayers ended and everyone began to make their way out of the tent, Faizan walked up to Zainah as she left the tent with Leila.

"Can I speak with you?" he asked her.

She looked at him as though he had asked her to jump off a cliff. She started to shake her head but he said, "It's about my birth father. Please."

She looked at Leila. "I'll join you in the tent soon."

Leila smiled and left them alone.

He pointed at the raised platform near the front of the tent. "Can we sit there and talk?"

She sighed and then nodded. She followed him to the front and they sat side by side on the platform. He looked around. Everyone had left the tent. It was now just the two of them here. He turned to face her and found that she was gazing around the tent too. She turned to him, worry clouding her features.

"I can't stay for long," she said.

He nodded and began. "The man I told you about who knows how to find people, he found out that my birth father is dead."

Zainah gasped and bit her lip. "I'm so sorry, Faizan." She put her hand on his shoulder and said, "I know how important it was for you to find him. I can't say how sorry I am."

For a few seconds, he didn't say anything, torn between the renewed sadness of his father's death and relishing her touch. She finally withdrew her hand and he went on. "He did, however, give me some good news. My father has three daughters." He smiled. "I have three sisters, Zainah. They live in a small town in America."

She beamed at him. "That's great."

"There is more good news," he said. "Khalid, the man I asked to look for my father, he told me that my sisters have been searching for me."

"They have?" Zainah's eyes widened in surprise. "Wow! That is so good to hear, Faizan." Her eyes searched his. "What are you planning to do about it now?"

He answered, "The oldest is getting married soon. Part of the reason why they wanted to find me as soon as possible was because they wanted me to be at the wedding. It's still two weeks away. I want to go and surprise them there."

Zainah nodded. Her eyes sparkled as she said, "I think it's a great idea. They will be so happy to meet you." She studied his face for a short moment and asked, "But how are you going to get to America? Even though your birth father is an American, you don't have an American passport." She shook her head. "Do you even have a passport?"

He shrugged. "I know a guy."

She raised her brows, but he was thankful she didn't pursue the issue.

"I'm so happy for you, Faizan," she said, smiling widely. And then she suddenly sobered.

"What is it?" he asked her, worried by the troubled expression on her face.

She shook her head quickly and then wore her smile again, but it didn't look so genuine this time. "It's nothing."

He studied her face, trying to read what was wrong, but he couldn't. He finally gave up.

"I take it you are leaving soon?"

He nodded, and then an unexpected wave of pain went through him at the thought that he would be separated from her before long. He held back a groan and then frowned as he noticed the expression on her face had turned immeasurably sad. And then he knew why she looked troubled. It was because he was leaving. His heart soared. She would miss him. From the expression on her face, he could see she didn't really want him to go. He tentatively took her hands in his. When she didn't withdraw her hands, hope grew in him; hope that she would reconsider and decide to be with him.

He said softly, "Zainah, if you just say the word now, I won't go. I'll leave it all to stay here with you."

"No… no!" she stood. "Don't do that. I meant it when I told you I couldn't break my vow. Besides, I would not be able to live with myself if I hindered you from going to see your long-lost family. You deserve to see your sisters, and I wouldn't take that away from you."

He gazed at her for a long moment, his heart breaking. He wanted to see the sisters he had never met. He wanted to hear stories about his father and feel like part of a real family. But more than all that, he wanted Zainah. He loved her so much, it hurt physically. He studied the expression on her face. She looked resolute, and he knew she wasn't going to change her mind.

He sighed and nodded. There was no use saying anything more, as her mind was made up. Besides, he couldn't, in good conscience, try to talk her out of fulfilling her vow to God. There was no hope for a romantic relationship with her. He had to go, and permanently too, or he would go crazy with longing.

She stood up and smiled down at him. "Again, I'm happy for you." She stood there for a few seconds more and it seemed like she was about to say something else. But she didn't. She sighed loudly, turned around, and quickly left the tent.

He watched the entrance of the tent for a long time, his heart heavy. And then he reached into his pocket and pulled out a small piece of paper. He opened it and looked at it. He had scribbled down a name and number which Khalid had provided for him. It was the number of one of his sister's fiancé. A guy named Ken. Faizan didn't even want to know how Khalid had gotten the man's personal number. He was only grateful that he had.

Faizan stood, left the tent, and headed for Miriam's. The woman would wonder at his recent phone calls, which all seemed urgent, but this call was an extremely important step towards finally being reunited with his sisters.

He had found out his sister and the man she was about to marry were police officers. At first, he had been hesitant because of that, but he had committed everything to God. He had an ugly past and that was a fact he couldn't change. He would not lie about his past if he was asked. If the Lord intended for him to pay the price for his involvement with Al-Muharib now, then so be it. If not, the Lord would protect him. He only hoped that his sister's fiancé could keep a secret.

*****

Audrey smiled at Ken as they took their seats in the posh Green Valley restaurant called Baker's Field. The place was packed. Thankfully, with her connections, she had booked seats for them even though it was a last-minute booking.

Ken's eyes moved around the place and then he said, "Who knew such a place existed in a small town like this? It's a pity Rosefield doesn't have this sort of place. I would have brought you here a long time ago."

Audrey chuckled. "You can blame the absence of this exact restaurant in Rosefield on a guy named Frank. He is the owner of the restaurant and a childhood friend."

Ken lifted his eyebrows as he looked at her. "Is it the same Frank you and Sienna were teasing Trisha about the other day?"

"Yes. He's been away from Rosefield for some time, but he used to live there with his family when we were young. He was our family friend and completely smitten with Trisha. Sometimes I think part of the reason he left Rosefield was because Trisha married Stan. He says it's not true, but I think it is."

Ken had an amused smile on his face. "Well... now Trisha is single again, maybe he will finally get a chance with her."

"Trisha says she isn't ready for a relationship." Audrey looked around the restaurant, noting the sophisticated décor. "I wonder if he's here today? It would be nice to see him, as I haven't seen him in a while. He's usually away because he wants to start a chain of restaurants. I think he has already started one in Boise and is probably there now."

As though Frank had heard them talking about him, he appeared from behind a counter and walked toward them.

Audrey smiled widely. "Frank!" He reached them, and she stood to hug him tightly. "How are you?" she asked. "Haven't seen you in a long time."

"I've been in Boise," he answered. "But I was in Rosefield a few weeks ago." He looked at Ken and smiled. He put out his hand, and Ken shook it. "Good to see you again."

"Likewise." Ken waved his hand around. "You have a great place here. I was just telling Audrey that it's a pity Rosefield doesn't have a restaurant like this."

"And I told Ken it was because of Trisha you decided to move to Green Valley. You set this place up here rather than your own town."

Frank chuckled. "You know that's untrue, Audrey. Green Valley is just a better choice for my restaurant at this time. That doesn't mean I won't set one up in Rosefield one day."

"Audrey shook her head. "Umm… I still think it's about Trisha."

Frank said soberly, "Talking about Trisha, I saw her when I came to Rosefield. She told me you guys went to Spain for a vacation."

"Yes. We had a nice time. Bryan and Sienna also came with us."

Frank nodded. "Don't let me keep you from your dinner any longer." He looked around. "All the waiters are busy now with the other guests, but I'll make sure one comes to you as soon as possible." He looked at Audrey and smiled. "In fact, why don't I take your order myself? I'll make sure your food gets to you in no time, too."

He took a menu from a passing waiter and handed it to Audrey. "Your request is my command, mademoiselle," he said, his green eyes shining.

Audrey looked at the menu list and then reeled out her order.

Ken grinned at her and then looked up at Frank. "I'll have what she is having."

Frank nodded as he scribbled their orders. He beamed again at Audrey and Ken and then told them a waiter would be out with their food as soon as possible.

When he was gone, Ken said, "Nice guy. Have you sent his invite for the wedding?"

"Not yet. I will send the remaining invites, including his, tomorrow." She took Ken's hand on the table. "Can you believe it, babe? The wedding is in just two weeks!"

He stared into her eyes. "Two weeks and two days. I've been counting the days." He said softly, "I can't wait to marry you, Audrey."

"I can't wait either, Ken." She threaded their fingers together and said, "Soon, I will be Mrs. Baylor. Best of all, we will finally be able to live together."

He laughed. "In two homes. One in Miami and the other in Rosefield."

"Yes," she said. "When do you want to have kids? As soon as we are married or in a year or so?"

He caressed the back of her hand with his thumb. "In five years. So I can enjoy as much of you as I can."

She felt herself blushing and breathed, "I want that too… but you can't be serious, Ken. Do you really want to wait five years before we start having kids?"

"All right. Whenever you are ready, I will be, too."

"Then it's settled. We will start having our children in a year. It amazes me that Sienna and Bryan want to start having kids right away. They are young and can afford to wait for another year or two."

Ken shrugged. "People are different and have different goals."

Audrey nodded. "That's true. Sienna has always wanted to be a mother, while I didn't even think I was ever going to get married until I met you."

"I swept you off your feet, didn't I?"

She shook her head and laughed at the naughty expression on his face. "Yes… yes you did."

They stared lovingly into each other's eyes for a full minute, and then the magical moment was broken when a waiter came with their drinks and set them on the table.

They sipped the drinks as they chatted about the wedding and then about their future plans. Ken's phone began to ring and at first he ignored it. It continued and he frowned.

"I'm sorry, Audrey. I forgot to turn it off." He picked up the cell phone from the table. "I'll do that now."

"No, don't worry about it. Just answer it. It might be important."

"Are you sure?" he asked.

"I am. Go ahead and answer the call."

He lifted the phone to his ear and said, "Hello, who is this?"

His eyes grew as round as saucers.

Her heart did a flip and she asked, "Who is it?" The expression on his face was alarming.

He held up a finger. "Just a minute, Audrey." He stood and walked out of the restaurant with the phone still to his ear.

She sat staring, her pulse racing with worry. What was wrong now? She tried to calm herself. Maybe the concern she'd seen on his face had to do with work. Nothing more. Still, she couldn't stop her stomach from clenching with fear.

Minutes later, he came back and sat down in front of her. His expression had mostly returned to normal. But she still detected a slight discomfort in his demeanor.

"Who was that?" she asked.

He smiled widely. "No one important. Just work."

"You forget I'm also a policewoman. What happened at work?"

He sighed. "It's a case I've been working on, that's all. It will probably be transferred to the CIA, and that will be that."

His tone was firm, like he was telling her not to ask any more questions. She knew him well enough to know there was something he wasn't telling her. Something that didn't just involve whatever case he was working on. It involved her, too. She could see it from the way he was avoiding her eyes. She smiled at him, choosing to let it go... for now.

Their food arrived some minutes later and they tucked in. By the time the second course came, the awkwardness between them, caused by the phone call, had vanished. Still, she made a mental note to discover what he was hiding, but as discreetly as possible.

*****

Hassan nodded as Khalid told him he had found out the particular town in America where Faizan's sisters lived. "And you have given him that information?" Hassan asked Khalid.

"Yes, and I'm sure he is going to the wedding."

"And did you find out what date the wedding is and when Faizan has decided to travel?"

"Yes. The wedding is in exactly one week and Faizan will be traveling as soon as possible."

"Thank you, Khalid. Your help has been invaluable."

"Anything for the brotherhood."

After the call, Hassan paced his cave. Previously, he'd decided that he would personally go to America and kill Faizan alone, but now he realized that wasn't enough punishment for the man who had betrayed the group. Besides, why kill just one man when he could get the whole lot?

He rubbed his beard as a new plan unfolded in his mind. He could send someone to carry out the plan he was thinking about, but he had learned not to delegate an important job to anyone. He would have to do it himself.

He ran the plan over in his mind. He would go to America using a false passport and visa. Once he got to the wedding venue in the small-town Khalid had told him about, he would plant a bomb before any of the guests arrived. After he'd made sure Faizan was at the venue, at just the right time, he would detonate the bomb and kill everyone there.

EIGHTEEN

Trisha carried baby Ruby out of her crib and then smiled when the doorbell rang.

Must be Paula, she thought. Paula had promised to come by to babysit Ruby once again. Trisha had to go to Audrey's in a few hours to help with the final plans for the wedding. It was in just a few days, and the closer it got, the more stressed out Audrey had become and the more she needed her sisters' help.

Trisha carried her sleeping baby to the living room and went to open the door. She bit back a groan at the sight of Frank standing there, flowers in his hand. It was not red roses like Stan used to bring her, but pink lilies, a favorite of hers when they were little children.

"Hi, Trisha," he said, smiling.

Once again, she noticed how handsome he was. He looked so tall and broad-shouldered in a light green polo shirt. His green eyes sparkled and looked irresistible as they matched the shirt perfectly. She forced herself to smile and said, "Hey,

Frank, I wasn't expecting you. When did you come to Rosefield?"

"Yesterday," he replied. He looked past her into the house, and Trisha's eyes widened in embarrassment. "Sorry... please come in." She stood aside so he could enter the house. When he did, she told him to take a seat.

He started to sit on the sofa near the door and then straightened again. He held out the flowers and then put down his hand, clearly noticing that her own hands were full.

She smiled and nodded at the vase on the dining table. The flowers there needed changing so he might as well do that too. He quickly went to the dining table to exchange the flowers, while she sat and looked down at Ruby.

Frank came back to the living room, but rather than sit on the love seat, he sat down on the couch beside her. He looked down at the baby in her arms and cooed at her.

Trisha frowned when her heart suddenly skipped a beat as he shifted a little closer to her. She could smell the enticing spicy fragrance of his cologne mixed with something delicious that made her mouth water. Without wanting to, she searched her mind for the origin of the smell until it came to her. Cinnamon pie. How come he smelled like her favorite dessert? She remembered the last time she had spoken with him he had said he was now a chef.

That might explain why.

In order to steer her mind away from her strange wayward thoughts, she asked, "How is your restaurant, Frank?"

"Umm… good, but which one?"

Her mouth opened for a few seconds, and then she covered it. "I'm sorry… umm… I didn't remember you told me you have several now. I guess what I should ask is how are your restaurants?"

He ran his fingers slowly through his hair, and she couldn't look away. It looked so lush now. He answered, "Two of them are great, one is so-so, and the last one is struggling a little."

He began to tell her about the restaurants, the peculiar problems he had with starting a new franchise in a big city, and the challenges of running each of them. At first, she listened absent-mindedly, thinking she would be bored with the tedious details of the day-to-day running of the restaurants, but she soon became absorbed in his stories. In between their conversation, she excused herself and carried Ruby to her room. She quickly but gently laid Ruby in her crib and went back to the living room.

She continued to listen to Frank's story with fascination until he'd finished. Shaking her head, she said with amazement, "And I thought running a bookstore in this small town was challenging!" She smiled at him. "I admire your persistence and entrepreneurial spirit, Mr. Kessler."

He tilted his head toward her, chuckled and said, "I didn't know you still remembered my last name, Trisha."

Trisha shook her head at the humorous expression on his face. "Very funny, Frank. Of course I remember your last name." She looked away as the intensity in his eyes as he watched her suddenly made her shy. She felt herself withering as she remembered again the incident that had happened years before which had filled her with so much guilt. Every time she saw him, she remembered and guilt gripped her heart. That day, however, it felt more like a chokehold than a grip. The fact that he had never married and that Audrey insisted it was because of her only made the guilt worse.

She sighed and suddenly couldn't take the guilt anymore. She had to face it with him here and see if she could find some type of absolution. She turned to him again and looked into his eyes. Even though the intense look in his eyes made her uncomfortable, she didn't look away this time. "Frank, I want to tell you something."

His eyes sparkled as he looked quizzically at her. "What is it?"

"You remember the day we went out on a date as teenagers? The surprise one you had organized for me?"

"How could I ever forget?"

She pressed her lips tightly together. The pleasant expression had disappeared from his face, replaced by a haunted look. "I've never forgotten that day, either," she said. "It fills me with so much guilt every time I remember what happened… especially as… umm… as Stan and I are no longer together."

His eyes searched hers. "It was such a long time ago, Trish. You shouldn't let that incident make you feel guilty. I still remember the events of the day clearly but I don't let it fill me with the hurt it did for a few years after. Even though it hurt terribly when you chose Stan over me on our date, I have let it go."

She smiled sadly and said, "But have you really, Frank?" She didn't want to say what was really on her mind, but she had to. For her sake and his. "I apologized then, but I always knew it wasn't enough. The way I blew you off that day, even after all you planned for me... wasn't right."

He shook his head. "You can't help who you love..."

"No, let me finish." She put a hand on his arm. "I hurt you terribly, and I'm almost certain you haven't gotten past that day. I just don't know what I can do to help you do that... but I could introduce you to one of my friends." She plowed on in spite of the incredulous look on his face. "I have this friend, Isla, who is single and very pretty. She also loves cooking. I think you two might make a good match."

He blinked and then leaned back on his seat. She held her breath and waited for him to say something while she warred with her feelings on the inside. In spite of how hard she tried, she couldn't shut down the conflicting voices in her mind.

Do you really want him to date someone else?

The least I can do for him is set him up with Isla since I don't want to date anyone now.

You'll be hard-pressed finding someone else who loves you like he does.

But I don't feel the same way he does, and I can't force myself to.

Are you sure that's true? You don't like him, even a little?

She shut her eyes as the troubling thoughts raged in her and then opened them again. Her eyes widened as she found him staring at her, the expression on his face a mixture of sadness and disbelief.

"Trisha," he said softly, "it's crazy that you think I would want to date a friend of yours as a replacement for you. The truth is that I don't want anyone else. I can't date anyone else. You are the only one I want, Trisha Gardner."

Her heart raced madly at his words and the way he gazed at her, as though she was his world. She bit her lip, unable to speak. After a full minute, she said, "I don't know what to say, Frank."

"Say you will go out with me… or at least that you will think about it."

"I just don't know…"

"Just like I said, you don't have to give me an answer now, just promise you will think about it. There's no rush. I have waited for years, and I will wait for you forever if I have to."

She couldn't breathe as she stared into his eyes. The love she saw in them literally took her breath away. Without thinking, she reached out and cupped his face. She felt tears shimmering in her eyes as she said, "I don't deserve your love, Frank."

The tears fell down her cheeks, and he reached out and wiped them away with his fingers. "I love you, Trisha. I will always love you."

She suddenly couldn't hold back. Without thinking, she drew him close and kissed his cheeks and then his nose. She trembled at the new feelings coursing through her. He searched her eyes and then took her in his arms. Her pulse raced madly as he tilted her head for what she knew would be an earth-shattering kiss. But just before their lips met, the doorbell rang and she jerked back. She quickly stood, took a deep breath and thanked God for the interruption. She would have done something she would have regretted later on.

She didn't look at him as she hurried to the door. Opening it, she found Paula standing there with both her kids. She grinned at Paula and opened the door wide for her and the children to enter.

The children ran into the house and Paula said, "We came for a play date with Ruby." She came in, saw Frank, grinned at Trisha and whispered, "Frank Kessler is here?" She winked at Trisha and asked mischievously, "Did I interrupt something?"

Trisha shook her head quickly, "No... no, nothing. Frank just stopped by to see Ruby, that's all." She looked at Frank, hoping he would take Paula's arrival as his cue to leave, but already, he was playing with Evan, Paula's four-year-old son. His baby sister, Jessica, stood watching them and giggling.

Trisha watched him playfully arm wrestle the child and Paula laughed. "He takes to children quickly."

Trisha nodded dumbly. She couldn't take her eyes off him.

Paula giggled and snapped her fingers. When Trisha forced her eyes away from Frank to look at her, Paula whispered, "Are you sure he just came to see the baby...? Because I think there is more. And that would be fine with me."

"There isn't more," Trisha said and sighed wearily. She was tired of people insinuating that she and Frank would be perfect together. First it was Audrey, and now Paula.

"Why not?" Paula pretended to whine. "He is

super cute, and he seems to be great with kids."

Trisha rolled her eyes. "He'll soon catch us watching him and whispering. And then he will think we are crazy for sure."

"I doubt he will think we are crazy," Paula said. "He was taken with you when we were young, and I think he would be pleased to see Trisha Gardner ogling him."

"I am not ogling him!" Trisha exclaimed, and then pressed her lips tightly together when Frank looked up at them. Evan took the opportunity to pull Frank's hand down and then raised his hands and yelled in triumph.

Frank groaned and Paula chuckled. "As I said, Trisha, he's really handsome and good with children. If you ask me, he's a great catch. If I wasn't already happily married, I would date him!"

"Paula!"

Paula laughed softly. "Well, you had better scoop him up before someone else does."

Trisha sighed again, but as she watched Frank continue to play with the children, she wondered if she shouldn't just give in to his advances. She could feel herself beginning to fall for him.

She immediately resisted the thought. After the way Stan had treated her in their marriage and after their drawn-out divorce, the last thing she needed was to be in a relationship. As Paula said, Frank was a great catch. It was better he moved on and found someone else to love, because she wasn't sure when or if she would ever be ready to date again.

*****

Lauren raised her hands in triumph as she read the email before her. She'd checked her email every day, eager to hear back from the different schools she'd secretly applied to. Now, one of them had written back and invited her for an interview. She felt invigorated as she thought about working again. She wouldn't think about Richie for now or his reaction when she told him about the job. All she could think about right now was preparing for the interview.

She finally closed her email and looked up from her computer. A troubling thought came to her and she sighed wearily. It wasn't just letting Richie know if she got the job that she had to worry about. She first had to tell him about the interview. Would he let her go? He hardly let her out of his sight. How would she allow her to go?

Well, he was welcome to come along with her if he wanted to, but she needed to go for the interview. It was in a few days. That meant she had to tell him about it now.

She put her laptop aside, stood up from the bed, and went to find him downstairs. He wasn't in the living room or the guest room. She went into the kitchen and found him there. She blinked in surprise as she found him fixing himself a sandwich. He never cooked or even made sandwiches. That job belonged to her. He did all the grocery shopping while she prepared all their meals. The days when he brought breakfast in bed for her or cooked her special dinners were over.

"You're fixing yourself lunch?" she asked him.

"Yes, as you can see. That's exactly what I am doing."

She asked curiously, "Why?"

"Because!"

She shrugged. What did she care if he decided he wanted to make lunch for himself? She said to him, "I have something to tell you."

He put the chicken sandwich on a plate and asked without looking at her, "What is it?"

She said without fumbling, "I applied for a teaching position and just received an invitation to an interview at the school. It's in less than a week, and I would like to go."

He put the plate down on the kitchen island and looked up at her. As usual, he had an angry expression on his face. "We've talked about this, Lauren. You are not going to any job interview."

Lauren glared at him. "I have to go. I need to work, Richie. I need to get out of this house."

"I said you are not going to get a job, and that is final!"

Lauren's shoulders stiffened and anger swelled in her belly. She said defiantly, "I am going to that interview, Richie. Whether you like it or not!"

He laughed and then shook his head. "Let me see you go."

She sighed. Anger and defiance were not going to work in this case. She had to try to plead with him. She walked up to him and put her arms around him. Looking into his eyes, she said, "Richie, I haven't really asked you for anything since I came back. This time I am asking… no, begging. Please let me go for that interview."

His eyes studied hers for a long moment, and then he uncurled her arms from his waist and stepped away from her. "You are trying to manipulate me." He frowned. "It's not going to work, so just forget it. You are not getting a job." He carried his plate of sandwich and walked out of the kitchen.

For a long moment, she stood there, looking at the wall in front of her. Her stomach boiled with rage, but she told herself to calm down. If she gave in to her anger, it would end really badly. What do I do? She asked herself.

She gazed out the window while thinking about how to get out of the prison that was her home. The easiest way would be to call Ken, find out if he was back in Miami, and tell him what had been happening with Richie. But she still didn't want that. She wouldn't be able to live with herself if either of the men got hurt, and it would likely be her husband. She also didn't want Richie in jail.

If only Richie would allow her to get a job, she would be content to stay with him. She still loved him, in spite of his violent ways. At least she wouldn't be home all day where it would be easy for him to torment her. Plus, her life would have a sense of purpose and direction. But he'd plainly refused and she didn't see him changing his mind.

She kept thinking of a way to escape as she stood gazing out the window, but she came up with nothing. And then as she turned around, something occurred to her, and she turned back to the window.

She stepped forward and touched the panes. This particular window in the kitchen was never opened. The one opposite it was the window she and Richie usually opened in the mornings. She twisted the handle. It creaked slightly as she pushed it open. Leaning forward, she stuck her head out and looked around. Grassy land stretched out before her eyes. On the left side, which she couldn't see from where she stood, was the path that led to the main road.

She gasped as she heard footsteps approaching the kitchen and quickly shut the window and twisted the handle to lock it.

Richie came in with an empty plate, looked at her, and then dropped the plate in the sink. He left the kitchen without speaking or looking at her again and she breathed a huge sigh of relief. She looked at the window again. In a few days' time, the night before her interview, she would climb out of this window. Finding a motel to stay in overnight would be easy enough. The next day, she would attend her interview and then come back. Richie would be mad when he found out, but it was a risk she had to take.

As for convincing Richie to allow her work if she got the job, maybe they could come to a compromise. She would agree to have a baby in a few months, if he would just let her work.

But even as she thought about that, she felt sickened at the thought of having a baby with him now when he was so violent.

She sighed wearily and decided she would cross that bridge when she got there. For now, her main concern was to get to that interview, no matter what.

*****

Zainah's stomach clenched as Faizan entered her tent. She stood and bit her lip. She'd been trying not to think of this day. Since he'd told her days before that he would be leaving soon, she'd been unable to sleep well. She had dreaded the day he would come to tell her it was time to leave. Now, looking at him with a small bag clearly containing the few clothes and personal items he'd been given, she knew that day had come. A sob rose in her throat, but she managed to push it down.

He walked up to her and said, "I'm leaving now, Zainah. I just wanted to thank you for everything you have done for me before I go."

The finality in his voice pierced her heart, and tears threatened to slip down her face. She was grateful the other women she shared the tent with had all gone to the morning prayers. He must have gone there and not found her before deciding to come here. Somehow she'd guessed he might leave that day and the thought had made her physically unwell and unable to attend the prayers.

She forced a smile and said haltingly, "It wasn't just me. Many of the women in this camp helped to nurture you back to health."

"It's not just my physical health. You also gave me the greatest gift anyone could receive—my relationship with Christ. I am truly grateful and I will always remember that."

She nodded, unable to speak.

He gazed at her for a long moment, his eyes studying her face closely.

She knew he was taking her in, memorizing her features so he would not forget her. She couldn't help but do the same. After a long moment, he pulled his eyes away from her. "So, I have to go now. Again, thank you for everything." His voice was choked with emotion. He started to turn away from her, and she suddenly felt dizzy with dread. She would never see him again, she was sure of that.

She leaned on the tent pillar, feeling like she was about to pass out. "Wait, Faizan," she said weakly.

He turned back to her. "Yes?"

She couldn't restrain the tears anymore and they fell down her cheeks. "I just wanted…" she swallowed the sob in her throat so she could clearly tell him what she wanted to say. "I just want to let you know that I love you, very much."

She sucked in her breath sharply when tears began to slip down his cheeks. She couldn't hold it in anymore and began to sob loudly, unable to control herself.

He took her in his arms and she cried, wetting his shirt with her tears. He let her cry, rubbing her back comfortingly and telling her he loved her with everything that was in him. After a few minutes, she pulled back and wiped her tears with her hand. "I'm sorry," she said, seeing the tortured look on his face. "I wish things could be different." She began to cry again.

He took hold of her shoulders and said gruffly, "I know I can't change your mind. And I wouldn't even dare to at this point, knowing you made a vow to God. But promise me that you won't forget about me; that you will keep me in your prayers always."

She nodded. "I could never forget about you. And I promise to always pray for you, Faizan."

He kissed her forehead and then stepped back from her. "I will miss you."

She smiled sadly. "And I will miss you."

"Goodbye, Zainah."

She hesitated to say the final goodbye as her heart tore into shreds. She took a deep breath and then said, "Goodbye, Faizan. God be with you always."

He turned around and walked out of the tent.

She ran out and watched him climb up on his camel and then head off into the desert. Her breath came quickly as she watched him going farther and farther away.

Go after him, her heart cried.

But she knew it would be the wrong thing to do. She stood crying silently until he disappeared from sight, and then she fell to her knees in the sand and wept loudly.

NINETEEN

Lauren slowly removed Richie's hand from her body and sat up. Quietly, she began to slide out of bed while looking at Richie. He moved, and she froze for a few seconds. She held her breath and watched his face for a brief moment, and then she quickly but silently slipped out of bed.

Hastily, she put on a sweater and a pair of jeans, which she had folded in her tote bag during the day. She picked up the bag from the floor beside the bed and tiptoed across the room. Without looking back, she slowly twisted the doorknob and opened the door. She stepped out of the bedroom and stealthily went down the stairs.

Walking quietly to the kitchen, she made to switch the light on and then changed her mind. She turned on her phone flashlight instead, went to the window and twisted the handle. She pushed the window open and then threw her bag out. There was a full moon in the sky and the back porch was well lit. She started to climb out of the window, but just as she got one leg out, the kitchen lights came on.

Her heart jumped at the sight of her husband staring at her with a look of astonishment on his face.

"What in the world, Lauren?" Richie exclaimed, staring at her with eyes wide.

Lauren gasped when Richie reached her in a flash and began to pull her back into the house. She decided there was no use trying to resist and let him pull her in.

"What the heck do you think you are doing?" he spat out, his eyes flashing with rage.

She shut her eyes as disappointment and fear took hold of her. She had thought for sure she would be able to get away tonight, at least for her interview. Apparently, there was no escaping Richie, not even for a few hours.

He took a hold of her shoulders and shook her hard. "Answer me!"

She opened her eyes and looked at his angry face. She said softly, "I wanted to go for my interview, Richie."

He clutched her hand and began to drag her out of the kitchen.

"I need to get my bag!" she cried out. "I left it out there."

He kept pulling her with him, his hand like an iron clasp around hers.

"Please, Richie!"

He turned around and yelled, "Stop begging!" They got to the living room, and he flung her to the side.

She screamed as she fell onto the coffee table. She heard a loud crunching sound and knew she had broken something. Pain screamed through her right arm and she turned to look at it. There was a cut running from her shoulder to her elbow. Blood seeped out of the wound.

She looked up at him, and for the first time since they'd gotten married her heart filled with an intense dislike that bordered on hatred.

His eyes were focused on her bleeding arm. He snarled at her. "Look what you made me do." He pointed at her arm. "If you weren't so stupid, that wouldn't have happened." He stood threateningly over her, and she thought he was going to pounce on her. He stared at her with disdain and then huffed away.

Tears streamed down her face as she sat on the ground. Not tears of pain because of her arm, but of self-loathing. How could she still live with this man? Even though she had tried to escape several times and he had caught her, ultimately, she hadn't tried hard enough. Her excuse had been that she still loved him, but she couldn't stay with him anymore. He'd been hurting her physically and emotionally. One day, he might kill her. This time, she was going to call Ken. Hopefully, he would be in Miami now. And if Ken shot her husband in the process of trying to get her out, then so be it.

*****

The next night, Lauren woke up and, without looking at Richie who was beside her, picked up her phone from the bedside table. She silently climbed out of the bed, left the room, and went down the stairs.

She went into the living room and took a deep breath before calling Ken's number. She glanced at the clock on the wall. It was a few minutes to one in the morning. It was terribly late. She knew he would be asleep now, but she was desperate.

As his phone began to ring, she prayed desperately that he was in Miami and that he would pick up. When she heard his voice say, "Hello," she breathed a huge sigh of relief.

"Ken, are you in Miami?" she whispered.

"Yes," he said, sounding groggy and confused. "Lauren, why are you calling so late in the night? Is something wrong?"

"I can't talk for long. I need your help, Ken. Richie has been abusing me again, and I need to get out."

Ken's voice was colored with anger as he said, "I am going to kill that beast!"

"No, Ken. Please don't do anything rash for my sake. I just need help getting out of the house since Richie won't let me leave."

"I'm coming over right away."

"No, no need. You can come tomorrow."

"Are you sure about that?"

"He is sleeping now. I'm safe… at least until he wakes up."

She began to hear footsteps coming down the stairs and her heart drummed. "I have to go, Ken. See you tomorrow." She ended the call just as Richie came into the living room.

"What are you doing here, Lauren?" he asked, frowning at her.

"Umm… I just came down to get a glass of water."

"In the living room?" He came closer and she

put her hand behind her so he wouldn't see her cell phone.

He regarded her closely and then asked, "What do you have in your hand?"

She shook her head. "Nothing!"

He grabbed the hand she'd hidden behind her back and scowled. "Who were you calling, Lauren?" he asked in a cold voice that chilled her.

"I was just browsing on my phone, that's all."

He grabbed her phone. She tried to take it back, but he pushed her away. He clicked on the phone and it lit up. His eyes glittered with anger as he stared at it. He looked up at her, and then a string of curses escaped his lips. "You called your ex?" he said with a look of hatred in his eyes that she had never seen before.

She couldn't speak.

He said again, with his voice raised this time, "You called your ex-fiancé, Lauren!"

"I only…" She sucked in her breath sharply as he lunged at her. He grabbed her throat and pinned her against the wall. She struggled against his tight grip, but his strength overpowered her. He yanked her hands behind her back and tied them together with a lamp's electric cord. As she tried to writhe out of the cord, he wrapped another lamp's cord around her ankles.

He ran out of the room. Lauren continued to struggle to break out of her restraints. But before she knew it, Richie was back with some duct tape that he put over her mouth. Now her muffled screams could barely be heard.

Richie seemed to be enjoying watching Lauren fight to get out of the tight knots he had put on her wrists and ankles. When she would make some progress in undoing them, he would bend down and retighten them.

After about twenty minutes of agony on the floor, just when Richie starting to kick Lauren's back, he froze when a loud voice yelled from outside the house, "Open up! Police!"

His eyes widened in surprise and fear. "You called the police?" he snarled.

The door suddenly burst open, and two policemen came in, their guns raised.

"Let her go right now!" Ken said, appearing from behind the policemen. He had his gun leveled at Richie. "Gently!"

Richie roared angrily, and then began to push her aside.

"I said gently!" Ken barked at him.

He let her go, and she took huge gulps of air.

"Put your hands in the air," Ken said. "Now!"

Her heart pounded as she looked at Ken. The rage in his eyes scared her. He looked like he wanted to shoot Richie. She had said she didn't care, but she did. "Please don't hurt him," she pleaded.

"Go and get your things, Lauren," Ken ordered.

Lauren looked at Richie once more and then hurried up to the bedroom. Her body trembled as she packed a few things into a duffel bag. As she left the room, she turned and glanced at it one more time. She didn't know if she would ever return to this house again. Even though she would miss living here, she definitely would not miss the constant violence and fear that had marked her stay.

She went downstairs again and bit her lip, about to cry at the sight before her. Richie was on the ground struggling while one of the policemen held him down and started handcuffing him. She watched with pain in her heart as the policeman hauled him up and led him out of the house.

Ken touched her shoulder. "Are you okay?"

She turned to him, feeling weak and overcome with conflicting emotions, and buried her face into his chest.

He held her as she wept. When she lifted her head, she smiled through her tears and said, "Thank you."

Ken smiled back. "Let's go."

She said to him, "What will happen to Richie?"

"He is going to jail where he belongs."

She put aside the heartache she felt at the news and asked, "Where am I going to stay?"

"With me."

"But I don't want your fiancée to be angry with you the way she was the last time I came to stay at your house. Maybe I should just stay here. I'll be safe since Richie has been arrested."

He looked at her with a thoughtful expression on his face and then nodded. "Okay. But I will be leaving for Rosefield in a few days for my wedding. Do you want to come back with me? Richie might get out on bail soon. I wouldn't feel right leaving you here when he does."

She sighed as she thought about it. Really, there was nothing keeping her here. She'd come to love Rosefield in the months she'd lived there. She loved the Gibsons. Most of all, she had to admit her marriage was over. She smiled sadly at Ken and said, "I think I will go back to Rosefield with you."

"Great decision," he said, smiling at her.

*****

Ken arrived at Fresno's, a cafe near the airport in Boise and then glanced at his watch. It was almost noon; the specific time the stranger had said he would meet him there.

Ken clearly recalled the day the man had called him. At first, he had been doubtful until the man had told him some things that he had no business knowing unless he was who he said he was. To say he had been astonished was an understatement. The worst or best part—depending on what the outcome of their meeting would be—was that he had been with Audrey at the restaurant. From the look on her face, he had known she was suspicious. However, he also knew she could never imagine what the phone call had been about. He only hoped when she found out, she would understand why he hadn't told her about it and not hold it against him.

He called over a waiter and ordered a cup of coffee and doughnuts. When the waiter left, he gave his partner, Mike, who was seated two tables away from him, a discreet nod. He had told Mike about the strange call immediately after it came through. It was just in case everything turned out to be bogus or dangerous, and he needed to make arrests on the spot.

He glanced at his watch again and saw it was time. As he looked up, a tall man with an arrogant bearing and a bushy beard began to make his way toward him. Ken eyed and assessed him as he approached.

It can't be him, Ken thought. But when the man

came and stood in front of him, every remaining doubt he'd had about the guy's identity disappeared. He looked almost identical to the pictures Audrey had shown him of her father. Unless Phil Gardner had been resurrected from the dead, this man was his son, and therefore Audrey, Trisha, and Sienna's brother; the brother they had gone to Spain to find.

The only troubling part about him was that Ken had done a background check when the man who called himself Faizan had called. He had found no real evidence of his existence past the age of twelve. Ken intended to know why. He wouldn't expose the sisters to a stranger without being sure they were safe with him. Aside from the fact that he hadn't been a hundred percent sure the man was Audrey's brother when he had first called, that was another reason why he hadn't told Audrey about it.

Ken pointed at the chair opposite his. "Sit!" he said in a commanding voice and then amended his command and said, "Please."

The man called Faizan sat.

Ken smiled and extended his hand. "Faizan, right?"

"Yes," Faizan shook his hand.

Ken said, "Umm… you have to forgive my hesitancy in this. As a police officer, I'm used to making sure I investigate everything I am involved in thoroughly."

"I understand," Faizan said in a deep voice.

"So, I see the uncanny resemblance between you and Audrey's… umm… Mr. Phil Gardner. Still, I need to make sure that you do not in any way present a threat to my soon-to-be wife and her sisters."

"I also understand that." Faizan paused and

looked intently at Ken for a few seconds and then he continued speaking. "That is why I am going to tell you everything about my life, including a terrorist plot I suspect is brewing right now. One that concerns you and I personally. After I finish, you can do whatever you want with me. I am in Christ's hands now. I only ask that I am allowed to see my sisters."

At the words "terrorist plot", Ken sat up straight. He frowned deeply and leaned forward. "Go ahead," he said. "Tell me everything. I'm listening."

*****

Audrey opened her eyes to the sun streaming through the windows. Someone had come into her room and opened the curtains. She rubbed her eyes, sat up and saw Trisha at the end of her bed, grinning down at her.

"It's your wedding day!" Trisha exclaimed.

Audrey nodded as her heart soared. "That it is!" she said, smiling widely. She took in a deep breath and uttered a silent prayer to the Lord. The day she had been waiting for had finally arrived. She imagined Ken in his hotel room not far from her house, waking up with a huge smile on his face, anticipating the time in the church when they would be pronounced man and wife. Her body trembled with excitement as she thought about finally being able to spend forever with him.

Trisha sat beside her on the bed. "Sienna will arrive anytime now with the bridesmaids' dresses. When will the other bridesmaids come?"

Audrey looked at the clock on the wall. It was

almost nine. "Since we have to leave for the church by three o'clock at the latest, I think they will all be here by one," she said.

"It's so funny but super cool how you chose Sienna and I to both be your maids of honor."

Audrey shrugged. "It's my wedding and so I can do whatever I want to. 'Sides, as you know, I am not a very conventional person."

"I know," Trisha said. "And what about your hair and makeup people? When will they arrive?"

"By noon, I think." She shook her head. "I don't know why Sienna bothered to hire them for me. I can easily do my own hair and makeup."

Trisha chuckled. "Sure you can."

Audrey looked at her. "You don't think I can?"

"I know you can't. You don't even wear makeup at all."

"Well… you or Sienna could have helped me with it."

"Why would we do that when you can afford to hire the best makeup artist? It's your special day, Audrey. You deserve the best today."

Audrey shrugged and changed the subject. They sat talking about all the wedding planning they had done. They laughed at some of the things that had been bungled by a few vendors, like the bridesmaids' dresses that had arrived in different styles than what they had initially ordered. It was the reason why they still didn't have them. One of Audrey's bridesmaids had had to send all the dresses back to be fixed.

Half an hour later, Sienna arrived, carrying a garment bag with her. Hanging it up in front of the wardrobe, she came and hugged Audrey first and then Trisha. She beamed and said, "Can you believe it, Audrey? After all the months of planning, your wedding day is finally here."

They squealed, and Audrey ran her fingers through her short hair. She sighed wistfully. "I don't have to listen with chagrin to your 'making babies' talk anymore, Sienna."

Sienna winked at her. "Yes, you will be too busy making yours with Ken."

They both laughed.

Trisha shook her head. "You girls are so naughty."

They laughed again, and then the conversation moved to talk about the men in their lives. Audrey talked about Ken with longing. He had arrived at Rosefield the day before, but she had only spoken to him on the phone. She hadn't seen him yet. He is such a good man, she thought. But he was also very persistent. She hadn't found out what it was he was keeping from her, but she had decided to let it go. She trusted him completely. In due time, he would let her know what it was.

"I can't wait to see Ken," she said.

"Where is Bryan, Sienna?"

"He's gone to Ken's hotel room. He'll change into his suit there and stay until the other groomsmen are ready to leave for the church."

Audrey looked at Trisha. She had a faraway look in her eyes. She felt slightly sorry for her sister. She and Sienna had the loves of their lives with them, but Trisha had no one but her baby now. She had to feel a little left out.

"I'm sorry, Trisha."

Trisha frowned and looked at her. "For what?"

"I've been so preoccupied with my wedding planning that I haven't asked how you are coping. Do you get lonely sometimes without Stan?"

Trisha thinned her lips and then sighed. "Sometimes. But I'd rather be lonely than have the type of relationship I had with Stan. I think I am truly over romantic relationships."

Sienna held her hand. "That can't be true. You just need a break. Soon, you will be ready to start dating again. You have so much love to give. I don't see you single for too long."

Trisha shook her head. "I just can't imagine dating anyone ever again."

Audrey smiled sadly. "I know I sound like a broken record, but what about Frank? He's perfect for you, Trish."

Trisha held up her hand. "Don't start, Audrey! Frank and I are friends, just like you two are. Nothing more will develop between us."

Audrey raised her hand. She wanted to tease Trisha and say, "the lady doth protest too much…", but she held her peace. She was beginning to learn from Ken not to say everything that was on her mind. All she could do was pray for Trish and Frank and ask that God's will alone would be done. If they were meant to be together, the Lord would make it happen. If not, then God knew who to bring into Trisha's life that would make her happy. Audrey also prayed silently that the Lord would bring someone special for Frank.

They talked about their expectations for the wedding. Sienna let out a long sigh. "If only we had found Rafael," she said.

"I know. It would have been the perfect complement to my wedding day," Audrey added.

They continued chatting and laughing until hours later when the doorbell rang. Audrey frowned and looked up at the clock. It was a few minutes to midday. She gasped. "Wow! We've been talking for hours! It must be the hairdresser and makeup artist."

She stood and started to put on her robe so she could go and open the door for the hair and makeup people.

"Just sit and relax, Audrey. I'll go and open the door," Sienna said.

A minute later, Sienna came into the room with a thin man and a young woman with bright red hair.

"This is Ben, Audrey," Sienna said. "As I told you before, he used to do my makeup when I modeled. And this is Yvonne. She's a great hairdresser. She's done my hair on many occasions. You are in safe hands."

Audrey nodded and greeted them.

Ten minutes later, she was sitting in front of the mirror as the redhead started on her hair. Forty minutes later, as she was finishing up with Audrey's hair, the first bridesmaid, Audrey's friend from back in the police academy, arrived.

Soon, the room was teeming with Audrey's female friends. Some were trying on their dresses, while others were in different parts of the room waiting to get their hair and makeup done. The room was noisy as her friends chattered and laughed.

Audrey stared into the mirror as her makeup was being done. She smiled at the chaos in the room. It was a glorious chaos, one she'd never dreamt of.

Finally, an hour later, she really looked in the mirror as the makeup artist stepped back. Her hair was swept back in a chignon and her makeup was a simple dewy look that made her complexion glow. She smiled, pleased at the result.

"You look great," everyone in the room told her.

She got up just as Sienna brought her dress to her: her mother's old wedding dress, which was now hers. Her heart beat fast as she put the dress on and Trisha helped her zip it up. She turned to look into the mirror as Sienna put her tiara on.

A hush fell over the room as she stared at herself in the mirror. Tears pooled in her eyes. She turned around, slightly worried at the silence. No one had said a word since she'd put on the gown. And then she saw tears in the eyes of her sisters and friends, and her heart soared.

Her bridesmaids gathered around her, kissing her cheeks and letting her know she was the most beautiful bride they had ever seen. She felt overwhelmed by their love and compliments.

After they had dispersed, the two people whose opinions, apart from Ken, meant the most to her in the world, came and stood next to her. Sienna and Trisha kissed her cheeks. "You look amazing," Trisha said through her tears. "Mom would have been so proud of you."

Sienna said in a voice choked with emotion, "Ken won't be able to take his eyes, or his hands, off you, Audrey."

Audrey laughed. "Sienna!"

"I'm just saying," Sienna grinned.

Audrey smiled widely as she hugged her sisters and then glanced around the room at her friends.

They were all here for her, to take part in her very special day. She felt tears of gratitude welling up in her eyes and blinked them back. She couldn't afford to ruin her makeup. Her heart filled with thanksgiving to the Lord and she felt blessed beyond measure. She lifted her voice in silent prayer and asked the Lord to bless her union with Ken.

*****

Hassan positioned himself on the roof of the town hall, a distance away from the church where the wedding was going to take place. He hefted his gun on his shoulders and looked through his binoculars, assessing the movement and number of guests at the venue. Before he'd arrived, he had decided this was going to be a suicide mission. But he hadn't known the bride and groom were disgusting police officers. He wondered why Khalid had not mentioned it.

But it didn't matter now. Even though the place was swarming with policemen, they didn't look like they were on alert. They all looked relaxed, like guests of the couple, come to partake in their union.

Hassan grinned. This was even better than he'd imagined. Even though he'd had to change his plan and instead plant a bomb in the church, this meant he would also get to take out the whole town's police officers. Every guest who escaped the blast in the church, he would mow down with his gun.

He cocked his rifle, pointed it in the direction of the church again, and waited. Apart from the policemen, some guests had arrived already. Some were even now exiting their cars and entering the church. He would wait another thirty minutes to make sure all the guests were inside. Once the bride entered and the doors closed, he would detonate the bomb he had carefully planted in the church basement the day before.

He grinned again as his body shook with the excited anticipation. He'd gotten word that Faizan had arrived the day before and confirmed that the former Al-Muharib leader would be attending the wedding. It was a perfect ending to Faizan, Hassan thought. The amount of damage he would do here would be very satisfying. Everyone would hear of this and fear. He couldn't wait.

He stilled his body and watched the church intently. He had to wait for all the infidels to enter their place of worship. And then he would do what he was born to do.

TWENTY

Audrey took a deep breath as the driver parked in front of her church, the New Day Fellowship. She turned to look out the window and then turned back to Trisha and Sienna. who sat in the backseat of the car with her.

Trisha, who was right next to her and dressed in a lavender silk gown, beamed. "It's time, Audrey."

Audrey nodded and smiled. Her heart was racing madly with nervous anticipation and excitement. She would finally get to see Ken and be joined to him as his wife. She shut her eyes, whispered a brief prayer of thanksgiving to the Lord, and then grinned at her sisters.

"Well… what are we waiting for? Let's go!" She couldn't contain her joy and squealed, "I'm so excited!"

Sienna and Trisha giggled.

The driver opened the door and Audrey stepped out of the car. Sienna and Trisha hugged her again, and then Trisha handed her the bouquet. "In about an hour or so, you will be Mrs. Baylor," Trisha said.

Audrey nodded. Sienna arranged her veil properly and then kissed her cheek. They both held her hands, as she had decided they would also be the ones giving her away. It was another tradition she was breaking. She'd wanted it to be their brother, Rafael, but since they hadn't been able to find him, she couldn't think of any other person or, in this case, persons she would want to give her away but her dear sisters.

Audrey's heart drummed as she stood with Sienna and Trisha in front of the church, waiting.

"I miss Mom and Dad," she said to her sisters. "I wish they were here." Her eyes filled with tears.

Sienna nodded with tears in her eyes.

Trisha shook her head. "Don't cry, Audrey… or you'll make me cry, too. And I don't want to." She took a handkerchief from her purse and began to dab the corners of Audrey's eyes. "Besides, you'll ruin your beautiful makeup if you keep crying."

Audrey nodded and exhaled. "I'm okay now, Trisha. I won't cry any longer." The wedding song suddenly started and her heart soared. Sienna handed Audrey her bouquet as the doors of the church were flung open.

She walked into the church and then gasped when she saw Ken at the altar. He looked so handsome in his charcoal tuxedo. He looked overcome as he gazed at her, and she felt exactly the same way he looked.

Suddenly, she couldn't see anyone else in the church except for him. She smiled and mouthed, "I love you."

He did the same.

She focused her eyes on his face and didn't turn

away until she was at the altar. Sienna and Trisha went to take their seats and Ken held her hands.

"I can't believe we're finally here," she whispered to him.

He nodded with tears in his eyes and whispered, "You look amazing, Audrey!"

"Thanks," she said quietly. She briefly turned to look at the preacher and then turned her eyes back to Ken. He was beaming at her, his eyes full of love for her.

She felt like weeping with tears of joy and wonder, but she bit back the emotion. As she gazed at Ken, she willed the preacher to hurry up so she could finally be married to the love of her life, to the dear man standing beside her with a smile that could light up the whole of Rosefield.

*****

Hassan smiled as the doors of the church were finally shut. It was time to detonate the bomb. He brought out the small explosive timer in his backpack, placed his thumb on the red button, and grinned. It was time to destroy the unbelievers. He yelled, "God is most great!" and then pressed the button, his heart dancing with anticipation of the loud blast and the destruction he would bring.

His eyes widened in surprise and disappointment as he looked at the church, still standing. There had been no blast.

What is this?

He pressed the button again, but still nothing.

His heart filled with panic. Something had gone wrong with the bomb or this device... he wasn't sure. Rage filled him and he almost roared. He controlled himself and positioned his gun to shoot anyone who came out of the church. If he had been set up, he would at least get a few people before he was caught.

He suddenly froze as a loud, familiar voice said from behind him, "Give it up, Hassan. It's over."

It can't be!

He slowly turned around and his jaw dropped. It was Faizan and a horde of American policemen with guns pointed at him.

He roared with anger. "You traitor! How did you know?"

"Khalid told me about your plans," Faizan said. "He owes me a huge favor."

Hassan held up his gun and pointed it at Faizan. If he was going down, he would take this traitorous fool with him. First, though, he had to plan and find an opportunity to strike and make sure he killed the man. To delay, he asked with a derisive sneer, "What did these fools offer you to make you give up your own brother?"

"You are no brother of mine. My brothers and sisters are in that church right there. Your plan to harm them has failed."

"So, you are saying you didn't make a deal with our enemies?"

"I made a deal with the American federal agents to reveal every terrorist cell I know. And yes, in exchange, I will get a permanent residency here and my freedom. But that wasn't why I did it. I did it to stop all the evil bloodshed, Hassan. As we speak, special agents in Algeria are hunting down all the Al-Muharib men in the desert as I gave them the location as well."

Hassan's vision blurred as he shook with rage. The man standing before him wasn't fit to live a second longer. Without thinking, he lunged at him in anger and then felt an excruciating pain go through his chest. He looked down at his chest and saw blood seeping out of a hole. He had been shot.

He lifted his gun and aimed it at Faizan.

Another agonizing pain shot through him. This time, blood poured down his shoulders, soaking his shirt. His mind began to go blank, and he cursed before trying to fire his gun. But he couldn't see anymore and he felt dizzy. He staggered and then fell.

Just before he went into the darkness, he cursed Faizan again and asked to be received into paradise as a martyr. That was all he wanted.

*****

Faizan waited at the back of the reception hall for Ken to say the secret word they had both agreed on. It was almost time for the groom's toast to the bride and Ken had told him to walk up to the stage immediately and say the words, "Surprise guest."

He stared at the stage where his three sisters—the bride, whose name Ken had told him was Audrey, and the two other ladies dressed in a similar purple gown—were standing.

After the unfortunate fiasco with Hassan, he had gone to the church, his emotions alternating between excitement and sadness; excitement at the thought that he would soon meet his sisters, and sadness because of Hassan, whose soul was lost.

He sat at the back of the church so as not to garner too much attention and craned his neck to see the bride.

At first, he couldn't see her clearly. But after the minister pronounced them 'man and wife', they began to walk down the aisle and she emerged, dressed in all white, beautiful as could be. Without warning, a sob rose in his throat and he almost reached out to touch her. At the last minute, he controlled himself and watched her glide down the aisle. And then he saw two other women who looked like the bride, walking behind her and he almost lost it. Instantly, he knew they were his other sisters. He couldn't take his eyes off them as they walked past him, and then he sighed deeply after they had left the church.

He came out of his reverie and glanced around; the venue was teeming with guests. Most of the guests were seated, but some walked around the hall, chatting with people. There were so many police officers that at first, he felt nervous. His reaction was due to years of being on the opposite side of the law. He had to remind himself he had nothing to fear now.

He stood, partly hidden by a purple drape in the reception hall, and waited, his eyes planted on his sisters. A minute later, Ken stood and hit his glass with a spoon. A hush fell over the hall and Ken grinned.

He began to talk about Audrey, how stubborn she was, which drew laughter from the crowd. And then he said with tears in his eyes, "But she is the most beautiful person, inside and out, that I know. She is compassionate and kind, and she's the girl you want to be in your corner if you ever get into a fight."

People laughed again.

He continued to declare his love for his bride and then he said, "I have a huge surprise for you, Audrey." He smiled down at her and she raised her brows.

Faizan wasn't sure it was time for him to reveal himself. They had agreed on the words "surprise guest," not just "surprise." He decided to wait.

Ken looked at the other ladies, Faizan's other sisters, sitting next to Audrey. "The surprise is also for you two, Trisha and Sienna." They stared at him with quizzical expressions on their faces. He looked away from them and faced the spot where Faizan stood.

Faizan's heart pounded as Ken said, "It's a surprise guest, actually; a perfect gift from God for this day."

Faizan took a deep breath and then walked out from behind the curtain. Murmurs rose throughout the hall as Faizan walked up to the stage. He beamed first at Audrey and then at his other two sisters, Trisha and Sienna.

The sisters stood up and stared at him, their mouths wide open, their eyes as round as saucers.

"He looks just like Dad!" his sister, who looked like she was the youngest, cried.

Loud whispers filled the hall.

Audrey turned to Ken with her brows furrowed and asked, "Who is he, Ken?"

Ken pointed at Faizan and smiled. "Let him tell you."

"Who are you?" Audrey demanded, staring at

him intently, tears in her eyes.

The third sister cried out, "Are you Rafael… our brother?"

Faizan smiled widely at his sisters as his heart pounded and he nodded. "Yes… my name was Rafael when I was younger, but it's now Faizan. I am your brother."

Pandemonium broke out in the hall, but Faizan had eyes only for the three beautiful women who stood before him.

He didn't have the chance to brace himself before the ladies rushed him and gathered him in a tight hug. They cried loudly, their tears wetting his shirt, and he cried with them until all their tears mingled together. He held each of them tightly, not wanting to let them go, but Audrey pulled away and took his face in her hands.

"See his eyes," she turned to her sisters and then looked back at him. "Exactly like Dad's."

"I have the same eyes," Trisha said, and laughed as she touched his cheek.

Audrey hugged him again and he rubbed her back. Sienna took over, but she cried loudly and didn't let him go until Trisha pulled her away. "You'll cut off his circulation soon," Trisha teased.

Faizan drank it all in as joy overwhelmed him. He kissed each of their cheeks and then at last, they led him to the stage. They sat him between them, and Audrey exclaimed, "This is the best wedding gift in the whole world!" She looked at Ken and shook her head. "So, this is what you've been hiding."

He nodded, looking pleased with himself.

People all over the hall came to greet Faizan and

asked him a multitude of questions, many of which he had no answers to. After an hour, when all the excitement had finally died down, the wedding reception continued.

Faizan smiled when Trisha took one of his hands and Sienna the other. His hands remained in theirs until an older lady asked him to dance.

He grinned and wanted to tell her he didn't know how, but his sisters encouraged him to go.

He danced for a short time with her and then someone else asked him as well.

The night progressed with everyone dancing together. Faizan grinned throughout. He couldn't remember when he'd last had so much fun.

The reception finally came to a close around midnight. His sisters took hold of his hands, and they all went out of the hall together. They found a park bench a few feet away from the church and sat down on it.

Trisha said, "Whew! Finally, we are alone with you." She grinned at him.

Audrey nodded. "Can you tell us everything about yourself?"

He looked at their faces, glowing under the street light, and wondered what they would say if he revealed his past to them. Would they judge him and reject him? He didn't say anything for a full minute, and then he felt the tugging of the Spirit in his heart. He immediately knew what he must do. He had to tell them everything—all the ugliness, as well as his new faith in Christ. He had promised the Lord he would not lie anymore. If his sisters rejected him, then so be it.

He opened his mouth and told them all of it,

starting from his birth mother's death, to his arrival at the wedding after giving his heart to Christ.

After he'd finished, nobody spoke for a long time and his emotions roiled with worry. He couldn't look at them, fearful that they would not want to have anything to do with him. And then he gasped as Sienna reached out and hugged him tight.

Trisha and Audrey wrapped their arms around him and held him.

He smiled as a rush of relief flooded him. Thank you, Lord, he whispered. He settled into their arms and relished their love. His mind suddenly went to Zainah, and for a brief minute he let in the sadness that enveloped him every time he thought about her. And then he shook it away. This was a special moment, and even though he missed Zainah with everything in him, he would not let it mar this time with his sisters. For the first time in his life, he belonged to a truly loving family.

*****

Zainah looked up and found herself in a field of red and white roses. Standing in the distance was the same man she'd seen in a dream some months before. Even though she'd not seen his face then, she knew he was the one. She also knew she was dreaming now.

She heard the same voice, which she wasn't sure was the Lord's, say, "That is your husband!"

She shook her head and then said, "I can't get married. I made a vow of chastity to the Lord." She covered her eyes as a bright light suddenly began to shine out of nowhere. She felt an overwhelming sense of love surround her. She closed her eyes and trembled with pleasure as waves of love washed over her, and then the familiar voice said softly, "Zainah, I never asked you to make that vow of chastity."

Her eyes widened in surprise as she immediately knew without a shadow of a doubt that the voice belonged to the Lord. She swallowed a sob and said, "But I thought it was what you wanted of me, Lord. I was making marriage a god, and I felt you wanted me to sacrifice the desire at the altar… for you."

The Lord laughed softly, and Zainah smiled in amazement. She didn't know God laughed, but she liked the sound of it. She laughed along.

"I never asked you to do that for me," the Lord said, his voice ringing with amusement.

Zainah sighed and asked, "What do you want me to do now, Lord?"

The bright light suddenly vanished. At first, she thought she had said something wrong and offended the Lord, but the man she'd seen in the distance began to approach her and then her eyes widened in disbelief and exhilaration. She could now see his features clearly. It was Faizan.

"Faizan!" she exclaimed.

He smiled as he reached her.

Joy flooded her heart, and she reached out her hand to take his. He reached his out, but he was still too far away and she couldn't reach.

"Come closer," she said to him.

He looked at her with a sad expression on his face, but he didn't move.

She tried to walk to him, but her feet felt heavy. She cried out, "Come closer, Faizan!"

Still he didn't move.

She struggled to go to him, but her feet refused to obey. She kept crying out desperately for him to come to her, but it was no use. He either couldn't hear her or he didn't want to come. Tears streamed down her face as she prayed desperately to God, asking Him to help Faizan come to her.

She kept crying and pleading with Faizan to move closer until she suddenly sat up on her sleeping mat. She took a deep breath and looked around her, disoriented. She was sleeping in her tent. Leila was a few feet from her, and the other women, on the other side of the room, were sleeping.

Zainah exhaled again and then whispered, "Faizan." She touched her cheeks and found she was crying. She shut her eyes and began to pray that the Lord would bring Faizan back to her, because she loved him with all her heart. She knew without a doubt that she wanted to spend the rest of her life with him. She wanted to be his wife.

*****

Audrey stirred as she felt a hand on her cheeks. She smiled and slowly opened her eyes.

"Good morning, sleepyhead," Ken said, grinning at her. He kissed her hair and then softly kissed her lips. "I love the way you look this morning," he said.

She shifted closer to him on the bed and kissed him passionately. She drew back and said, "So, what are we going to do this bright new morning? It's our honeymoon. We can't stay in bed all day like we did yesterday."

He pretended to grumble. "Why not?"

She laughed at the look on his face and then kissed his cheek. "Because there is a whole wide world, or should I say city, to explore. Madrid is waiting."

"We explored it all when we came here months ago." He pulled her into his arms, but she chuckled and shook her head. "Ken, we really have to get up now."

He smiled and pulled back. "Okay. Where do we go today?"

They talked about their plans to see other tourist destinations they hadn't seen the first time they were here. They had finally decided to come for their honeymoon just so they could enjoy the place as a couple. They had chosen the same hotel and penthouse room they'd stayed in when they'd come earlier in the year. This time, they took the room Sienna and Bryan had stayed in.

Ken finally rolled out of bed and went into the bathroom. Audrey lay on her back and sighed with contentment. A deep sense of peace and joy overwhelmed her, the way it had since she'd married Ken. She lifted up her voice to the Lord in thanks for giving her all the desires of her heart. Their brother, Faizan, in a miracle only God could have orchestrated, had been found and had actually attended her wedding. Best of all, she had finally married the love of her life. Now she and Ken belonged fully to each other and could spend as much time as they liked together. The wait had been hard, but worth it.

She opened her eyes again when she felt a soft touch on her lips and smiled. She had unknowingly dozed off, but Ken had awakened her with a kiss.

"I didn't know I had fallen asleep again," she said. She stretched out and yawned. "I guess I have to get up now." She looked up at him and her heart raced with an overwhelming desire for him. He was wiping his hair with a towel and looking down at her like she was his whole world. She grabbed his hand, pulled him down on the bed, and kissed him again.

When they came up for air, he shook his head and grinned. "I thought you wanted us to go out now?"

"We have many more days to explore the city." She shrugged and ran her fingers through his hair. "All I want to do is spend today exploring you. Only you."

He smiled tenderly at her and took her in his arms. She trembled as she excitedly anticipated his kiss. But before he claimed her lips again, he said softly, "I love you, Audrey, with all that I am."

"And I love you, Ken. More than anything in this world. More than life itself."

As they kissed, she sighed with pleasure. Earlier in the year, when she'd been disappointed about having to postpone their wedding, he'd told her that the wait would only make their union sweeter. And it had indeed. Much more than she could ever imagine. And the best thing was that she now had forever to spend with this wonderful man. He was a true gift from God.

A LOOK AT:

LOVE MEANS EVERYTHING

Connecting with her brother Faizan has taught Audrey the importance of family, and she's ready to create her own. But her career is on track, and she's finally doing the work she was born to do. When her inner conflict starts to fray the threads of her relationship Audrey knows she has a choice to make, but God's guiding voice has gone strangely silent. If that weren't bad enough, Audrey longs to see her brother start his new life in the U.S., but an old flame from his past refuses to let him go.

All Trisha ever wanted was a stable, loving home for herself and her daughter—but even the simplest desires can prove dangerous. As her head and her heart go to war, Trisha must make a choice that will shape the lives of those she loves forever.

From New York's cut-throat fashion world to the quiet of God's service, Sienna's new reality is unrecognizable. But the husband who holds her heart struggles to find his way, and when he claims to have finally discovered a path forward, the announcement shatters Sienna's contented existence. To make good on the oath she made to God, Sienna will have to make tremendous sacrifices.

COMING FEBRUARY 2020

ABOUT THE AUTHOR

Like the characters in her stories, Emma Easter juggles a range of identities.

In the low-income community where she works, Easter is known as a family medicine physician who treats patients of all ages and backgrounds.

College friends see her as an accomplished musician, having studied and mastered five classical instruments—but behind closed doors, she's just as comfortable rocking an air guitar to Creed. And when she isn't giving her heart, soul, and sanity to her three young children she's indulging in her most secret identity of all: meeting new characters, crafting fresh plots, and exploring every corner of her imagination.

Across all these different roles, one cohesive thread has tied everything together: her faith and love of Jesus Christ.

Find more great titles by Emma Easter and Christian Kindle News at https://christiankindle-news.com/our-authors/emma-easter/